Y0-BUA-336

**More Praise For
Dorothy Salisbury Davis**

"Davis is a skillful tale-weaver."
Chicago Tribune

"Davis has special appeal to more sophisticated
crime fiction fans."
Minneapolis Star and Tribune

Also by Dorothy Salisbury Davis:

A GENTLE MURDERER
A GENTLEMAN CALLED*
A DEATH IN THE LIFE
DEATH OF AN OLD SINNER*
THE HABIT OF FEAR
LULLABY OF MURDER
THE PALE BETRAYER
SCARLET NIGHT
TALES FOR A STORMY NIGHT:
   The Collected Crime Stories
WHERE THE DARK STREETS GO

*Published by Ballantine Books

BLACK SHEEP, WHITE LAMB

Dorothy Salisbury Davis

BALLANTINE BOOKS • NEW YORK

Copyright © 1963 by Dorothy Salisbury Davis

All rights reserved under International and Pan-American Copyright Conventions. Published in the United States of America by Ballantine Books, a division of Random House, Inc., New York, and simultaneously in Canada by Random House of Canada Limited, Toronto. Originally published by Charles Scribner's Sons in 1963.

No part of this book may be reproduced in any form without permission of Charles Scribner's Sons.

ISBN 0-345-34664-5

Manufactured in the United States of America

First Ballantine Books Edition: March 1991

For Sarah

1

At nine-forty-five Georgie Rocco and Phil Daley strolled out
of the *Crazy Cat*, a casual departure as though boredom had
set in for each of them simultaneously. Rocco's girl called
after him: "Luck, Georgie."

Georgie glanced at her in the crackled mirror behind the
counter and gave the familiar sign, the letter "o" shaped
with his thumb and forefinger. Rosie tossed her head and
then swept her hair out from under the ruff of her sweater.
She straightened her back. This had the effect of shooting
her breasts out beneath the sweater like artillery pieces under
camouflage. Georgie threw her a dirty look—for all the good
that did, but he had something more important to think about.

On the street, Phil Daley looked round at the shorter boy,
scowling. "What did she mean, good luck?"

"Stay loose," Georgie Rocco said. "She thinks I'm playing poker or something." He lit a cigaret and sucked in a
long drag of smoke, which he spewed defiantly toward the
stars.

The muddle of noise, brassy talk, showy laughter, and
music with a hard beat was muted when the shop door closed
behind them. The clangor of somebody banging on pipes had
the effect of getting it toned down even further. Georgie
Rocco jerked his head toward the shop and grinned. His
partner just stood, kicking one shabby shoe against the other.
"For Chris' sake, relax," Georgie said.

Inside, Pete lowered the jukebox volume.

The *Crazy Cat* was a decent sort of place hung with faded
college pennants and smelling all year round of the kerosene
space heater. It was run by Pete Morietti, a religious old
gentleman who felt that he did the community a service by

1

keeping a shop where the kids could meet and drink soda and play the jukebox. There were worse places in Hillside. It was a one-factory, three-church town. Its taverns were more numerous. Pete was a little deaf so that he could say in all sincerity he did not allow bad language or indecent talk in his place. Nor could he hear the added volume when one of the boys would slip his hand behind the jukebox and juice it up. Whenever the people who lived upstairs hammered on the water pipes, Pete could hear that and he would get up and scurry across the room to adjust the machine. Every time the service man came to change the records, Pete complained of the way the volume control had of slipping.

Georgie Rocco flicked his cigaret halfway across the street and watched it roll with the wind. "See you," he said and eased himself into the phone booth that stood within a few feet of the shop. He had to close and reopen the door and close it again before the light went on, and that night he wanted the light on.

Phil Daley started down the street, trying to amble. It was too cold to amble even if he could do it while thinking about it. His legs felt as jerky as a toy soldier's. He cursed the fat slob of a Georgie Rocco who had got him into this, and himself for not having the guts to get out of it. He went on, starting up and slowing down. He couldn't see a soul on the street except Billy Skillet who was pounding with a stick on the hall door for somebody to come out and get him. Why the hell didn't they? The poor bastard had no legs—just an iron platform with rollers to get around on. If they didn't come out for him Daley was either going to have to break his time plan to help him or go around by the alley on the river side and that way Mike Pekarik, the third partner, wouldn't see him. He couldn't help him anyway. Billy Skillet was one of the first guys the police would go to. He perched day and night like a crow on his platform, seeing everybody who went by, looking for a handout he'd take but wouldn't ask for. Then Big Molly came out and got him, her nightgown popping up in the wind like a chicken's tail when she bent

over to lift him up the stoop. Phil Daley wiped his face on
the sleeve of his jacket. Sweating in October.

In the phone booth Georgie Rocco had dialed Daley's
number, knowing he would get no answer. He let the phone
ring while he improvised a conversation—if it could be called
that: it consisted of reading aloud the initials scratched in the
phone booth, and substituting obscenities for the milder
words that plighted boys to girls, girls to boys. He had to
open the booth for air. The light went out. He closed it
quickly and hoped Pekarik hadn't seen it. Not that it was so
important that they get to the car at the same time; but you
had to make guys like Daley and Pekarik think so. You had
to plan every step for them, key them up. The sweat began
to ooze out around his neck. Like the football coach said:
Nerves were all right, they were fine. They keyed you up.
It's what you did with them. Georgie would have given anything to be team quarterback. He was a guard, and the
second-string at that. Too fat. Too damned much starch in
his food. No meat, no vegetables. Pasta, pasta, pasta!

He banged the receiver down on the hook and stepped out
of the booth. He turned up his jacket collar, for the wind
caught at his sweaty neck like a hand just out of ice water.

Phil Daley turned off the main street, his shadow running
a skinny zig-zag ahead of him until it disappeared in the
darkness. At the same time, further down the street, Mike
Pekarik crossed from the Triple-X filling station, walked to
the river's edge, turned then at a right angle and followed
Daley where he had doubled back in the direction of the
Crazy Cat, but at the rear of the buildings. Daley heard Pekarik whistling. Whistling! As Daley passed an alley through
which he could see to the main street, something darted out
of the dark into the light and then into darkness again before
he could see what it was. He paused, hearing the scuffle. The
low snarl, then the sudden screech of mating cats stiffened
him. Pekarik passed him, still whistling.

"Shut up," Daley said, catching up with him.

The cats had started every dog in the town yammering.

Georgie Rocco moved along the outside wall of the *Crazy*

Cat toward the factory parking lot. Once away from the building he lost the sound and throb of music in the steady, increasingly louder hum of the plant machinery. The frost silvered the tops of the cars belonging to the workmen on the night shift. At the edge of the lot Mike Pekarik's car was waiting, Mike having left it there earlier, its nose headed toward the exit. Rocco, passing, gave it an affectionate pat on the trunk. He opened the door on the driver's side and drew from beneath the seat a homemade blackjack, a large screwdriver wadded round with electrical tape. He tested the weapon in the palm of his hand lovingly, for it was his own creation.

The three boys met at the empty boxcar on the siding, some five hundred feet from the office. That close to the main building they found the machinery hum a real nuisance. It made a stranger to it want to whack himself on the ear as though the sound was in his own head. Rocco had warned his partners of this: he had also told them it would muffle any noise they made when they got near the office.

Georgie gave the others a final pep talk: "All you got to remember—take your time. Easy, slow, sure. After he opens it, we still got almost an hour."

For the tenth time Mike Pekarik asked: "How can you be sure he'll open it that early?"

"I told you, he does everything regular, like your old man going to the can."

Every Friday night for a month, Georgie Rocco had watched the office manager from outside the window of the small frame building attached to the factory. MacAndrews was indeed a man of habit. As Rocco had told his partners, he was the kind of guy who polished his shoes every night before he went to bed. Georgie had used psychology planning the robbery.

He took a nylon stocking from his pocket. The others got theirs out. "Put it on careful," he said.

They had rehearsed this, the donning of the stocking disguises, bringing the foot of the hose tightly round from the back and tucking it in with several thicknesses just under the nose.

"It stinks of perfume," Daley said. "He'll smell us coming."

Pekarik giggled.

"Want me to smack you one?" Rocco said. "They ain't going to smell once we're wearing them outdoors for a while."

When they were ready, Georgie Rocco gave the signal. He caught himself saying a Hail Mary and stopped in the middle of it. They moved up one at a time to their prearranged positions, Mike Pekarik at the side of one office window, Phil Daley at the other, Georgie at the door. MacAndrews, his chin in his hand, was poring over the bookkeeper's ledger, his back to the door. He turned a page. When the timeclock brayed ten, MacAndrews looked up at the clock, checked his watch and, even as Georgie had predicted, went to the iron safe at the side of his desk and began to twist the dial of the combination lock. MacAndrews was a company man. Every Friday night at the hour of ten he took upon himself to double-check against the books the cashier's figures on the pay envelopes the men would receive coming off the night shift at eleven. At eleven the Hillside police chief would be on hand. At ten MacAndrews was alone. In all his years of checking, he had found but one discrepancy: the company had once overpaid Georgie Rocco's father—since dead—by seventy-eight cents.

The moment the safe door swung open, Pekarik waved his hand.

Georgie's careful instructions to Pekarik had been to wait until MacAndrews returned to his desk with the box of pay envelopes and to give the signal the minute the office manager sat down. But Mike was excited as well as nervous. He had never in his life known a moment such as this; he could hardly believe his eyes when he saw the safe door open, and he waved his hand, thinking to confirm Georgie's prediction of what MacAndrews would do, forgetting at the instant that he was giving the prearranged signal. Georgie started confidently into the office. Phil Daley wanted to run right then, seeing Rocco move too soon, but his distrust of Georgie if he were caught prevented his flight. He followed him into the office and Pekarik followed Daley.

Rocco saw instantly the mistake, but he was by then beyond escape. His own partners blocked the doorway, and he knew his backside was of a size to make him easily recognizable in retreat. MacAndrews was bent over, reaching into the safe. Georgie plunged ahead because there wasn't any escape. He had to strike his blow at a moving target. He struck hard and then again for he thought MacAndrews had seen him. MacAndrews hit the cement floor head-first, the sound like the cracking of a boiled egg on the sink. And he lay absolutely still where he had fallen. Georgie looked down at him, fascinated, then at Pekarik. "Stupid bastard!"

Phil Daley moved toward the prone figure shakily. He stooped down to where he could look at his face. The blood had begun to trickle from the sockets of MacAndrews' eyes. Daley looked away fast. "You killed him, Georgie. You said you were going to tap him."

"He ain't dead," Rocco said.

Pekarik began to whimper, his chin quivering beneath the stocking mask.

Daley said, "We better get going." He straightened up and, acting out of fear more than calculation, he closed the safe door, kicking it shut. The sound of its metallic clank gave him confidence. Still Rocco and Pekarik stood. "Will you get out of here? Nobody'll know what happened." He gave Rocco a shove, starting him toward the door. He pushed him outside. Pekarik scurried past both of them. Daley closed the office door, using his coat pocket to smear any prints on the doorknob. A few feet away a blast of steam exhaust spurted from the factory vent and the boys skittered down the walk in greater terror. Daley snatched the stocking from his head and led the way to the boxcar. He could run faster than Georgie Rocco, and just now he thought he could think faster.

In the shadow of the boxcar he said, "Nothing's missing

back there, see? They won't know what happened if one of us don't tell them. A fight maybe. Nobody liked Mac-Andrews."

Georgie and Pekarik wagged their heads. Daley went on, "Georgie, you ain't seen Mike all night, me not after we left the *Crazy Cat*. Mike and me are going up to my place now and we'll be playing gin when my old man gets home."

"What about me?" Georgie said. "I'm the guy that needs the alibi." He turned on Mike and began to swear at him again for his stupidity.

"Cut it out!" Daley ordered.

Georgie did.

"You got a sister home," Daley said. "Get her to alibi you."

"She'd rather turn me in!"

"Georgie, get yourself whatever alibi you can," Daley said, and then with careful logic: "We ain't seen you at all. If we ain't seen you, we don't know what you did back there. That way, nobody is going to tell anybody anything. Mike and me are going to take the car and drive up to my place like we never seen you at all."

Rocco was still holding his handmade blackjack. "What'll I do with this?"

Daley was beginning to feel the pleasure of superiority. "You got a big mouth, Georgie. Why don't you swallow it?"

The cowards, the bastards. Rocco heaped his under-breath abuses on Pekarik and Daley as he started home the back way as far as the river, then past the fire station and up the hill through the school grounds. What he wanted to do was cry or to go back to the *Crazy Cat* and pretend nothing had happened. But he could feel the blackjack in his pocket, hard and a dead weight. Jesus. He hadn't meant to kill him. He'd been scared; that was all. Jesus. Jesus, Mary, and Joseph. He had to stop for breath. Climbing the hill so fast had given him a pain in his chest. Looking down, he saw a couple of cars go by. He'd been lucky there, anyway. Nobody'd seen him. A dead, sleepy town—outside. Inside—back of the

Triple-X Garage—things were going on all right, and there'd
be a poker game at Big Molly's along with other things—if
you could just get inside. But for that you had to have money
. . . and a tight lip. Another car went by. It was getting closer
and closer to eleven. And MacAndrews lying there. Georgie
got the picture again, clear as if it were happening all over
again. Christ, what it felt like to hit him. And he'd hit him
the second time because he knew he'd hurt him; it was to
make him stop hurting he'd hit him again. Georgie heard his
own little squeaks of agony that he couldn't keep inside himself, and began to run again. If Jo was home alone . . . not
that he could tell her. What he'd have to tell her was a story
about a girl he'd been with. That was it. He'd tell her all
about it and make her listen, all kinds of crap about her
letting him paw her. Jo'd want to kill him, but if they asked
her questions later she wouldn't be able to tell that on him so
she wouldn't say anything. She might even say he was home.

He was less than a block from home coming out of the
school yard. The light was on in the living room. That meant
Martin was there, Jo's boy friend. That was better maybe.
He'd go round to the basement and pretend he'd been down
there for an hour, spying on them. What was to spy? All they
did was sit and plan, then go into a clinch and then break up
like in an old TV movie. Man, talk about squares!

But it was not Martin Scully who was sitting in the living
room with Johanna; a man, Georgie saw as soon as he got
near the house, but it wasn't Martin. With Martin there she'd
have pulled the blinds down. Georgie stood on tiptoe at the
side window. It was the priest, Father Walsh. Christ, what
was he doing there at that hour? The first thing Georgie
thought of was that his mother must be dead. But she was
getting better. It wasn't serious, what she was in the hospital
for, just some women's trouble. She was coming home next
week: that's what they'd said.

He moistened his lips. If she was dead that meant they'd
called up the *Crazy Cat* looking for him. That meant . . .
But Jo wasn't crying. She was just sitting there talking—
serious. They were talking about him, that's what it was. Jo

had that pious look. And Father Walsh had the look he always got when he wanted you to see things his way, maybe not as bad as you thought they were. He was a good guy for a priest—and a smooth looker. He could really send some of the girls. And, brother, didn't he know it!

But there they sat jazzing, and any minute the factory whistle was going to blow . . . Georgie took the screwdriver from his pocket and peeled the electrical tape off the handle. He balled the tape up and buried it under the leaves by the hydrangea bush. Later he'd find a place for it—the Hudson River. He threw the screwdriver under the front steps. Afterwards he'd put it back where it belonged with his father's tools in the basement.

Father Walsh got up then. So did Johanna. Georgie looked around to see where the priest had left his car. He saw it up a ways across the street, in front of old lady Tonelli's. Two birds with one stone. He called on the old lady every week or so. She wouldn't have Father de Gasso, the pastor, who could speak Italian with her. Father Walsh—she wanted the young one. What a dame she was. Christ, would he never leave? They were standing, Johanna and him, in the hall just at the living room door. What happened then Georgie could hardly believe he was seeing: his sister in the priest's arms. They were holding onto each other, her hands at the back of his head; it was a real bubie-rubbing clinch! After the first shock of what he was seeing, thrill after thrill rocketed through Georgie's body. He had to hang onto the windowsill. Then the priest pried Jo's hands away. Georgie realized he was going to get himself the tightest alibi there was this side of innocence.

Quickly and quietly he rounded the porch and went up the steps. They both started round when he threw the door open.

"You ought to pull down the blinds sometimes, sis." Then in mock surprise: "Oh . . . good evening, Father. I thought it was Martin in here with Jo . . . Gee, excuse me!"

He clumped noisily up the stairs and flopped on his bed, jacket, shoes and all.

* * *

Downstairs, Johanna said, "I'm very sorry, Father."

The priest took his topcoat from where it lay over the banister. He said, "Goodnight, Johanna," and went out. He was on the steps, putting on his coat, when the siren alert for the ambulance sounded. The factory whistle had not blown yet; this was the worst hour for industrial accidents at the plant, the last of each shift. The men were tired and hurrying to finish a quota. At the Graham plant they still worked on an incentive plan.

The priest was halfway down the hill when the ambulance passed the intersection below and following it a car the priest thought would be Dr. Tagliaferro's. He drove into the plant grounds to see if he was needed.

Kearns stopped him at the office door. "Looks like a heart attack," the police chief said. "I come round my usual time and found him. I know for a fact he's been complaining. Doc?"

Tagliaferro was kneeling over the stricken man. "He gave his skull a hell of a crack going down, I'll say that."

The two ambulance drivers waited just inside the office door, their white coats bulging over their street clothes. They were discussing the time it had taken them to make it to the plant. Outside, the circling red light from the ambulance played across the dirty building like an invisible hand daubing on paint.

"Is he dead?" the priest asked.

"Dead when I got here," Kearns said. He amended, "Though it'll take Doc to make it official."

"Might as well take him up now to Toby's," Tagliaferro said, straightening up. "Can't do a post mortem on him here."

The priest turned to go. MacAndrews had not been a Catholic. "May his soul and all the souls of the faithful departed rest in peace," he murmured.

"Father, will you speak to the men with me?" Kearns said. "They'll be coming off work and expecting their pay."

The two men walked across the gravel to the plant door, reaching it as the whistle blew.

Kearns waited until the men lined up as was their custom on pay night. "I'm sorry to have to tell you, Mr. Mac-Andrews has had an accident—his heart, I'd say." The men watched stonily while Kearns took a handkerchief from his pocket and blew his nose. "Mac was a friend of mine," he said by way of explanation. "You'll have to wait till tomorrow for your pay. That's all."

2

Georgie lay on the bed, smoking his next-to-last cigaret, and stared at the ceiling where the paint was chipped off in the shape of a bat. What a dump. For this his father had worked all his life at the Graham plant. Twenty years it had taken him to pay for it, twenty years of spaghetti to pay off four thousand dollars. It made him die happy, knowing it was paid for. Christ!

He listened, thinking he'd heard Johanna's step on the stairs. He'd made up his mind to wait for her to come up to him and start explaining. But could he wait? He'd heard the single wail of the ambulance siren, going toward the plant. Then the eleven o'clock whistle. What was going on down there? Old Kearns must have found him. Somebody did. Georgie tried to see himself answering old blotchy-faced Kearns' questions. "Yes, sir," he'd say, and "No, sir." If you said "sir" to Kearns you could tell him anything. Only Kearns wasn't going to ask him questions, not unless he was going to ask maybe forty kids the same questions. Georgie didn't trust Pekarik. He didn't trust anybody. Except Pekarik and Daley were in on it. They'd be . . . accessories. Daley turned out to be a cool one. Talk about loose, kicking the safe closed like that. They could've grabbed a couple of envelopes first. Georgie didn't have the price of a pack of cigarets. Or petty cash, at least. There ought to have been a few bucks for stamps in the safe.

Georgie listened again. All he could hear was Jo's alarm clock ticking through the wall. Like paper the walls were, stuck together with adhesive tape. He looked at his hands. He could feel a stickiness on them from the electrical tape. Tar or whatever it was. He could even smell it. Or maybe

12

that was just nicotine. He rolled off the bed, deciding to wash his hands anyway. He took a last drag off the cigaret that burned it right down to where it yellowed his thumbnail.

In the bathroom mirror he examined his face. Chubby, red-cheeked. Christ, it looked like a baby's backside. But he opened his dark eyes wide and rehearsed his story: "I must've got home maybe ten o'clock. I know it was. Father Walsh was here and I was thinking he was out late for him, having to get up for the early Mass and everything. He was in talking with Jo so I went down to the basement for a while. I didn't want to interrupt. I figured they were talking about her and Martin maybe. I mean, they got to get married some time . . ." He grinned at himself, satisfied. It would go pretty good if he could make kind of a joke out of it.

He turned off the bathroom light and looked out in time to see the police chief's car streak up the River Road. No sirens. Just the red light circling round and round on the top. Where the hell was he going in that direction? For Doc Tagliaferro? Doc's car was always cracked up at the wrong time. But what did they need Doc for?

Georgie went down the stairs. His sister was sitting in the living room, waiting like he'd waited upstairs. Only she didn't have the right. Rubbing herself up against the priest. His sister with a priest. And there she sat knitting. Like Lady La Farge in the French Revolution. He just leaned against the door frame and watched for a couple of minutes. He couldn't see her eyes; she didn't dare look up at him, just the long lashes blinking, fluttering. Two red spots were burning in her cheeks. She moistened her lips so that from where he stood they sparkled with the spittle. If there was another girl as pretty as his sister in Hillside, he'd never seen her. When the genes decided who was going to get what in this family, Johanna got there first—in more ways than one. And after him they'd quit. He'd often wondered how they'd just quit, going to church and all. Jo had tried to explain it to him. Rhythm. Man, if you could believe that, you could believe anything.

He ambled into the room and stood over his sister. He

reached down and caught a strand of wool, tugged it, and pulled out her last row of stitches. Jo looked up at him. She'd been crying. And damn well she'd ought to have been crying!

"You're the deep one, ain't you, sis?"

Johanna put the knitting away. "Please don't say anything, Georgie."

"Say anything! Who's going to say it then—the priest? Hah!"

Johanna got up and began to walk back and forth across the napless carpet. She kept rubbing her hands together as though they were cold. "It just happened in a minute. It wasn't anything really. We'd been talking about mother—you . . ."

"I'll bet."

"We were, Georgie. I can't help being worried, the way you stay out at night . . ."

"I didn't stay out long enough tonight, did I?"

His sister pressed her teeth into her lip and tried to look at him without letting the tears come out of her eyes. "You stayed out too long," she said. "If you'd been home . . ."

He interrupted. "Now don't start blaming me, Jo. It so happens I was home. Early. When I saw you and the priest in here I went down to the basement. I didn't think he was ever going to leave. Didn't you hear me down there?"

"No," she said. "I never hear you down there." The words were bitter. She well knew he was in the habit of trying to hear what she and Martin were saying, listening at the ventilator. But he'd got across exactly what he wanted.

He felt that he could afford to be tolerant. "I don't exactly blame you, Jo, him being that good-looking. I know a lot of girls who'd like to go into a clinch with him."

Johanna's head shot back, her eyes flashing.

"Well, that's what you did, didn't you?" Georgie said.

"You make it sound so dirty."

"*I* make it! Look, sis, it was you and him—like that." Georgie put his hands together, flat, and then rubbed one of them against the other. "If that ain't dirty, what is, for Christ sake?"

"Don't Georgie, please."

"I got a right, Jo. I'm your brother. And ma in the hospital. What about old Martin?"

"Georgie, understand something. Just try . . . maybe the way I try to understand you . . ."

"Yeah."

"Will you just listen for a minute?" She drew a deep breath, trying to compose herself. "Father Walsh said something tonight—just as we were standing out there. He said, 'We are all at the mercy of God as well as of one another. And for that we can be grateful. He has so much more of it than we have.' "

"What does that mean?"

"It means . . . I don't know how to explain if you don't understand it. But when he said it—after what we'd been talking about—about how cruel people are, even if they don't intend to be—it hurt me inside seeing all of a sudden how much he understood, and couldn't do anything. Even him. And that's his life. Alone. It was just like a great, hollow cave out there, and him standing at the end of it. I swear to you, Georgie, what I wanted to do just at that minute, was run to meet him, to help him. But he was right there, next to me. He didn't know. It must have been a terrible shock to him. Temptation—that's what it must have been to him. But it all happened in just a few seconds, and it was all over. I was ashamed as I've never been in my life."

"What about old Martin? You going to tell him about it?"

Johanna shook her head. Her eyes were closed. "I don't want ever to have to tell anyone about it, ever again in my life."

"I wish I could get away with things like that," George said. Everything was going the way he wanted, but the moment it did, he wanted more, the personal inside gratification that came of being ahead in the game. "I mean, talk about making excuses for yourself. That's what you're always telling me I'm doing, isn't it?"

"I'm not making excuses—not for myself. I'm deeply,

heartily sorry it ever happened.'' Her eyes were wide on his again.

Georgie wet his lips. "I thought you said nothing happened, huh? How about it? You're always wanting me to tell the truth, Jo. How about trying it on yourself for a change? You liked it, didn't you—right smack belly-rubbing with a priest?''

Johanna stared at him with fear or hate or something in her eyes he couldn't just dig. Or maybe he'd got to her in a way he'd never been able to before. Then she turned her back on him and hid her face in her hands, just sobbing but not making any noise.

Georgie took his last cigaret from his pocket and lit it. When Jo lifted her head and turned to face him again, he said, "I mean with old Martin, Jo . . . but with the priest. That's spooky.''

Jo flew at him, her temper raging. She hammered him with her fists about the shoulders and arms where he threw them up to protect his hair. But she got to it anyway, and having knocked the cigaret from his hand, she dug her fingers into his hair, pulling and shaking his head with all her strength.

Georgie broke her grip, striking out at her with both his arms. She stumbled backwards halfway across the room. He had to look around to find his cigaret and then to stamp it out where it was burning the rug, his last cigaret.

Johanna ran from the room and up the stairs. He heard the squeal of the casters when she threw herself on the bed. He went to the mantel where a framed picture of his father stood, and turned it so that he could use the glass as a mirror. With his pocket comb he restored his hair to the two meticulous crests in which he wore it. If he'd had the price of a package of cigarets he'd have gone down to the Comfort Tavern. They wouldn't let him inside the door for anything else. Instead he picked up the one he had stepped on, reshaped it, and lit it. He sat for a while and enjoyed it after the first ashy drag. It was some night . . . to have come out on top of. But Johanna and Padre Walsh. It'd be a lot of Christian Doctrine old Walsh would teach him after this. He thought then what it would be like to go and tell the priest in confession about what he'd done that night, earlier. MacAndrews. He began to get excited just thinking about it. And that had been nagging at him all night back of his mind, having to tell some priest. But he probably couldn't trust Walsh—after what he'd seen him doing. If Walsh could slip like that with a girl, how could you be sure he wouldn't slip on something else? Like the seal of the confessional? It was a hell of a thing if you couldn't depend on a priest even.

Georgie pulled at his cigaret. Nothing. It was dead, the ember gone. He leaped out of the chair, realizing that the burning end of it had fallen somewhere. He could smell it then, the smell of burnt cloth. He dug out the faded cushion and saw where it was burning its way into the upholstery at the side of the chair. He watched it, fascinated. His imagination caught fire much faster—the drama of a fire alarm at that hour breaking on top of whatever was already happening down in the village. He saw himself publicly accounting his version of what had happened in the house that night, his sister having to confirm it . . . the way he told it. Nobody would even think of connecting him then with the MacAndrews business. And if Pekarik and Daley knew he was safe, they'd be sewed up for good. Daley would ride with the engine, and Georgie would see to it he heard him tell his story. And what the hell worth was the house, always getting the money that should have been spent on the family who lived in it? It was insured. Like some people—worth more dead than alive.

Georgie could not wait for the slow charity of an accident. He struck a match and held it to the window drapery where it hung in ancient and brittle folds behind the chair. The flames slithered upward. The catch was instantaneous, almost too quick even for him. He ran outdoors and got the screwdriver from beneath the porch steps. He took it down to the basement and put it on the rack; it was the only one of his father's tools to have been taken from its place since the old man's death. Georgie forced himself to wait. A few seconds, just, he told himself, to be sure it got a good start.

When he could smell the smoke he ran around the house and up the stairs, shouting to his sister. Johanna, coming down, met him in the hall. The living room was already churning with yellow smoke and the red, darting flames. They left the house together, but Georgie ran ahead. He had dreamed as long as he'd known what the box was for of turning in a fire alarm. But just as he broke the glass, the town siren began to wail. Someone had already called the fire department.

3

County Detective Raymond Bassett was about ready to turn off the lights and go upstairs when the phone rang. It was after one o'clock. His wife and the four children had a good part of their night's sleep behind them. But he had got home late from a meeting at the D.A.'s office, one of those noisy, ill-disciplined meetings of politicians, citizen representatives, and local police chiefs where everybody wanted to be heard but nobody spoke to the point. He was not a good sleeper at best, and after these affairs he had to, so to speak, read himself out of them when he got home. He picked up his tie from the table and used it as a bookmark while he answered the phone.

"That you, Bassett? This is Harry Toby."

Toby had been one of the few sensible men present at the meeting tonight. It was an odd thing about undertakers, Bassett thought: They were generally sensible, sound-reasoning men. It no doubt came of their dealing with the ultimate fact of life.

"I don't suppose you've had a report of MacAndrews' death," Toby went on. "He was the night manager at the Graham plant in Hillside. Remember, we were talking about him tonight?"

"Yes," Bassett said. The meeting had been called over reports of gambling in the county. MacAndrews, though not present, had been one of the complainants. Kearns, the Hillside police chief, had made an ass of himself at the meeting, first denying that he knew of any gambling in the village and then admitting that MacAndrews had complained of it several times to him. Kearns had had to leave the meeting early: pay night at the plant.

19

"Well, he had an accident over there tonight. Cracked his skull on the cement floor. Anyway, the body was waiting here for me when I got home from the meeting and I've just had a look at him. He's got two nasty lumps on the back of his head as well as the fracture in front. Like from a lead pipe or something like that."

Bassett cradled the phone between his head and his shoulder and automatically began to button his shirt. "You think it's connected with our business tonight, is that it?"

"I wouldn't say that," Toby said. "But the thing is, I can't get hold of anybody in Hillside. There's a big fire down there, the operator says."

"I'll get things rolling," Bassett said. "Get the coroner first, but don't do anything on him till we get some pictures, eh?"

"Right."

Bassett took the time to go to the kitchen for a cup of strong cold coffee. It was always there. If it were still there in the morning his wife would throw it out and assume he had got to bed at a decent hour.

Jurisdiction. He was always having to back into a case, and generally after it was well mucked up. He would take his oath that wherever MacAndrews had been killed it might as well have been in Grand Central Station for the traffic through it since. He began making phone calls. He was exceeding his authority, he well knew, but he counted on opening up the Pontiac and getting to Kearns himself before the first of the state technical trucks could reach the scene. They had ten miles to roll, he but five. He gave the locations and then instructions to stand by until the local officer was on hand. Then he called his own boss and got the okay to do what he had already done.

The roads were all but deserted. He did not need to use his siren, the only police equipment he had. It was his own car. In a way, the fire might prove fortuitous: It would keep the volunteers occupied. Then he thought what a hell of a note it was to be grateful that somebody's house was burning down—just so he could do his job better.

Bassett had to park a block from the blaze and walk; the Hillside police car was parked crosswise to block the street to traffic. Bassett opened the door of the car. Inside, the radio was on, county police central droning the usual communications. Bassett went on. Fire equipment from Anders Cove, the next town, was on hand as well as the two Hillside engines. Twenty or so men were working furiously, bravely, for the fire was whipping out of the upstairs windows, and it wasn't safe on the roof of the frame house at all, but men were up there all the same, chopping holes, while others dragged the hoses to their furthest reach, not quite far enough. It was an awesome sight, at once terrible and magnificent—like some primeval battle, man against nature. Other men were hosing the next house, for the wind was coming up from the north, carrying sparks like skyrockets in the night. A younger batch of volunteers was keeping back the people of the neighborhood who had come out in their nightclothes under their coats. Bassett wondered if there was a killer in this crowd. It was too soon to speculate on that, but he realized that if there were, the fire might not be so fortuitous for a policeman after all. With all this excitement, nobody was going to remember any other odd thing in the town with any degree of reliability.

Kearns was easily discovered. He stood between the fire trucks, his hands behind his back, his feet spread, his body tilted forward attentively, and with a great, dead cigar in his mouth.

"Kearns," Bassett said.

Kearns squinted at him to see who it was and shifted the cigar to the other side of his mouth. "Bad one, isn't it?"

"Toby's been trying to get hold of you," Bassett said.

Kearns grunted and jerked his head toward the police car. "Why didn't he try the radio?"

Bassett said, "Well, I was on hand." It was better to do it the easy way. Bassett was not a man who yearned after authority. In fact, he did not yearn after police work, having got into it accidentally. He had been trained as a sociologist. But that was before the war.

"What'd he want?"

"MacAndrews seems to have got a couple of raps on the back of his head."

Kearns took the cigar from his mouth, looked at it, and threw it away. "That a fact?" he said.

The two men walked toward the cars, neither of them actually having taken the lead.

"Funny," Kearns said. "There didn't look to have been anything like that happen. Pay night, of course. But the payroll wasn't touched. We got the day man down to open the safe. Maybe that's why he got it, because he wouldn't open up. Mac wasn't a guy to scare easy."

"Well, let's have another look now," Bassett said. "I assumed you'd want the technical boys to go over the place when you found out. So I rolled them out."

The police chief hesitated for only a moment. "Sure," he said. "Thanks."

Kearns was no less competent than the majority of men in positions like his. The job paid no great fortune, but more than he could have earned at the plant. He had taken a course at the State Police School, getting the appointment. He was honest, except possibly in the ways politicians sometimes have to balance facts against factions.

Hillside was a factory town, skirted round in recent years by commuters from New York City who settled in the houses owned by families in the Hudson Valley long before the Graham plant had been built, or in homes they built themselves, carving terraces out of the mountainside. But the core of the village population was in the people who had moved in with the factory, two generations before, primarily Italian, but with a sprinkling of other nationalities, largely intermarried by now. It was a town proud of its autonomy, delivering a strong one-party vote, working-class conservative, and ruggedly determined to keep its independence. It would not consolidate with other areas in school, police, or sanitation facilities. It was a town determined to take care of its own.

They had almost reached the car when a great hulk of a

boy ran up to them, calling to Kearns. "Chief, have you seen my sister?"

"No. Wouldn't she be in with the women at Lodini's?"

"I didn't look there," he said, and wiped his dirty face with the back of his sleeve. "You'd think she'd be out here helping, wouldn't you?"

"Not much for a girl to do, Georgie," Kearns said.

The boy loped back toward the fire.

"Not much for anybody to do," Kearns added. "Want to take your own car?"

"I'll go down with you," Bassett said. He might want to use the radio. "The boy's house?"

In the car Kearns said, "Most of the houses along here are tinderboxes. Bad wiring, junk. Getting as bad as Moontown—that's the colored section."

"Moontown," Bassett said.

"Got its name from Prohibition. That's where the gambling is they were talking about tonight. Those people live on it—and religion."

"What else have they got?" Bassett said.

"Oh, I don't know. They get the same at the plant as a white man now. Get laid off a little sooner maybe. That's all."

"What about the union?"

"They belong to it—some of them."

Bassett was trying to think of everything he knew about Hillside. He lived on the other side of the mountain himself, near the county seat where he worked. "That's autonomous, too, isn't it?"

"The union? It's independent if that's what you mean."

"Any of the national boys ever come in and try to organize?"

"Nope. They don't come where they ain't invited."

"That's pretty much the truth, isn't it?" Bassett mused. He was getting a little sour on trade unionism himself these days. Whether the unions were getting fat or he was, he wasn't sure. Both probably.

"Young Martin Scully tried to get them in here a couple

of years back. It didn't win him any popularity contest for a while, I'll tell you that." Kearns slowed down and looked both ways before driving across the main street. There wasn't a car in sight. "Matter of fact, he had a fist fight with MacAndrews over it. The real old-fashioned kind you ain't seen in years. We got the high school athletic coach to referee it . . . out back of the plant." Kearns turned past the *Crazy Cat*, now all in darkness. "I was just thinking, I won twenty bucks on Mac."

"He beat the younger man?" Bassett said. He knew MacAndrews had to have been well into his fifties.

"No. But I had good odds on him to stay to the sixth round. And that's what he did. It cost him a new dental plate but he hung on. Those of us coming out ahead on him chipped in for his new choppers."

But all the gambling in Hillside was done in Moontown, Bassett thought. He said, "Was there bad blood between him and the young fellow after that?"

"Hell, no," the police chief said. "That's how you get rid of bad blood, spill a little of it. Get it out of your system."

"Might be an idea all the same to have a talk with him," Bassett said. "Don't you think?"

"Don't see where it'll do any harm. He's up at the fire right now—first ladder man."

"No hurry," Bassett said. The technical truck had just rolled in behind them. "What's his name again?"

"Scully. Martin Scully. His father used to be the druggist here in town. Married one of the Tonelli girls. They were killed in an auto accident when Martin was a kid. Funny how close things are in this town—Martin goes with Johanna Rocco—and that's her house they aren't going to be able to save a stick of."

If Martin Scully were one of the firemen he'd seen on the roof, Bassett thought, he'd be lucky if they saved a stick of him.

4

Georgie ran from one operation to another, lending his weight and pull to the hose, his hands to the ladders; he got hold of one of the fire axes and came within an inch of splitting a man's head with his backswing. Joe Lodini, the fire chief, took the axe from him and ordered him out of the area.

"It's my house," Georgie said.

"That don't give you the privilege of helping it burn down."

"That's what you think, man," Georgie murmured, but under his breath. He faded back into the crowd, but only for a moment. When Daley and Martin Scully started to maneuver the ladders to the south, Georgie could not resist the impulse to help them. He succeeded only in trampling on their feet.

Daley swore at him.

"Watch it, brother," Georgie warned him. "Just watch it."

Daley was too surprised to say anything, Rocco telling him to watch it.

Scully said, "Where's Johanna? Somebody ought to be taking care of her just now, Georgie."

"Yeah," George said, again under his breath. "She needs taking care of, all right." But he fell back to the fringe of the operation, to where he could watch from between the fire trucks. His feet were freezing. How the guys could stand it in rubber boots, he didn't know. He'd gone hunting in rubber boots once; he could have shot off his own toes and they would have felt better.

A scream went up from the crowd as a section of the roof collapsed in a torrent of sparks. It was the section of the house from which Martin Scully and Daley had just moved the ladder. It passed through Georgie's mind that if anything happened to Daley, if he was killed, well . . . He looked around then to see if Pekarik was in the crowd. Not him. He'd be home with the blankets over his head, chicken all the way through. What had been real dumb was messing around with him in the first place.

Shortly after two o'clock the fire was declared under control. By then an odd piece of furniture that wouldn't burn, such as the brass bedstead in his mother's room, stood gaunt as a skeleton. And the upstairs bathroom. It made Georgie sick, looking at the sink and the toilet bowl and the knob-footed tub, not because of the way they looked now, but because of his memories of them—the water-stained bowl that Jo couldn't get clean no matter what—she spent more money on Sani-Flush than he was allowed for cigarets—the chipped tub, and the torn linoleum with the goddamned red paint under it like somebody'd bled to death.

As soon as he declared the fire under control, Chief Lodini said, "Now where's young Rocco? Let's find out what happened here."

Georgie faded back of the trucks and galloped down the other side of the street to Lodini's house. He wanted to tell his story once and with Johanna there to confirm it. He went round to the kitchen door at the side of the house; a couple of times he had already been there, looking in on Jo who was taking it like she did her father's death, just sitting and staring. She could cry over the priest all right, but not over her own family. It was hard to dig girls. All the women were yapping, a half-dozen of them maybe. The big round table was stacked with coffee mugs. He could smell the coffee outside. The men would be coming along soon. He'd meant to say something to Daley, to be sure he'd be there when he was telling his story. The trouble with Daley, with all the fire gang, after they'd come off a job you couldn't speak to them. You'd think they'd just raised the flag on Iwo Jima or something.

The women, all except Jo, looked around when George

came in. Mrs. Lodini got up from the table and made him sit down while she got him coffee.

Georgie put his hand on Jo's shoulder and gave her an awkward hug. The women sounded like Ferucci's chickens with the clucking of their tongues and their babble of sympathy. Georgie felt he was making a good impression on them.

"You aren't hurt?" Jo said.

If only he was hurt, Georgie thought, he'd have her eating out of his hand. But the men would be coming up soon. He couldn't play it both ways. "Naw," he said with bravura. "But it's all over and there ain't much left, Jo."

"Never mind," Mrs. Gerosa said, and patted his hand. "We got lots of things for you, clothes and blankets and dishes."

Things the Salvation Army wouldn't take for bums off the street. And what she'd like to give to him, Georgie thought: slow poison. He wasn't good enough for her Rosie. And where the hell was Rosie? Some girl friend who didn't show up when a guy's house burned down. Only her old man wouldn't let her, probably, with the fire gang around. He blew up if anybody just whistled at her. "That's very kind of you, Mrs. Gerosa." He started to rise when Mrs. Lodini brought him coffee.

"Don't get up," she said. "Sugar and milk?"

"No, thank you," he said. "I'm in football training."

"Grandma Tonelli invited us to stay at her house," Johanna said.

Mrs. Tonelli was no relation to them; she was Martin's grandmother and she had a lot of other grandchildren living outside Hillside, but everybody in the town called her Grandma Tonelli. Georgie didn't like the old lady much, except that she had money. That fascinated him. But she had the dark, sharp eyes of a bird and a bird's way of pecking at you for information. She loved to know everything that was going on. She was the only person he knew who could send for the priest and have him come when she wasn't sick even.

"Can we go up soon, Georgie?" Johanna asked.

"Sure," Georgie said, "but I think Mr. Lodini wants to talk to us. You know, how it started and all that. And old Martin, he wants to see you." He watched the little dilation at his sister's nostrils, the dropping of her eyes after one startled look at him. Georgie poured it on: "Jeez, was he the hero tonight. The way he was trying to get up the ladder to your room—you'd 've thought you were in it, I mean."

"Reckless," Mrs. Gerosa said. "Like all the Tonellis. They do not care that for life, you would think." She snapped her fingers.

"*Life* is like that," Mrs. Lodini also snapped her fingers. "You heard about Mr. MacAndrews tonight. At his desk one minute. Dead the next. Who can tell when he gets up in the morning where he'll lie down at night?"

Georgie's heart began to pound. He hid his face behind the great mug of coffee, spilling it when he burned his lip.

"I found a penny today," Mrs. Gerosa said solemnly. "It was black like the heart of a miser . . ." She said the word in Italian, unsure of it in English, but everybody at the table, even Georgie, understood it. "I said to myself, MacAndrews must have lost it. And I threw it away. Yes! I threw it as far as I could. Men," she nodded morosely. "All men!" Then she reached across to Johanna and caught her hand. "Except your Martin. He has courage."

Johanna merely stared at her.

Someone across the table grunted. "Wait till he has a houseful of kids. Courage is what you lose a little every time you get another baby."

Georgie wanted them to talk about MacAndrews. Why didn't they talk more? Wasn't it something to talk about? Or wasn't old Kearns telling what really happened to him?

Mrs. Gerosa said to Johanna, "How cold your hand is. But your heart, it will soon be warm, eh? That is all that matters." She nodded knowingly toward the door. The sound of the men's approach confirmed her meaning: Martin's coming. The flashing light of the ladder truck played across the room as the truck was turned around, and even as the men came in, the low moan of the siren could be heard as the driver headed it down to the station house. The pumps and hoses would have to stay on for a while.

The women withdrew from the table as the men came in slowly, for they stopped at the door to remove their boots. Martin Scully went to Johanna directly. He was in his late twenties, good-looking but not in the way of most Hillsiders: his hair was light brown and his eyes blue. Georgie thought he looked like he'd been on an all-night bender just now, his eyes bloodshot and watery from the smoke. Georgie hung close to his sister.

Martin took her hands. She didn't seem anxious to give them, Georgie thought. "I'm sorry this had to happen to you, Jo," Scully said. "We tried our damndest . . ." He shook his head.

"I know," she said. Georgie thought she was trying to get her hands back.

"And I'm sorry about not calling you earlier," Martin said. "But every time I looked out, the booth was loaded with kids." Scully lived over the drugstore that had been his father's across the street from the *Crazy Cat*.

That was a lie, Georgie thought. The booth had been empty at a quarter to ten when he used it. He wondered for the first time if maybe old Martin didn't have another girl. What a laugh that would be, with Jo stiff-arming him right now.

Lodini, a powerfully built man, a garage mechanic by trade, fire chief by the election of his peers, strode across the room. "Where's the coffee?" he said to his wife, who plainly was hurrying to serve it. "Couldn't you hear us coming?"

He was always irritable with himself and his men after a fire they had not been able to bring under control, and he always took it out on the women.

"Beats hell how that thing got so far out ahead of us," he said, sitting down heavily at the table. "Rocco! Sit down here." He gave an imperative gesture.

Georgie looked at him, and moved with deliberate slowness, saying to himself: stay loose. He wasn't going to act like it was his fault Lodini and his men couldn't save a house. He was tempted even to take the offensive, to let him have a complaint or two right now. After all, he didn't have a shirt to his name now, not even the suit of his father's, which had just been made over for him; fifteen bucks old Gerosa had charged. No wonder his wife had pots and pans and blankets and stuff to give away. Georgie looked around. Where the hell was Daley? He saw him then, getting coffee from Mrs. Gerosa. He'd be listening.

Lodini deliberately glowered up at him over the rim of his coffee mug. After a long swallow, Lodini put down the cup. "Sit," he said to Georgie. Then he called Johanna. Georgie, with elaborate and clumsy politeness, got up to give his chair to his sister, and took the one next to her.

"Any idea how it got started?" Lodini said, looking from one of them to the other.

Johanna shook her head that she did not. She looked like a frightened rabbit, Georgie thought, like one that was caught in a trap but not dead yet.

"Georgie?" Lodini said.

"I think maybe . . . I don't know, but . . . let me tell you what happened tonight."

Johanna took her hands from the table and held them tightly in her lap.

"Go ahead."

Georgie ran his tongue around his lips. His mouth had suddenly gone dry. "Well, sir . . . I was hanging around the *Crazy Cat* earlier, you know, with the kids. I was supposed to be home early. It was maybe nine-thirty, quarter to ten when I got up home, but Jo was talking with the priest, with Father Walsh, so I went down to the basement and puttered around."

Lodini was drumming his fingers on the table, but Georgie didn't care now. He'd got started, the spit was wetting his mouth and he was going to come out all right. He was sure of himself, just saying Father Walsh's name, passing that part and seeing his sister take a deep breath. Man, did he know how she felt!

". . . Anyway, as soon as he was gone, Jo started giving me hell. I mean, maybe she's right. She's over-protective—

that's what the guidance councilor at school calls it. But it always makes me sore. You know, I'm no kid . . ."

"Get on with what happened," Lodini said.

"I'm coming to that. Jo was giving me hell, you know, about girls and all that jazz, and then I got on her about Martin not showing up being the reason she was sore at me. I must've said something I didn't mean, 'cause all of a sudden, Jo came at me like she was going to beat me up, trying to wallop me. I was smoking a cigaret, see, and she knocked it out of my hand. I thought I stamped out the sparks, but maybe that's how it started. Jo, she ran upstairs then, and I went back down to turn out the basement light. I was down there for a while and I smelled smoke. When I got upstairs the whole living room was full of smoke. Jo must've smelled it too, because she was coming down. We both ran outdoors—and I smashed open the glass on the alarm box and pulled the lever." He shrugged. "Maybe that isn't what started it, but it could've been."

Lodini said, "Kids your age shouldn't smoke."

Georgie said, "I know. Jo always says it's a bad habit of mine."

Martin Scully, knowing the many times Georgie had tried to eavesdrop on him and Johanna through the basement vent, asked, "What were you doing in the basement that was so important, Georgie?"

Georgie wasn't prepared for that question. "What's it of your business?" But realizing that he couldn't afford any mystery about himself, he took care of it in a way that would shut Martin up in a hurry. "If you gotta know, I relieve myself in the drain down there sometimes instead of going upstairs to the bathroom."

Lodini said dryly, but without intended humor, "It must've been a slow leak."

Martin laughed, though he was immediately ashamed for having done it in front of Johanna, but there was nothing pleased him more than to see Georgie, who made up his hair like a girl in front of a mirror, discomfited.

Georgie got up and walked over to Daley. "Gimme a cig-aret, will you?"

Daley obliged him, even started to light it for him. Georgie waited for that, a tribute to his authority.

Martin said, addressing himself to Lodini, "What's this about MacAndrews? Somebody was saying on the truck he was dead?"

Georgie and Daley looked at each other. Georgie steadied Daley's hand where it jerked away just as he'd struck the match.

"Keeled over and cracked his skull," Lodini said. "That's what I heard from Kearns. Heart attack."

A murmur of talk picked up in the room, turning on the death of MacAndrews and what it would mean at the plant.

Georgie said, loud enough for only Daley to hear, "I'll be a son of a bitch."

Daley looked as though he was going to bust out laughing or crying. Georgie gave him a soft punch in the ribs, a good-natured, but telling punch, and went back to his sister's side.

Lodini said, "You'd better call your insurance man in the morning, Johanna. Got a place to stay tonight?"

Johanna roused herself, trying to throw off the numbness that had settled on her while Georgie had told his story, part right and part wrong, but what matter? What he could have told . . . She shuddered. "Grandma Tonelli's," she said.

Martin said, "I'll take you up when you're ready, Jo. The boys can take my gear back to the station."

"I'll take it down for you," Georgie said. "Please, Marty, let me do it?" It was well known that he dearly loved to hang out around the fire station, and that night above all, he wanted to know everything that was going on.

"Okay, kid," Scully said, like he was patting him on the head, Georgie thought.

Jo was about to protest. She wasn't so keen on being alone with old Martin, Georgie figured, not after what happened between her and the priest. He knew his sister pretty well, a lot better than she knew him anyway, than anybody knew him. But he said ingratiatingly, "I'll come right back, sis. I promise."

5

Johanna thought she wanted more than anything else just to be alone. But she didn't want that either, she realized. Those few minutes alone after Father Walsh had gone, waiting for Georgie to come downstairs, had been too terrible. Not to understand other people—her mother, Georgie, even Martin sometimes—was bad enough, but not to understand herself was the worst of all. She had been truthful, trying to explain to Georgie—up to a point. She had meant to be entirely truthful, but when he described what he had seen, the way he put it—belly-rubbing with the priest—she knew that in his crude, sickening way, he was right. Father Walsh had put his arm around her, and she had felt . . . the same thing as when Martin had first kissed her.

Martin put Mrs. Lodini's shawl about her shoulders and doing it gave her shoulders a little squeeze. She wanted to pull away from him, to run, to hide. But where?

They went out from Lodini's, and she walked up the street, past the smoldering ruin on which the hoses were still playing water. Hell's own fury, fire. How just and quick God's judgment. She stumbled and recovered herself, shying away from the hand Martin extended to help her.

"Don't look back," Martin said. "It's like when your father died, Jo. You've got to look ahead and keep going that way."

If only it could be that way, not having to look back. Martin could say that: all his sins were clean, easily told in confession, she was sure, and therefore easily forgotten. She could not help but think of all the people going back innocently to sleep, seeing the lights going out in all the houses round.

"It could have been worse, you know," Martin said as they turned onto Mrs. Tonelli's flagstone walk. "Going up that fast if you'd been asleep . . . My God, Jo!" He made her stop by himself stopping. "We've got each other. That's all that counts, isn't it?"

She nodded. The wish that what she told was not a lie was as close now as she could come to telling the truth.

"Right," Martin said, and catching her hand he turned her round and pulled her into his arms. Mute and numb, she yielded to the embrace. Then fiercely, hoping an act of the will might also compel the heart, she forced herself to respond as in times past she had done so willingly. But memory of the dark moment still intruded, and even with Martin she felt degrading and degraded.

A tapping at the window above drew their attention. They looked up. The old lady was gesturing, a silhouette against the light. They went inside quickly.

"Such affairs should be conducted in private," she said. The truth was that she loved to spy on young lovers, her petulance of the moment due to the fact that she had not been able to see well enough where they had been standing in the shadows.

From childhood Johanna had been a little afraid of Mrs. Tonelli. She could not remember her except as a wrinkled old woman who commanded what she wanted, her dark eyes fierce even when her intention was merry. There were tales in the village of how beautiful she had been as a girl, emigrating from Italy with a man her social inferior whom she drove to success. She was still elegant in manner. Her children, except for Martin's mother who had died, had long since moved away from Hillside. She boasted of their independence whatever her true feelings about their having left her house. Now she lived alone, having only a servant who came in by day. She was parsimonious and rich by the standards of the community, and an offer of generosity from her automatically put the recipient on guard.

Mrs. Tonelli took them to the dining room first to show

the clothes she had laid out on the table. The room was pungent with the smell of mothballs.

"You have kept me waiting," she said. "You will take what you need."

"I'm sorry," Johanna said. "We had to stay. Mr. Lodini wanted to talk to us."

"And where is the fat one now?" To Martin she said, "Remember your Uncle Pedro?" She indicated the boy's clothing on the table. "He was that size at Georgie's age, the only one, and he grew out of it."

"Georgie will come soon," Johanna said. "You are very kind, Mrs. Tonelli."

"Your mother will also come here," Mrs. Tonelli said. "She has had her operation. After her recuperation, she will come. I cannot have an invalid. Tell me, Johanna, how much insurance?"

"I don't know."

"Your brother will know," the old lady said with a dry laugh. "Oh, yes, he will know." She went to the door of the room and caught up her long silk dressing gown, a graceful motion despite the rheumatic hand. "I have put out two of my nightgowns on the stairs. You will have the rooms over the kitchen."

Johanna murmured her thanks.

"Martin, get me my cane, and then go home."

He got her cane from where it hung near the hall door. "I'll go in a minute, Grandma."

Their eyes met. Their wills had clashed before. She had raised Martin after his parents' death. She had had the means to educate him as he had wanted to be educated—in the law. But she had refused. Pharmacy, yes. She had wanted him to go into his father's business, foreseeing him then spending out at least her lifetime in the village. At eighteen he had moved out of her house, ten years before. He visited her at least once a week, but what existed between them was a kind of armed truce. And she never failed to ask him how much closer he was now to being a lawyer.

The old lady went out, repeating mockingly, "In a minute, in a minute."

Johanna and Martin listened to the rasp of her slippers along the floor, diminishing. When there was only silence, Martin said, "We're going to get married, Jo. As soon as they can publish the banns."

Johanna found herself now having to think out each thing separately as though in a thick weariness: where she was, where she was to sleep . . . now this—the banns of matrimony; if anyone knows just cause why Johanna Rocco and Martin Joseph Scully should not marry . . .

Her mind simply broke away on the thought. "I've got to see mother first thing in the morning and tell her what happened. Why doesn't Georgie come?"

"Damn Georgie! Did you hear what I said to you?" Martin shook her as he might a child, gently but firmly. And she was a child in ways, or what was left of one at nineteen in Hillside.

"Yes, Martin, I heard you . . . thank you . . ."

"Don't thank me. Do you love me, or don't you? The world didn't come to an end tonight. Maybe this was a good thing. You and I can start from here. Our whole lives."

"Could we leave Hillside?" She scarcely knew she asked the question, yet it stirred in her a quickening of hope for the first time in many hours.

"Why?" Martin said, for of all the dreams they had shared, foremost was Martin's hope of doing something worthwhile for the town, of breaking the feudal hold of the Graham factory. Suddenly he was angry. "Jo, you've got more courage than this. What's the matter with you? Sure, your house burned down. It's tough, it's hard. You lost a lot of things you loved, but you didn't lose people. It's people that count, not things. What the hell are things but what makes us greedy, selfish? Look around this room—that what-not there . . ." He pointed to the Victorian glass cabinet, the elegant dishes and glassware gleaming behind the concave doors. "What good is it to the old lady? It's people she needs—like you and me. Only she'd like to put us in there with all those gadgets. That's what it means to care about things. That's not for you and me, Jo. We've got work to do in this world. Haven't we?"

"You sound like a Communist," she said, her purpose to stop him, even to hurt him.

"I don't care what I sound like. I know what I am and so do you. Or do you?"

"I know . . . nothing. Really nothing. Please go, Martin, or your grandmother will come back. Please!"

Martin just looked at her. There was the sound in the hall of a door opening, the scuffling of feet, the closing of the door.

"Is that you, Georgie?" Johanna cried out, her voice on the thin edge of hysteria.

Martin strode to the dining room door and threw it open. The boy was in the hall. He had been in front of the mirror when he heard Johanna's voice, and turned, gaping, when Martin opened the door.

Martin said, "Your sister's looking for you."

Georgie shuffled toward them. "They wouldn't let me on the truck," he said. "Bastards."

Martin said nothing. He went out and deliberately closed the door soundlessly behind him.

6

There had been little hope of finding anything in the way of footprints by the time Bassett and the technicians reached the Graham plant. Cement and fine gravel, the latter shuffled by many feet. A number of fingerprints were lifted within the office, but Bassett knew how long a chance it was that any of them would prove significant.

Kearns, failing in his attempt to describe the position in which he had found the night manager, simulated it himself, carefully spreading his handkerchief over the spot where the murdered man's head had struck the floor before putting his own head down. The photographer shot him from several angles. A picture for posterity, if nothing else. It could no longer be said with certainty that the swivel chair from which MacAndrews had risen—or tumbled—was in its original position. What Bassett did note was that MacAndrews had had the time sheets open on the desk, a pad and pencil beside them. The wastebasket yielded several pieces of paper from the same pad, a few minutes' comparison and study of which told him that MacAndrews had, during the evening, gone over the bookkeeper's record of the men's earnings. It told him something about MacAndrews, at least.

While Bassett was rooting in the wastebasket, Kearns was on the telephone, trying to narrow the time of MacAndrews' death. Dr. Tagliaferro had placed it between nine and eleven. Kearns called the shop foreman. The foreman had talked with the office manager sometime around eight o'clock. He then remembered that Jack Moss had gone off work two hours early, sick. Moss had tried to hold out till quitting time, but unable to make it, had clocked out at nine.

"It would be right on the hour," Kearns explained to Bassett, "so that he wouldn't be docked for more than two hours' pay."

"Would he have come in here to MacAndrews for his pay tonight?"

"I don't know that Mac would've given it to him," Kearns said, which did not precisely answer Bassett's question, but which again told him something about MacAndrews. "Likely he'd have gone home and had his wife come back at eleven for it."

On a hunch, Bassett asked, "Moss lives in Moontown?"

"Yeah," Kearns said, and taking a lead quite the opposite from Bassett's reasoning, he went on, "Moss is a big guy, strong as an ox. Kind of sour, too."

Bassett said, "Was his wife here at eleven?"

"Don't remember seeing her. But that don't mean she wasn't here. I mean, if Moss had done this thing, he'd 've gone home and sent his wife up anyway. You know, to cover up."

"We've got a lot of ifs in there," Bassett said. "Am I right that the men weren't paid tonight because of what happened?"

"That's right."

"The payroll is still in the safe?"

Kearns nodded.

"Do you have the combination?"

"No. I just got the day man down to check it—you know, just to be sure." He rubbed the back of his neck. "I see what you mean. If Moss got his money, that means he saw the rest of it in there, too, didn't he?"

"One more if," Bassett said, trying to conceal his impatience. Kearns wanted it both ways—on Moss—if he didn't get his money he was suspect, and if he did get it, he was suspect. It was not that Kearns was malicious: He was simply at the moment groping his way along the blind alley of prejudice without even knowing he was in its neighborhood. But by the same token, Bassett cautioned himself, the fact that Moss was a Negro was no grounds for presumption of innocence. "Does he drive to work?" Bassett was thinking of the availability of a weapon, a pipe or possibly a wrench.

"Don't know for sure. I think he rides with somebody."

"Then he'd have had to walk home tonight?"

"Can't really say," Kearns said.

"We'd better check him out tonight—just to be on the safe side," Bassett said.

"Better let me do it," Kearns said. "Those people are kind of touchy with strangers."

Bassett called the county coroner at Toby's funeral home, who had by then had time for at least a superficial examination of the wound. He would say no more than that the weapon was pipe-like—except of smaller bore than the standard plumbing equipment.

"The back end of a wrench, maybe?" Bassett suggested.

"Could be . . . ." The examiner thought about it. "No . . . more round. Like the barrel of a pistol—a big one. Damn it, I'm not qualified to say exactly."

"I understand," Bassett said. "Let's lift a piece of the scalp when you're through and have the lab boys give it the works. Was he bald?"

"No, a fine head of sandy hair."

"Good," Bassett said. Sometimes things clung to hair—dust, powder, anything sticky. And hair, especially soaked with blood, was likely also to cling.

Bassett went outdoors. It was almost two o'clock. The smell of smoke was on the wind. They were having quite a fire up the hill. He watched Kearns drive off, presumably on his way to have his talk with Moss. He remembered then that his own car was parked at the top of a good steep hill. There was just so much a man could do in one night. A late half-moon hung like a Christmas bauble alongside the plant smokestack.

Bassett walked a few steps from the office door and looked back. Through the two windows he could see the technicians finishing up. It would have been a simple matter for his assailant to have observed MacAndrews at his desk from outdoors, to have ascertained that he was alone. That he had been struck on the back of the head suggested that he had been taken by surprise. But what motive—the safe unopened? He then set himself to conjecturing the path of approach. There was but one door to the office shed although it was attached to the main building. If his assailant had come from the plant he would have come out the main door, some fifty feet away, and walked directly along the building, past the south wall of the shed, no doubt pausing to observe MacAndrews at his desk. To have approached the office from the street, he would have had to come along the drive from the parking lot or the railroad track adjacent to it. One lone boxcar sat on the tracks. To the north a Cyclone fence bordered the Graham grounds, also to the west. The northern and eastern walls of the plant were on the river. The gates to the parking lot and the railroad track lay open. He supposed that when or if the plant was shut down for an extensive time the gates were kept closed. There was no indication that that had happened for some time: The salt-river dampness had corroded the hinges.

Bassett turned back toward the plant, this time walking along the tracks, the beam of his flashlight running before him. A puzzling thing: the rails shone brightly in the moonlight for some distance. Abruptly then they were rusted, and some thirty feet beyond the rusted section sat the solitary boxcar. Bassett went on toward the car. A remarkable accumulation of beer cans lay along the track bed, some of them of recent deposit, more already settled under the long grass. The glisten of frost shone over everything. Before he reached the boxcar, Bassett speculated on its use: It was a perfect setup for gambling. There were no foot tracks in the frost, except his own, and they would vanish within an hour, he suspected, but trailing his light along the ground at the side of the car, he picked up something curious in its beam: a nylon stocking. Bassett took his time about disturbing it. He would not say it had lain there long, not as long as the beer cans and empty cigaret packages. It was damp to his touch, but not wet, and he suspected that if it had been there for any length of time it would have settled, like the other debris, under the grass. He laid his own handkerchief on the ground and gingerly lifted the stocking into it and put it in his pocket. He proceeded then to satisfy his earlier curiosity. The boxcar was not locked, the door rolled easily, quietly. It had been greased far more recently than had the car wheels. The car was empty, the floor strewn with straw. Odd. There was a curious smell, too, one vaguely associated with his own youth—from the straw perhaps, a visit to the farm. Bassett hoisted himself into the car, and gently raked the straw with his foot. His flashlight picked up stains beneath the fresh straw—old blood stains if he was not mistaken. The walls of the car were hung with lanterns.

As Bassett closed the boxcar door, he heard the low groan of the fire siren and the sound of the truck's motor. The fire would be out, the engines returning to the stationhouse. He went back briefly to the plant office, giving the technicians the stocking to take to the laboratory and instructions on lifting specimens from the boxcar. He himself headed toward the firehouse.

The station doors were open, only one truck having returned. A dozen or so men were cleaning equipment, others working on the truck. A man behind a small bar at the rear of the station was drawing beer.

"All right," somebody shouted. "We worked our asses off, didn't we? We couldn't save it, so to hell with it."

They were a gloomy bunch of men at the moment, Bassett thought, wildly jealous of their reputation as the best volunteer fire company in the state. A plaque over the bar testified to their excellence. He would himself be a long time forgetting the magnificent abandon with which they had fought. The times were short on this kind of heroism.

Bassett went to the one man there he recognized, the ambulance attendant, who was standing at the bar. The man nodded to him and said to the one drawing beer, "Give my friend here a beer, Tony. He needs it."

Bassett was grateful to be called friend. He said, "Do they know yet that MacAndrews was murdered?"

"Naw. You could tell 'em their own mother was murdered and it wouldn't make any impression right now."

When a number of men had come to the bar, every one of them giving Bassett what he might almost have called the evil eye—it was not a time for welcoming strangers here either—the ambulance man said, "This here's the county detective—that's what you are, ain't you?"

Bassett nodded. "Ray Bassett," he said.

A couple of men muttered some sort of greeting and went on to their beer.

The ambulance man, a young fellow with a flare for the dramatic, said then, "Old MacAndrews was bumped off, it turns out. No natural causes."

It was a long moment before the news seemed to take on any significance for the men present. Bassett would have liked to know which of them was Martin Scully, if he was among them, before the announcement. But in a community like Hillside, he wanted to be careful of the moment at which he singled a man out for his attention.

"Bumped off?" Tony, the acting bartender, said. "You mean murdered?" He was looking at the detective.

"I'm afraid so," Bassett said.

Somebody down the bar gave a short laugh. "Ain't that like old Kearns? A heart attack. Holy Jeez."

"It could've looked like it," the ambulance man said, having shared the assumption with the police chief at the time. "And Der Tag didn't say any different."

Bassett was not going to criticize Kearns in his own town. "Were any of you fellows on the night shift at the plant?"

"I was," Tony said.

Another man raised a finger without looking up.

"Me and Angie," Tony added.

Bassett kept trying to eliminate without asking the direct question. "Do you all work at the plant?"

"Not me," somebody said. "I work in my father's grocery."

"And Daley," Tony said, nodding at the tall, stringy kid at the end of the bar who looked as though he should have been home in bed. "All he does is go hunting when the boatyard closes up. Some life!"

Phil Daley wet his lips. "Cut it out, Tony."

Bassett had eliminated five of eleven men. There had to be a quicker way of finding out what he wanted to know. Then he remembered something Kearns had told him abut Scully. "I don't suppose there's any way of getting into the drugstore at this hour of the night, is there?"

Tony stretched his neck. "Where's Scully? He just come down, didn't he?" He called out, "Hey, Scully!"

The blond young man came around from the far side of the truck. He was a good-looking boy, Bassett thought, and as he drew closer, not quite as young as he looked in the distance. There were lines already in his face, strong lines; he was by no means a callow youth. He spoke to Bassett, obviously having heard everything said at the bar. "I have a key to the building, but not to the store. I live up over it, that's all."

"All I wanted was aspirin," Bassett said lamely.

"Hell," Tony said with a sweep of his hand toward a shelf at the back of the bar, "I got Alka-Seltzer, Bromo-Seltzer, Ex-Lax, and Anacin right here."

Bassett said, "I'll have one of each, please."

The men laughed then. They were all young, they had to be to sprint with every fire, to work all day, and turn out night or day whenever the alarm sounded. They would not brood long over their inability to save the house that night; they would talk about it, argue about what went wrong, and drill to see that the same mistakes did not happen again. Bassett had had his good moment with them. He did not want to push for camaraderie. He wouldn't get it anyway.

One of the boys sidled along the bar until he was standing next to Bassett. "How come you're in on it?" he asked, gesturing with his glass. "We got our own police, ain't we?"

This was more like the reception Bassett had expected. "Well, I guess you could say it's like the fire company from Anders Cove turning out to give you a hand tonight. I just rolled in to see if Kearns could use some help."

Scully asked him, "You didn't want me for anything, did you?"

"Not particularly," Bassett said so that the others might also hear it.

"Then I'm going home. I've had it."

"So have I," Bassett said, and to those at the bar, "Thanks for the beer . . . and all the other jazz." He indicated the row of medications Tony had set before him. It seemed to be the right word. He had picked it up from his son.

He discovered, reaching the street, that Scully was waiting for him. "MacAndrews was murdered," he said, as though needing private confirmation before believing it. "What for?"

"That would be pretty valuable information right now," Bassett said. "He wasn't the most popular man in town, was he?"

A gust of wind whirled round their legs, sweeping the debris of the street against their ankles. Instinctively they withdrew into the entryway of the darkened store. Its bleak window displayed an assortment of hunting equipment: knives, rifles, boots . . . and two stuffed pheasants.

"He wasn't the most unpopular either," Scully said.

"He was unpopular with somebody tonight." Bassett thought about his car at the top of a long climb. This was no place for interrogation. Besides, he wanted to see a witness's face talking to him. "I'd like to talk to you, Scully, but not here."

"Want to come up to my place?"

"That would be better," Bassett said. It could not be much worse.

As they bent their head against a sudden shifting wind and strode into it, Kearns drove up to the police station across the street. Bassett got directions from Scully on where he lived, and stopped to see Kearns.

He slipped into the police car before Kearns got out of it. "Mind driving me up for my car?"

"Moss'd be in the clear, I think," Kearns said on the way. "Damn fool foreman didn't tell me he had an infected hand.

That's what's wrong with him, running poison through his system. Had the doctor with him, ten o'clock for near an hour. He couldn't swat flies with that hand.''

"Did he stop for his pay?"

"No. He was damn near delirious. High fever, and he walked all the way. Why wouldn't he stop at the station? Somebody there would have run him home.''

Bassett did not say anything. The rest of the way Kearns brooded over the man from Moontown who had failed to ask for help when he needed it. "It isn't right, you know,'' he said finally, "the way those people look on the police. They need a lot of educating in more ways than one.''

Bassett didn't answer. They drew up alongside his car. There was no sign of fire in the ruin down the street. Only occasional puffs of smoke. Two men still patrolled the area. Bassett chose his next words with care although they sounded casual: "I'll check in with you in the morning, shall I, Chief?''

"That'd be fine,'' Kearns said. "Think I ought to put on some more men? I got two part-time boys on the job now.''

"Let's wait and see if we need them,'' Bassett said. The depressing vision ran through his mind of their possibly putting the killer on police duty—at twelve dollars per day.

The question Bassett asked himself climbing the dusty stairs to Scully's rooms was what kept young people in a town like Hillside. Their parents, he could understand. First generation American, their roots were here—family, their friends, their gardens, and the only jobs most of them had ever held; church and village hall, firehouse and tavern, politics and palaver, trapping crabs off the pier in summer, TV in the winter and a little gambling all year round. It wasn't a bad life—as long as the factory kept running. In fact, take out the television and put in a little medieval pageantry, and you could fade twentieth century America into an ancient village on the Mediterranean, where men carved sandstone perhaps, or quarried marble . . . except for one thing: beauty. In all the times he had driven through the town, he had seen but one monument, that to the war dead, and it resembled nothing so much as a giant machine-cut tombstone. Youth, he had always thought, craved beauty. What did the youth of Hillside crave?

He tapped on Scully's door, half-hoping to be admitted to an apartment that would give the lie to his somber view of the town. He was surprised with his first glimpse of the place, but not in the way he had hoped. The living-bedroom was whisper clean, but as bare of ornamentation as a laundromat. Not a picture, not a lamp except one hung low from the ceiling over the large table Scully obviously used as a desk. Whatever Scully was, the detective thought, he was not given to the pursuit of creature comforts. The chairs were straight-backed, without cushions. The floor was painted black. But once in the room, Bassett changed his mind. Along the wall, from door to window, was one large bookcase, loaded. It was large enough to cover almost one whole wall. And large enough, Bassett knew, to cover quite a fair-sized prejudice in himself. It would take some mighty vivid proof to convince him that a book-man was capable of brutal murder. And yet . . . there was a neatness to MacAndrews' killing, such neatness that Kearns had not suspected for a moment that any violence had occurred. Bassett frowned, thinking of it—and from weariness. He was well into doing a second day's work in one. The apartment was damp and cold, the heat in the building long since turned down for the night.

"I got some coffee I can warm up," Scully said. "Okay?"

"That would be fine." Bassett took the moment the younger man was in the other room to estimate his interests: law and labor books mostly, some school textbooks kept over from his days of formal education . . . high school books, Bassett would guess. There was an odd sort of contrast in jackets and typeface that suggested their owner had made his own leap from the course of general studies to some pretty advanced tomes in industrial law.

He went to the window where he could look down on the main street of Hillside. A hardware store stood opposite, the village hall next to it, with the single white light burning over the door to the police station. To the south of the hardware store was an empty building—or rather, a store converted to living quarters, for the window front was curtained. And next to that was the *Crazy Cat*, whatever that was. The sign, its lettering purposely askew, swayed in the wind, the face of a cat, its definition just perceptible from where he stood, had been painted between the words "Crazy" and "Cat." And, Bassett thought wryly, he had supposed Hillside without benefit of art. Behind the street of one- and two-story buildings, the Graham plant brooded like a quiescent volcano, dribbling thin smoke into the wind from its single stack.

"What's the *Crazy Cat*?" he asked when Scully returned with two mugs of steaming coffee.

"That's where the kids hang out . . . when they're not in the phone booth." He nodded by way of emphasis and Bassett looked back to see the booth where it stood in the shadow of the building. "In summer you can't hear yourself think for the jukebox," Scully added.

Bassett sipped the coffee. It was strong, bitter, and hot, what he needed. "You don't work on the night shift?"

"I go on it next week," Scully said. "We change over every two weeks."

"What happens when there's a fire and you're at work?" He was remembering the timeclock at the plant.

Scully shrugged. "There's enough men off work generally. A second alarm and some of us clock out for it, depending on what we're working on."

"What do you do at the plant?"

"I run a machine that folds boxes," Scully said with a touch of cold pride.

Bassett said, "MacAndrews was rapped on the head with a small round pipe—or something like it. I was wondering what kind of tools were used in the plant."

"There's machinery. I guess the engineers would have all kinds of tools."

"I guess they would," Bassett said. "What time was the fire alarm tonight?"

"At eleven-thirty-five."

Bassett set his cup on the table, lifted it then, and wiped

the circle of moisture from where it would have marked the wood.

"That's all right," Scully said. "It's got a good coat of wax."

"You'll make some woman a good husband." He glanced at the younger man, offering the weak levity.

The lines at Scully's mouth tightened for an instant. "That'll be the day."

"Where were you tonight—until the time of the alarm?"

"Right in this room—from five o'clock on."

"Working?" Bassett glanced at the books and papers neatly stacked on the other side of the table.

"Working," Scully repeated. "Though a lot of people in this town wouldn't call it that."

"Anybody call you—or come to see you?"

"Nobody. I don't have a phone. When I can get to it I use that booby trap across the street."

"But not tonight?"

"What are you driving at, Mr. . . . ."

"Bassett, Ray Bassett. I'm trying to help you establish an alibi . . . to account for your time."

"Do I need one?"

Bassett shrugged. "Let's put it this way—I'm trying to eliminate all possible suspects. You had a fight a couple of years ago with MacAndrews."

"It didn't take you long to find that out, did it?"

"What I should like to know for now," Bassett said quietly, "is whether anything happened tonight—think back now— that would corroborate your statement that you were here, in this room, something, someone on the street, say . . ."

"I understand," Scully said. "I do my best not to hear what goes on out there." The belligerence had gone out of his voice. "I heard the ambulance go by on the way to the plant. You always wonder about that, who's lost a finger or what. That's the worst time for accidents, at the end of the shift. And I've got my own reasons for keeping track of them. We've got a safety record like the Battle of the Bulge."

It was a strange symbol for so young a man to make,

Bassett thought. Maybe not. Maybe he just knew someone who had been there. Oddly, Bassett himself had been.

Scully stopped abruptly, to Bassett's regret. He would have liked to hear him elaborate of his own will on the Graham operation. Nor did he want to get the boy's back up again if he could help it. He purposely asked and answered his own questions: "You didn't go over to the plant to see what happened? No, you've already said you were here till the fire."

"One of the things I've learned, Mr. Bassett, trying to get somewhere—in labor relations, I guess you'd call it—is not to telegraph my punches. They can't keep secrets about who gets hurt on the job at the plant. I'd have found out."

Bassett nodded. "How long was the ambulance there? Do you know?"

"Twenty minutes maybe. By then I'd decided it couldn't have been serious. Or else it was fatal." Scully laughed grimly. "I remember that went through my mind too. I know it was a few minutes after the night shift came off before the ambulance left. You can hear the parade of cars go by here."

"And it was pay night," Bassett prompted.

"That doesn't take long, ordinarily."

"Just what is the procedure. Do you mind telling me?"

"At eleven o'clock MacAndrews and Kearns would be waiting inside the plant door. MacAndrews would have the box of pay envelopes and call off the names alphabetically. That simple. Ten minutes, maybe."

Bassett thought for a moment. "And if a man were to question the computation of his wage?"

Scully grinned. "I don't remember a man ever doing it. Except MacAndrews . . . someone else's wage, that is. There's a story that he found a mistake of seventy-eight cents once in the bookkeeper's figures."

"A careful man, MacAndrews. Wasn't he?"

"That describes him."

"At the time he died he seems to have been checking over the time sheets. When's the payroll made up, do you know?"

"Friday noon, for both shifts. I got paid at three o'clock."

"MacAndrews himself would come on duty with the second shift?"

Scully nodded.

"I'm trying to follow this payroll operation from beginning to end," Bassett explained.

Scully asked suddenly, "Was there a robbery?"

"No. But what I'd like to make sure is that there wasn't one attempted." Bassett felt that he almost had something. Then it escaped his mind. "The precaution was taken of having Kearns on hand for the walk from the office to the plant. In the afternoon, too?"

Scully nodded. "The chief also escorted the paymaster from the bank every Friday morning. And he'd stay around for an hour or so—as long as it took the cashier to make up the envelopes. We've always kidded about whether they didn't throw him five or ten bucks—whatever was left over."

Bassett snapped his fingers. "How many men are on the night shift?"

"Maybe two hundred."

"Have you got some index cards?"

"Happens I do," Scully said.

"And a few sheets of paper." In the next few minutes Bassett experimented with the mere physical routine of fingering one card and a sheet of paper, a card and a sheet of paper. He concluded: "It would have taken him a half-hour to check the figures on the envelopes against the time sheets. And he wouldn't have been satisfied without doing that, would he?" It was an academic question. "And I know for a fact that Kearns was in a meeting at ten-thirty last night. He left it in order to be back here by eleven. That means that MacAndrews tonight—and probably every pay night— opened the safe and checked the pay envelopes against his own figures . . . before Kearns arrived on the scene at all."

Scully said thoughtfully, "I guess I knew that all along— without knowing that I knew it, if you know what I mean."

"I don't. Explain, please."

"Everybody took for granted he checked the pay envelopes. I just never got to thinking specifically about when he'd have done it."

Bassett felt let down: the mountain laboring to bring forth a mouse. Everybody took for granted . . . Everybody was a lot of people, even in Hillside.

Scully sensed his disappointment. He said, "But then it's always the particular use of general knowledge that starts things rolling, isn't it, sir?"

"Yes, quite right," Bassett said, and he realized from that moment on that he wanted to know Martin Scully better—whether in connection with his investigation or outside it. One such lad out of a population of twelve hundred wasn't so bad, he thought. He got up. "I think we'd better go on from here by daylight."

"That won't be long coming," Scully said.

At the door, Bassett said, "In the meantime, try to remember some little thing—a noise, a smell, something on the street—so that I can check you out on having been here for the time you say you were."

"I have remembered something," Scully said. "It was a quarter to ten when I suddenly remembered that I was supposed to call my girl. And, as I always do before going down to the phone booth, I looked out to see if anyone was using it. When it's empty I go at a sprint. I don't always make it, but I didn't even try last night. I looked out just in time to see Georgie Rocco settle into the booth, and I knew the phone was tied up for the night."

"George Rocco—a quarter to ten," Bassett repeated. He made a note of the name and the hour. "We always know more than we think we do—except when we know less. Goodnight, Scully."

"Goodnight, sir. I won't leave town."

Bassett laughed and started down the stairs.

"Not till they kick me out of it."

An addendum Bassett wanted to think more about—but not at four in the morning.

7

When Johanna awoke she knew almost at once where she was despite the strangeness of the room. She had slept very little but she was seeing the bedroom by daylight for the first time. A row of dolls sat atop the dresser, looking at her with eyes that had not changed since leaving the manufacturer, though time had faded their clothes and hair. She wondered if any child had seen them since perhaps Martin's mother was herself a child.

She could not remember when last she had slept in a strange bed. She had not been a visiting child. Her father had always wanted her home. He hadn't ever said so exactly, but the moment he came into the house, he always used to call out first, "Where's my Jo-Jo?" Sometimes, to tease him, she concealed herself behind the door and watched him. When he got no answer to his call he heaved a great sigh and went along to the kitchen to see if her mother was home. "Papa," she would then call out. And always now when she remembered him it was as he turned around, his whole face smiling. She could remember the smell of his clothes as she ran full-tilt into his arms and got a moment's quick enveloping hug. He always smelt a little like damp sawdust, for he had worked in the carpentry shop at the plant.

To avoid the glare of the sun just rising over the tops of the half-curtains, she sank herself deeper into the bed. She had not lowered the window shade. With that association she remembered the whole sweep of the night's happenings. "Oh, papa," she said and, turning over in the bed, buried her face in the pillow.

She was roused by a rap at the door and a strange voice

calling out, "Miss Johanna? Wake up, miss. Breakfast in ten minutes. You hear?"

"Yes."

She listened as the footsteps padded on, and a few seconds later the voice repeated, "Breakfast in ten minutes." Then, "George, I'm putting a clean shirt in the bathroom, hear? Mrs. Tonelli says you put it on."

Johanna realized that it was Ida Grey, Mrs. Tonelli's maid, who came from Moontown every morning on the seven-thirty bus. Johanna sometimes met her, panting and resting at the top of the hill, when she was going down herself to the seven-thirty Mass. Mrs. Grey was a large, friendly woman, one of whose three sons had been in high school with Johanna at the time he was drowned in the creek. After that had happened, Mrs. Grey would stop her now and then and say, "You knowed my son, Albie?"

"Yes," Johanna would say. "I'll say a prayer for him, Mrs. Grey."

"He don't need it, thank you. But you say it just the same."

Georgie was late getting down to breakfast. He hadn't meant to be, but he couldn't make up his mind whether or not to wear the shirt Mrs. Tonelli had sent up to him. He tried it on, but it wouldn't button at the neck. Otherwise it fit him well enough. He had played a lot of hunches lately; he decided to play one more and wore his own shirt, dirty as it was at the collar.

"I appreciate you offering it to me, Mrs. Tonelli," he explained when she asked him why he wasn't wearing the clean shirt, "but I got a funny feeling about wearing other people's clothes. I'm kind of like you that way, independent. I figure you got to be if you're going to get some place in life."

The old lady merely grunted, but Georgie thought she was not displeased. She sat at the head of the dining room table like in an English movie, with Johanna on one side and him on the other and enough empty space at the other end of the table to shoot pool on. Johanna lifted her napkin and, looking at him, dabbed her mouth with it. What the hell did she think he was going to do with his—blow his nose in it? He shook it out with a flourish and spread it over his lap. Mrs. Tonelli took the cover from the platter of scrambled eggs, and heaped two big spoonfuls of them on a plate. Mrs. Grey took the plate from her and set it before Georgie. Then she brought hot muffins from the kitchen. This was how to live. Man! Johanna had scarcely touched the eggs on her plate. At home, George would have offered to finish them. But not here. No, sir.

"I've called the post office," Johanna said. "Mr. Jacobi said I didn't have to come in. So the first thing we must do is go up to the hospital and tell mother what happened."

"Why? I mean won't it worry her if we tell her right away?"

"She'd hear about it anyway. It's better that we tell her."

'Okay," Georgie said. "Have you got any money, sis?"

He was aware that the old lady had been looking from one to the other of them. She was kind of like a kid watching a game of catch.

"No, but I get paid next week."

Georgie took a deep breath. "Mrs. Tonelli, could I borrow some money from you—enough to buy some clothes and toothbrushes and things?"

"Do you want to work for it?"

"No." Georgie amended quickly, "I mean, not today or tomorrow."

But the old lady laughed. "Not today, not tomorrow. What do you want to do today?"

"I've got to play football this afternoon. It's the biggest game of the year."

"Ah-ha. You want to be a hero."

"I might just be," Georgie said, a little offended.

"And you will get a scholarship to go to college?"

He was not sure the old girl wasn't pulling his leg.

But Johanna took her seriously. She took everybody seriously. "He could if he got better marks in school, and he could do that if he tried. He's very good in some things—like mathematics and science."

Very good if you called passing good, Georgie thought.
But he realized Jo was trying to build him up. Jo knew even
better than he did that Grandma Tonelli had money, money
she wasn't willing to spend on Martin. For just a moment
Georgie contemplated saying that he'd like to be a pharma-
cist. But that was just too corny.

"And good in football," the old lady said, nodding her
head vigorously as she sometimes did as though she couldn't
stop nodding it.

Georgie said, "There's more than one way to skin a cat."

Mrs. Tonelli steadied her head then and looked at him for
a long moment. He did not like to be looked at like that, as
though she was making sure she could see him inside and
out.

"No, Georgie," the old lady said at last, "there is only
one way for every person, their own way. But I am sure you
are able to skin a cat." She rang the little silver bell at the
side of her plate. When Mrs. Grey came to the dining room
door, she said, "Will you bring my pocketbook, Ida,
please?"

Georgie said, "You'd better get ready, Jo, if we're going
to make the next bus."

"Take the red sweater, Johanna," Mrs. Tonelli said. "You
need some color. I will put the other things away in case Mr.
Proud here changes his mind."

"Thank you," Jo said, and left them.

Georgie remembered his manners at the last moment and
scrambled to his feet. He sat down again when Johanna was
gone.

"How much insurance did you have on the house?" Mrs.
Tonelli asked.

He had no idea, but he said without hesitation, "Twelve
thousand dollars." He could always say later that he had
made a mistake.

"Twelve thousand dollars. That would make a very good
dowry."

"For who?" Georgie blurted out.

The old lady leaned across the table and gave him a poke

with her long, stiff forefinger. "Well, not for you, you bull calf." She laughed aloud and after a moment's hesitation, Georgie joined in the laughter.

Catherine Rocco was alone in the semi-private room when her children arrived at the hospital. They had had to get special permission to see her outside visiting hours, and asking it at the admissions desk, Johanna had been aware of an exchange of glances between the nurses. She could not understand why hospital people always acted so superior. She was sure they were pretending. Nobody could feel that superior all the time.

Jo and her brother never knew what to expect of their mother on normal occasions, much less confined to a hospital bed. The day before she had been sitting up, laughing, making jokes to the woman in the bed across the room, a woman whom it had hurt to laugh but who had laughed nonetheless. Now, although her bed had been partially raised, Mrs. Rocco lay back in the pillows and stared straight ahead as though she did not even see the children come into the room.

Georgie noticed the funny smell in the place. He hated hospitals even more than schools.

Johanna took in the bleakness of the room, the screen set back against the wall, the stripped bed opposite her mother's. She too noticed the smell, a little sweet, a little foul, and she suspected at once what had happened.

"Hello, mama." She went round the bed and, leaning down, brushed the cold forehead with her lips. Immediately she took a piece of tissue from the side table, saturated it with cologne from the bottle Martin had sent her mother, and patted the sick woman's cheeks and forehead with it.

The dark eyes, so much like her own, brightened, acknowledged and were grateful.

"She was terribly sick, mama," Johanna said quietly of the woman no longer occupying the bed across the room.

Her mother's eyes welled up with tears.

"Poor mama," Johanna said, and patted awkwardly at her arm.

Georgie stood gawking at the empty bed, finally catching on.

Mrs. Rocco motioned for some tissue. She wiped her eyes and blew her nose, wincing a little at the pain too hard a blow had caused her. "I said the prayers for the dead for her with Father Walsh. And nobody came but him."

"And you," Johanna said soothingly. She had a way, this girl, of making people know their own importance. "You were her friend."

"So soon," her mother said. "A few days only and we were friends. Time is a funny thing . . . a minute can be a lifetime. And what is a lifetime?" she sighed and answered herself: "A minute, that's all. Georgie, stop gawking and come here to me."

He shuffled slowly around the foot of the bed and stood at her side. "Hi, mama."

She looked him up and down, the powerful shoulders, the pink plump cheeks and pouty lips that made him remind her sometimes of the cherubic faces around the Virgin on painted holy cards. His hair looked to have been plastered onto his head. It made him stand up straight anyway, trying to keep it in place.

"Mrs. Moran was right, may she rest in peace. 'Oh-h-h, Mrs. Rocco,' " his mother tried to mimic the brogue of the departed Irishwoman, " " 'he's fadin' away to a ton.' ' "

"We had an accident at the house, mama," he said, wanting to get the worst over with as quickly as possible.

"Father Walsh already told me. It did not matter so much—after what happened there this morning." She nodded toward the empty bed.

"We haven't got along very well without you, mama, have we?" Johanna said.

Her mother lifted herself up carefully while Johanna fixed the pillows. In changing her position, Mrs. Rocco exposed one breast, round and plump, the nipple puckered. Georgie scowled but he could not take his eyes from it. His mother made a sound of mock reproval and drew her gown across her breast with exaggerated modesty. There was something close to mirth in her eyes, the eyes that but a moment before had been laden with the tears of mourning.

Georgie moistened his lips.

"It was an old house," his mother said. "We are not so old, I'm not." She ran her fingers through her dark hair that showed not a strand of grey. "Dr. Tagliaferro says it will not matter, my operation. Soon I will be younger than ever. Johanna, give me the mirror and the comb. In this hospital nobody takes care of the living. To the dead they come quick."

Her children watched her repair the brief ravages of sorrow for her friend. They were accustomed to the changes in her moods, and to her, sorrow was no more than a mood. Sometimes Johanna thought it even less—a pose. But for the sake of peace she had always gone along, even as her father before her, with the mood her mother fancied at the moment. Her tempers were too terrible.

She looked up suddenly at Johanna. "Why don't you wear a little lipstick?"

"I don't have any. We didn't have time last night to take anything, not even papa's picture."

Mrs. Rocco's eyes flashed at her daughter, suspicious of an implied rebuke. But she said, "Father Walsh said the fire happened very quickly."

"He ought to know," Georgie blurted out. "I mean, he was there just before it started."

The color shot up in Johanna's face. Nor was it missed by her mother who chose from that moment on to play yet another role. "So the priest was there? He didn't tell me that. What did he want, Johanna?"

"He just stopped after visiting Mrs. Tonelli. We're staying with Mrs. Tonelli, mama. She wants you to come also—as soon as you're better."

"Why did he stop to see you? To talk about me?"

Johanna shook her head.

"To talk about *me*, I'll bet," Georgie said, trying to mend a damage he, for once, had not intended to cause.

"About you he talks to me," his mother said, thumping

her breast as in a *mea culpa*. "What are they saying about me down there? Eh? What do they say so that a priest comes to talk to my daughter?"

Johanna shook her head. She tried not ever to hear what was said about her mother, and people tried not to say anything about Catherine Rocco in front of her children, suddenly in their presence putting on the smiles of innocence. But like all covert malice, the smiling subterfuge served only to accent it. And Johanna *had* talked with Father Walsh about her mother; there was a thread between that conversation and what had happened in the hall. She just realized it then, remembering beyond the instant. The priest had been very careful to say nothing ill of her mother, but at the same time to explain that she was still a young woman, that she ought to be able, nay, encouraged, to marry again. And all the while both he and Johanna knew, although no word of it was said between them, that marriage had never been a bond to Catherine Rocco. It had merely bound one man to her for as long as he had lived. That was where the mercy of God had come into their conversation which she so well remembered: "We are all at the mercy of God as well as of one another. And for that we can be grateful. He has so much more of it than we have."

"What do they say about my operation?" her mother demanded.

"I don't know, mama. I don't even know—if they know."

"Ho-ho, they know." Her mother nodded vigorously. "They would all like the same disease."

Johanna's face was flaming.

"Hey, what's going on?" Georgie said.

"You aren't old enough to know," his mother said. "And you are a boy, thank God. How is your girl friend?"

"All right, I guess." He hadn't thought much about Rosie since leaving her at the *Crazy Cat*, a million years ago.

Mrs. Rocco laughed. "I've forgotten who it is." She winked at her son. "And so have you. Tell the truth."

"No, I haven't. Rosie Gerosa."

"She is a lump." Georgie scowled. "All right, a lump of sugar," his mother added.

Georgie grinned. "Yeah."

"I think you're both being awful," Johanna said.

"Yeah?" Georgie said. It was an old alliance, his and his mother's.

Mrs. Rocco looked up at her daughter. "My little puritan. And how is Martin? Now there is a man. A knight. A shining knight in a paper box."

The scathing contempt implicit in the words cut Johanna to the quick. And frightened her. It was like being caught in a malignant dream, when these two got going, one topping the other. She was on the verge of admitting to herself that her mother was wicked. And Georgie had the same way, a way of making things dirty, which she held sacred. But she herself? Was she not flesh of their flesh—she, who could thrill to the touch of a priest's hand? She felt faint and caught up Martin's cologne, which she splashed in her hands. Holding them to her face, she was revived.

Georgie said, "I'm going to be sick to my stomach if I stay here, ma. This place smells awful."

"It's time for us to go anyway," Johanna said. "They don't allow visitors at this hour."

"They don't allow!" her mother mimicked. "Nobody allows in this world. But if you take what is coming to you, all of a sudden it is allowed. Mr. Mancuso has our insurance policy, Johanna. Call him up. We are going to need the money to find a place to live. And for clothes. Everything burned, eh?"

"Yes."

"All right. What was there to burn? It's not too late to start over."

"That's what Martin said."

"For Martin it is too late," her mother said with an impatient wave of her hand.

Johanna could not understand her mother's dislike of Martin; it was like a wound to the girl that her mother reopened with a sudden thrust every time it seemed about to heal. And

the worst of it was, in front of Martin her mother was her
most ingratiating, smiling, curious about his studies—and
that was what she made most fun of behind his back: a man
of twenty-eight studying books. She was even affectionate
toward him, flirtatious, so that Martin sometimes blushed
and Johanna felt ashamed.

"Ma, why can't we live with Mrs. Tonelli? She invited
us—you too," Georgie said. "Boy, real napkins on the table.
Like pillowcases. And a little bell. All she has to do is ring
it and Mrs. Grey comes in and says, 'yes, ma'am.' "

"When you have that much money everybody says, 'yes,
ma'am,' but not Catherine Rocco, not to any woman. I would
rather live in a barn as long as it was my own."

"So would I," Johanna said.

"Okay," Georgie said, a little pouty. "Come on, sis. I
got to be at the fieldhouse at one o'clock and we got things
to get first."

Johanna said, "Do you want me to bring you anything,
mama?"

"A million dollars. How about that?"

"Seriously," Johanna said.

"Seriously, Johanna . . ." Her mother looked at her with
a cold penetration. ". . . I am going to be ready to leave the
hospital in a day or two. Are you glad?"

"Of course, I'm glad."

"I don't know why you should be," her mother said, and
turned away her head.

Brother and sister walked the half-mile distance from the
hospital to the shopping district. It was actually the first time
they had been alone since the fire, Dr. Tagliaferro having
picked them up at the bus stop and given them a ride directly
to the hospital. There was something Georgie had to know
because a lot of things depended on it. "Jo, what did ma
mean about the priest?"

"I don't exactly know, Georgie. I don't always understand
mama myself."

"I mean, I didn't tell her," Georgie said. "I couldn't have, even if I wanted to."

"I know."

"What did she mean, then?"

Johanna drew a deep breath. "It's just that mama might want to get married again."

"Who to?"

"I don't know. Somebody."

"You don't just marry *anybody*."

"Sometimes you do!" Johanna cried out—half in anger, half in frustration. Not from anything said by her mother, by Father Walsh—but from silence itself, Martin's, the neighbors'—and from things half-said, and the flowers she had seen in her mother's room, she knew. She had known well enough not to ask who the flowers had come from, not even to comment on them. All the times before her operation, her mother had been going away—to doctors, she had said, to hospitals in the city where she had to stay a day or two, never long enough to visit. Johanna knew. Everybody knew now—except Georgie.

And Georgie at that point arrived at a sudden conclusion of his own. "Jo, ma's got a boy friend, hasn't she? That's what it's all about, ain't it?"

"Isn't it," Johanna corrected mechanically. "I think it is in a way."

"I'll kill him!"

"Oh, shut up, Georgie. You aren't going to kill anybody, and it doesn't help saying things like that."

Georgie stopped stock-still, going slowly over in his mind fragments of things he had heard and not understood between mother and daughter, and other things he had heard—about Dr. Tagliaferro, for example. "Did ma have an abortion, Jo?"

"You shouldn't even say such things. You don't know what you're talking about."

"I know plenty. I got ears. Old Doctor Tag—I've heard the guys talking about him. 'That abortionist.' I've heard it, Jo."

Blessedly for Johanna they had to be quiet for a moment,

approaching a woman who was waiting for her dog to make up his mind which side of the tree he most fancied. The woman said "Good morning" as they passed. Johanna answered her.

"That's just their way of talking about Dr. Tagliaferro," she tried to explain rationally when they were beyond the woman's hearing. "It's because he treats women for . . . internal troubles." She wasn't sure herself she knew what that meant, but it sounded knowing. "Even so, they shouldn't say that. Abortion is a terrible sin . . . and it's against the law."

"What's 'internal troubles'?"

Johanna drew a deep breath.

"All right," Georgie said. "What kind of an operation did ma have?"

"It's called a hysterectomy."

"What does that mean?"

"Well, for one thing," Johanna said, trying to be very careful, "if she was to get married again, she couldn't have any more children."

"Man!" Georgie plunged one fist into his other hand like a ball into a baseball mitt. He did it again. "The bastard!"

"Georgie!"

He glanced at her, his eyes aglint with fury. Excited with it. "You women sure split hairs, don't you? Oh, man . . ."

His sister shook her head.

"What's the difference between an abortion and a hyst . . . whatever it is?"

"There's a great difference. There is!"

"Nuts." He stopped again, abruptly, awkwardly, for he had been trying to pace his steps to his sister's. Johanna had to turn round to him. "You know where the difference is, sis?" He pecked at her forehead with a stubby finger. "In your upstairs room. In your head, I mean. That's where it is." Then with a rare bit of insight, he added, "And you can't stay there all your life."

8

County Detective Bassett slept until nine o'clock, an achievement ordinarily impossible among his houseful of youngsters. His wife had managed to keep the youngest in the kitchen, and the fact that it was Saturday took care of the older ones. The older they got the better they liked bed—in the morning. Bassett called his office and then Kearns whom he was pretty sure he wakened. Calls to the Hillside police station were, at certain hours, automatically put through to the chief's house. Bassett made out his schedule for the day only to have it changed at breakfast by his son. He had quite forgotten his promise to go to the football game that afternoon, and it was Newport's big game of the year . . . with Hillside.

"Well, that's neat anyway," he commented, hearing where they were to play.

"It'll be neat if we beat them," his son, John, corrected.

Bassett promised to be there. As usual, his wife inveighed against football as a barbarous sport. "I say that any game where the players have to wear armor for protection is just plain medieval."

"Armor she says," her son chided.

"Nor," said Bassett, leaving the table and giving her a light kiss on the forehead, "was there anything just plain about medievalism."

He thought about her views on football as he drove across the mountain, musing on what sports did not require armor. He was reminded of Martin Scully's barefisted fight with MacAndrews.

He sat in the car for a moment in front of the MacAndrews house. The house had been painted within the year, white

66

with green shutters. On the northern edge of the Hillside limits, it bore little in common with the houses at the heart of the village. It looked New England, and somehow virginal even from the outside. But that, Bassett thought, was because he knew that MacAndrews, a bachelor, had lived with his sister, a spinster named Grace. His visualization of her was as a tall, flat woman, thin-lipped, greying hair parted in the middle and gathered into a wren's nest at the back of her head. He rang the bell, noticing idly that the doors had recently been painted a thick black, grimly prophetic on the painter's part.

Except that her hair was white, he had been right on Miss MacAndrews' appearance—even to the center part. She was neither hostile nor warm in her greeting, but she opened the door to him and, seeing his identification, allowed him to enter. The house was as neat inside as out, the upholstered chairs primly decked in fresh antimacassars. The one ashtray in the room was a stand, the chrome recently polished—since MacAndrews' death, he would say. And obviously during his lifetime it had been the only place he was allowed to put his cigaret ashes. Bassett would have taken an oath that upstairs all MacAndrews' belongings were laid out, sorted for disposal.

He murmured his solicitations.

"I could have told them right off it was not a natural death," Miss MacAndrews said. She spread her skirt with the backs of her hands and sat down opposite him, choosing a straight chair. Bassett sat forward in his; to call any chair easy in this house would be a misnomer. "James was in sound health—for which we gave thanks to Almighty God every day of our lives." There were traces of a Scotch accent in her speech.

"Would you say he had enemies in the town?"

"Oh, he had them a-plenty. The Mafia were out for him, you know."

"The Mafia?"

"Don't pretend you haven't heard, Mr. Bassett, and you in the District Attorney's office. They run the gambling in

Hillside the same as in the rest of the country. And other things as well—if you know what I mean.''

"I'm not sure that I do," Bassett said, although he was fairly sure that when a woman like Miss MacAndrews referred to ''other things,'' it could only mean sex.

"Then you'll find them out from other than me," she said, confirming his suspicion.

"Your brother was opposed to the gambling?''

"Aren't you?'' she challenged.

He did not feel called upon to affirm his own virtue in this instance. He knew that MacAndrews had been one of the complainants to the District Attorney's office. "I was thinking—that unless I'm badly mistaken—it was going on all the same right under his nose.''

"It was, Mr. Bassett, and he could not do a thing about it. There are those who will tell you James was a company man—that's the Communist word for it, a company man. Because he was loyal to his employer. He *was* loyal, and that's a word they know nothing about. But he was also a man of his own principles, James. And when the company forbade his interference in the simple pleasures—their words, not mine!—of the workers, James obeyed his conscience and went to the District Attorney.''

"He seems to have made enemies on all sides,'' Bassett said, and hoped immediately that the irony had not come through in his voice.

"The righteous are as proud of their enemies as they are of their friends.''

Rather prouder, Bassett thought, but merely nodded assent. "I wonder if maybe you and I couldn't sort a few of them out individually, Miss MacAndrews . . .'' He waited, hoping she would volunteer names as readily as opinions. But whoever or whatever her and her brother's enemies, silence was not among them. The kitchen clock was no more at home with it than she was.

"What about this young fellow, Martin Scully?'' he finally prompted.

"Aye, there's one,'' she said. "Red as the flag of Russia.

It is my opinion—and I'm not the only one who thinks it—he's in the pay of the Communists. Mind, that's only opinion, I would not say it to everyone. But I ask you this: why would a young man with his abilities stay in a menial factory job in this day and age if there wasn't something—or somebody making it worth his while?''

"How long has he been in his present job, do you know, Miss MacAndrews?''

"Near ten years, I would say. I know it's seven since he started making trouble . . . secret meetings.'' She leaned forward and said the two words in a half-whisper.

They could not have been very secret, Bassett thought. "I'm not sure I understand,'' he said.

"One group and then another—hand-picked of the men—where he brought in the labor organizer to talk to them. If they'd all got together at the same time, you see, they'd have run the man out in a hurry. But in a small group they'd listen, and every one of them would be asked to say something. And one would take his cue from the other, building up his own importance. These people are children, Mr. Bassett. The priest or the politician can lead them anywhere.''

"Still,'' Bassett said, "it didn't come to much in the end, did it? The plant still isn't unionized.''

"It most certainly is, sir. They have their own union. James MacAndrews helped set it up for them.''

"Yes, of course. What I meant was, they have no outside affiliation.'' He intended the word "outside'' to conciliate her, giving it emphasis.

"They do not, but it's not for want of Mr. Scully's endeavor. He's in constant correspondence with this, that and the other of them, making reports and surveys—I dare say.''

Bassett was very much aware of the "I dare say,'' for it suddenly amended with caution an, until then, uninhibited flow of opinion and information. Someone had been providing MacAndrews with a regular account of Scully's activities.

"Do you honestly think, Miss MacAndrews, that Scully could have had anything to do with your brother's death?''

"I did not say that!" Her proud head quivered with the vehemence of her answer. "Whatever I think of Martin Scully—and I do not approve of his ideas for a minute—but I do not think he would strike a man behind his back. James had a certain respect for him, for all that they were enemies."

"They had an actual fist-fight once, didn't they?"

"They did, and it was a fair fight. James asked for it, and he got it. It was the only way he could keep the men's respect. From then on he was manager in person as well as in name."

Bassett nodded his understanding. "Did your brother say anything—or was there anything in his behavior to suggest that he was uneasy or perhaps even fearful lately?"

"I've already told you—the Mafia were out to get him."

"He had had some sort of warning?"

"He had. Did you notice our front door was recently painted?"

"I did," Bassett said.

"It was white till the day before yesterday. Sometime during Wednesday night a black hand was painted on it."

"Painted—or was it a handprint?"

"It was the size of a man's hand, if that's what you mean."

"Did you tell the police?"

"Mr. Kearns came to see it. James and he said it was a Halloween prank. But that was only to make me feel easier, I know."

"Well, we'll look into it just to be sure," Bassett said. He picked up his hat from where he had set it on the rug at the side of the chair. "If there's anything comes to your mind—or anything we can do, please call me—or the police chief."

She rose stiffly with him. "I don't suppose I'll need protection—now that they've got James."

"Unless you've got vital information, something that might lead to his killer, I shouldn't think so."

"I consider what I told you vital, Mr. Bassett."

He said soothingly, "I probably should have said 'specific' information."

"Isn't a black hand specific enough?"

Lord, lord, he thought: what would it be like to live year in year out with a woman who pecked over her obsessions like a crow at a corpse? "Not when it's been blacked out with a fresh coat of paint, Miss MacAndrews."

Nonetheless he drove slowly along the River Road watching for other evidences of pre-Halloween mischief. Not many youngsters successful in the perpetration of one prank can resist the temptation to try another, and yet another until they are caught. But Bassett saw none, and when he reached the Hillside police station, he asked Kearns about it.

"Oh, hell," the chief said. "I knew she'd tell you about that. She's been hipped for years on that subject—the Mafia. Everybody knows it. I can tell you for a fact, Bassett, it *was* a kid's prank."

"If you say so," Bassett said. He knew better than to antagonize Kearns by persistence over such an incident, but he would have liked to have had the matter more convincingly settled in his own mind.

Kearns was aware of his companion's doubts. In the car, while they were driving around to the Graham plant office, the chief said, "You got kids?"

"Four of them."

"What if one of your kids did a thing like that?"

"I'd give him a reason not to do it again," Bassett said.

"But being the police chief, you wouldn't advertise the fact that it was your own kid that did it?"

"No, I don't suppose I would."

"Some kids got big ears." Kearns' neck was showing high color.

Bassett grinned. "And big hands."

Kearns glanced at him and smiled, a broad, warm smile that would make up for many shortcomings.

A meeting with the New York representative of the Graham Company was not Bassett's notion of how best to proceed with the investigation of the murder, and several times during that half-hour session he was hard put to hold his temper. Kearns was treated as though he were in the company's employ, not that of the people of Hillside. The company wanted the murderer found not so much for justice's sake as to assure the stability of the plant. He heard for himself the dictum by which Graham had kept its employees in line for over a generation: "We're under pressure now from our shareholders to close this plant and move the entire operation south." It occurred to Bassett that just possibly history would pass Mr. Graham's spokesman: one day soon, his southern management might just have to threaten to move that operation to Hillside.

Six men in all were present at the meeting: the day manager, the night foreman, the mayor of Hillside, Chief Kearns, Bassett, and the man from the top office, Alden Royce by name. At a well chosen moment Bassett said, "I was just thinking about the Brinks robbery in Boston a few years ago—some two million dollars. But it didn't put Brinks out of business."

"Meaning?"

"We're by no means sure that there wasn't an attempted robbery here last night. That would seem the most likely motive—to an impartial investigator. If such was the case, MacAndrews may have died in the line of duty."

"That I have no doubt," Royce said, and added quickly, "that he died in the line of duty."

"Then why not vote his sister a compensatory tribute—and let the police get on with their work?"

Royce turned to the man sitting next to him. It happened to be the village mayor, Frank Covello. "Who is this man?" he said, referring to Bassett.

Covello wasn't sure himself. Bassett answered, "I'm a detective, working out of the District Attorney's office."

"Ah-ha," Royce said, as though now armed with a certain sinister knowledge of Bassett.

Bassett, giving not a damn for Royce or his operation north or south, nonetheless knew that to keep his own position sound in this case he had to justify himself with the local people. "I'm working under the instructions of Police Chief Kearns."

"Then one of the first things in which Mr. Kearns should instruct you, young man, is the economic realities of Hillside."

"Its economics are not my concern, sir. Nor, if I may say so, do I think they're Chief Kearns'."

Kearns rubbed the back of his heavy neck. "For a fact, that's so," he said. "In our house it's my wife that handles all that business."

Kearns' seeming obtuseness mollified the company executive—and Bassett, getting to know the police chief, doubted that the remark came out of obtuseness. No quicker snare was ever laid for an arrogant, facile man than to set him at table with a ponderous one.

Kearns, Bassett and Mayor Covello left the plant together.

Covello, a round, cheerful man who in his own home, and indeed in all things, was for peace at all costs, complained, "What does he want from us?"

"I was asking myself the same question," Bassett said. "Do they want to close the plant? Are they looking for an excuse?"

"No, I don't think it's that," Kearns said. "They're making money. Paid an extra dividend last quarter. The thing is, it pays them sometimes to slow down part of the Hillside operation. The thing about Hillside is, they don't have to work at capacity to make a profit. And the population here's been geared to capacity since the war. In other words we got more people than jobs to go around."

"I thought you didn't know anything about economics," Bassett said.

The chief grinned. "Is that economics?"

Bassett took a long look at the grounds of the plant, his first good view of them by daylight. He pointed to the single boxcar on the tracks. "Any idea what that's used for?" He had not yet received the laboratory report on the scrapings he had ordered taken from the stained floorboards.

"Getting out of date now, aren't they?" the mayor said. "The trucks have taken over. Not that I mind, of course, since that's my business." He turned a puckish sort of face up to Bassett's and stuck out his hand. "Glad to have met you." To Kearns he said, "Let me know if there's any way I can help out." He got into his car and drove off.

Bassett realized that neither man had answered his question on the boxcar. "I want to have another look over there by daylight."

Kearns nodded and followed him. Bassett had wondered if he would. He pointed out the beer cans, cigaret packages. Kearns said nothing. It was in the shadow of the car that the chief stooped down and picked up a woman's stocking. He scowled, looking at it. "What the hell is this?"

Bassett looked to see what he had. "Well! That makes a pair. I found one last night." He took a cellophane bag from his pocket and held it open so that Kearns could drop his find into it. "The other one's at the lab . . . I wonder if they're mates." He thought about it for a moment. "Interesting. Now . . . the boxcar."

"I can tell you what it's not used for," Kearns said.

Bassett looked at him.

"It's not used for hanging silk stockings outside of," Kearns said.

Bassett laughed. "Nylon," he said. "But I agree with you—silk stockings sound much better, don't they? Nothing sensuous about nylon."

At the last minute before Bassett would have rolled open the door, the police chief said, "I know what the car's used for."

Bassett turned back. "I . . . thought you might," he admitted. "What about the mayor? Was I putting him on the spot, too?"

"Man, you sure were. It's him raises the cocks up on the hill there."

It took Bassett a few seconds to grasp the significance of what Kearns had just told him; suddenly then he realized what the stains were: blood drawn from each other by fighting gamecocks. And the smell: it had been chicken dung!

"Jesus Christ," he said with considerable fervor.

* * *

Bassett and Kearns dropped in together to see Pete Morietti, owner of the *Crazy Cat*. Pete was scraping the grill at the back of the shop and the smell of cooking fat mingled with the faint fumes from the space heater. Both were odors associable with poverty in Bassett's mind, taking him back to his days of case work in the city tenements when he little dreamed he would wind up in law enforcement. The two men sat down at the counter. Pete, hard of hearing, was unaware that they were there. He had no other customers. A small, tinny radio was tuned in to the Italian Hour. The jukebox was silent.

Kearns said, "How did you get into police work?"

Bassett said, "I was just wondering the same thing myself. Why, the army made an M.P. of me. They kept me on the other side for a long time, working with refugees. When I got back I went to work out of the Kings County D.A.'s office—on juvenile delinquency. I was married—I have four youngsters. A few years ago I got caught in the crossfire of a gang war. My wife said enough. I wasn't going to be much use in that area any more, anyway. Nobody confides in a cop who's been beaten up; they figure he has a grudge. So we came out to a healthy environment."

Kearns grunted. "It's a hell of a way to make a living, ain't it?" Environment was something he thought very little about.

"Sometimes."

Kearns called out, "Hey, Pete!"

Morietti turned and squinted at them over the top of his glasses. He shuffled forward, bringing the grill pan and replacing it over the burners. He wiped the grease from his hands on his apron, and turned off the radio. Without asking, he brought two coffee mugs from under the counter and filled them with a thick, black brew. "Why don't you speak?" Pete pointed to his bad ear.

Kearns shouted an introduction.

"I can hear," Pete said, pointing then to his good ear. He

gave Bassett his hand across the counter—a cold hand that felt as boneless as rubber.

Kearns had promised that Morietti would be able to tell them very little. He was short-sighted as well as partially deaf, and he seemed likely to fulfill the chief's promise.

"They come and go like hungry cats," he explained. "Sometimes a dozen times a night. They got a path worn inside and out to the telephone booth. Who do they call, I sometimes wonder. Everybody's in here. But in and out, all night."

Slowly, with coaxing and prompting, the two policemen compiled a list of seventeen names, local teen-agers who Morietti was reasonably sure had been in the shop the night before. When he mentioned Georgie Rocco, he said, "The Rocco house burned to ashes, eh?"

The chief nodded.

"The wages of sin." The old man shook his head.

"Do you remember what time the boy left here?" Bassett asked, for Rocco was the youngster with whom he had to check out Martin Scully's story of wanting to use the phone booth.

Pete said, "The only time I know for sure is eleven o'clock. That's when I start to close up the shop." He thought for a moment. "At eleven o'clock his girl friend was still here, I can tell you that." He shrugged. "Maybe they had a fight."

"Or maybe he got a new girl," Bassett suggested.

Kearns said, "The kids in this town are pretty settled that way. They like going steady."

He and Kearns compiled a second list of names: three boys and two girls who had been in the shop at closing time. Bassett drank as much as he could of the bitter coffee, and they moved on.

The sun shone brightly on the motley fronts of the buildings facing east, making them if anything less attractive in daytime than at night. Here and there a cheap composition facade had been layered over the timbered walls fronting the streets. Incongruous, the gingerbread eaves of a prettier day in Hillside architecture remained on a building, giving it the aspect of a child-made valentine. All the store windows were streaked with soap, reminding Bassett again of the approach of Halloween. A few cars were parked along the street. A woman was going into the drugstore. The delivery boy for the Village Market was loading a station wagon. He waved at Kearns. Bassett remembered him from the firehouse the night before.

"What did Morietti mean—about the wages of sin? He was talking about the fire last night."

Kearns unwrapped a cigar and made a point to throw the cellophane into the waste container on which there was a sign HELP KEEP HILLSIDE CLEAN. God knows, help was needed to that purpose. "Well," he said, biting the nub off the cigar and spitting it out, "there's talk about the kid's mother. I went to high school with Catherine Rocco myself. Even in those days, she was what the fellows called easy—if you were the right fellow, that is. I never was myself. There always has been talk—even when her husband was alive. But I'll tell you this: she's raised one of the sweetest girls this or any other town ever saw—Johanna. I told you about her, didn't I—going with Martin Scully?"

"I guess you did mention it." Bassett was looking at the window of the laundromat across the street: open twenty-four hours a day. He watched a woman go in with a bag of clothes. "Let's have a look over there," he said.

The moment they walked in, the woman said, "I'm glad you're here, Mr. Kearns. Just look at this place. You should close it up if they don't keep it clean."

Her complaint was more than justified: half the machines were clogged with dirty water. In some of them work clothes seemed to have been abandoned halfway through the washing. Powdered soap lay in mounds like blue sand. Empty soda bottles were strewn everywhere.

"Is it always like this?" Bassett asked.

"Mister," the woman said, "I consider myself lucky if I don't have to wash my clothes over when I get them home."

Kearns looked at his watch. "I'm going over and get a warrant and close it up right now."

"Let's do it without a warrant," Bassett said. "Let's roll the technical crew down here—just on the chance that somebody dumped his dirty clothes here last night. Got a padlock?"

"I know where I can get one," Kearns said.

"Better save your wash for next week," Bassett said to the woman. "This place is temporarily closed."

"Where do you come from, mister?" the woman asked, hitching up her bag of wash.

"I live in Newport," Bassett said.

Inexplicably, the woman had got into a temper with him. "If you don't like the way we do things in Hillside, why don't you do your wash in your own town?"

And that, Bassett thought, was how things could be in Hillside.

While he waited for Kearns to return with the lock, he watched, grimly fascinated, while a man with no legs maneuvered himself across the street on what looked like roller skates beneath the platform on which his torso was supported. Kearns passed the cripple on his way back, bidding him time of day.

"Poor devil," Bassett said.

"Ah, Billy's happy enough—in his own way. He wouldn't thank you for sympathy. Or for much else either."

"How does he live?"

"Big Molly," Kearns said, and set about padlocking the door.

Bassett noticed the color at his neck again. "What does she do?"

Kearns threw him a covert glance. "Works for Billy," he said tersely.

From there Kearns began his check of the village taverns, working south from the police station. He had his best deputy working toward the town from the northern limits. Even if Bassett had had the time to make the tour with him, he knew it was a job better left to the local talent. He went himself to search for the boy, Georgie Rocco.

9

Mrs. Tonelli was in the habit of taking her daily walk just before her lunch. The sun was at its warmest at that hour, and she was at her most alert. After lunch she liked to nap, and after that on weekdays she could watch the children coming home from school. As soon as she left the house, she moved along at a good clip for a woman nearly eighty, to the scene of last night's fire. Fires frightened her, this one had particularly, the whole house so quickly destroyed. She slept downstairs, living alone. But even so it was not going to be safe for her to live alone much longer.

She poked a bit with her stick along the fringes of the ruin, then at a piece of furniture cast out by the firemen. She clucked her disapproval at what she saw, nothing worth risking lives over in the first place. Catherine Rocco had never been one for putting money into the house, not that she ever had much of it—from her husband at least. Twelve thousand dollars was a lot of insurance. But Gerry Mancuso could sell insurance on a blind man's eyes. She watched a mangy white dog scratching under the bushes. Hydrangea bushes: she remembered telling Johanna that there was too much lime in the ground for them there; they would blossom to a sick greenish pink and never come to their full color. Suddenly the Lodini bulldog streaked past her. He gave her a terrible fright. Then, in front of the mangy cur, he came to a bristling stop. The cur growled without letting go whatever it was he had in his mouth. From where she stood it looked like the inside of an old baseball. She could remember one of her boys once—she couldn't remember which one now—taking the hide off his baseball. The center of it had been bound round with black tape, round and round a little rubber pellet at the middle. She remembered his disappointment reaching the pellet.

The bulldog began edging closer, poising each foot in the air for a second before putting it down. The cur's hackle rose like a jagged knife. Mrs. Tonelli shouted at the dogs, orders to go home, to go away. She shouted at them in Italian then, all to no avail. The bull was circling, the cur twisting round to keep facing him.

A fight between boys or even men never failed to excite Mrs. Tonelli. In fact, although it made her a little ashamed of herself afterwards, she enjoyed a good hair-pulling between women, if she thought the subject was worth it. But the sight of dumb animals tearing at each other put her in a frenzy. She could not forgive Frank Covello his hobby of cock-raising. She had refused to vote for him for that reason, and told him so.

The bull narrowed the distance between himself and the cur. Mrs. Tonelli moved in on them, shouting and waving her stick, never giving a thought to her own safety. The bulldog charged; the cur dropped what he had in his mouth and shot up the street in full flight, the bull after him.

The old lady stood where she was for a few seconds, trying to regain her composure, to quiet her heartbeat. Then she picked her way among the debris and with the tip of her cane hooked out the cur dog's find: it was a ball of black tape. She looked down at it, frowning, for it occurred to her that it was electrical tape, and electrical tape was what stood between half the houses in Hillside and such combustion as had occurred here last night. The women were constantly on the alert for exposed wiring, their men regularly doing, each, his own electrical patchwork, taping the wires. But what was patched, she reasoned, could be unpatched; an insurance inspector, finding the tape, might just choose to make something of it. And possibly with reason! She thought about the cocky lump of a boy who had sat confidently at her breakfast table that morning and refused to wear other people's clothes. Without a stick save the rags on his back, without a dime for bus fare in his pocket, he had boldly asked her for a loan.

And when she had proposed to give him ten dollars, he had said it was not enough. No one had ever said that to her before, not a member of her own family: they took what she gave and said nothing . . . Or else took nothing and left her house which was the case with Martin. There was something about young Rocco she liked. Instinctively she knew that she shouldn't. It took no great knowledge of human nature to see that he was out to get what he could. But a certain excitement had come into the house with him. And in her own way, she was out herself to get what she could, while there was time left to enjoy it.

She saw Bassett's black sedan approaching slowly, its solitary occupant looking here and there as though unfamiliar with the neighborhood, and guessed that his was an official mission of some sort. Without a thought to the stiffness in her bones, she bent and scooped up the tape and tucked it into her coat pocket.

Bassett parked in front of the charred ruins and got out of the car. He was aware of the sharp black eyes upon him, measuring his car, the cut of his clothes. He tipped his hat. He would have done it in any case, but he knew a matriarch when he saw one.

"Could you tell me where the people are now who lived here?"

"At the county hospital," Mrs. Tonelli said. "The mother is ill. The children went up this morning to see her. Who are you?"

Bassett took off his hat. "I'm Raymond Bassett, a county detective."

"If you tell me what it is you want, perhaps I could help you."

"Nothing that can't wait," Bassett said. "A shame this, isn't it?" He indicated the ruin.

"Oh, a great shame," she said, petulant for his not having confided in her.

"But they fought hard to save it, the firemen did," Bassett said. "They're a brave lot of men."

"I saw it first," she said. "I live up there." She indicated the house, a rambling, well-kept Victorian relic of a more prosperous period in the village's history. "I called the fire department."

Bassett would have bet that she saw most things first, with those eagle eyes. "Did you?" he murmured. He looked at his watch.

Suddenly the old lady realized that he was not interested in the fire at all. A detective: his business would be what had happened at the plant, MacAndrews' death. She had heard from Mrs. Grey that MacAndrews had been murdered. That's what they were saying in Moontown. But no one she had talked to on the phone that morning seemed to know what had happened. Or if they did, they weren't saying. In fact, they didn't want to talk about it at all. None of her people liked MacAndrews. Some of them hated him. But so far as most of them were concerned, he *was* the Graham Company, and the Graham Company was their living. An ordinarily talkative community had, overnight, voluntarily imposed a rule of silence on itself. She felt a little sorry for the detective sent in from the outside—but not sorry enough to want to help him. She heard the bus stopping on the road below. The Roccos might well be returning on it. Curious as she was as to what this man wanted with them, she did not intend to make the introductions.

"It's time for my lunch," she said, and with a curt nod of her head, started across the street.

Absorbed in his own thoughts, Bassett wondered if he had offended her, her departure was so abrupt. "Can I help you?" he said, seeing her use of the cane.

"How?" she said, and twisted her head round to look at him.

He smiled sheepishly. "I can see you don't need help," he said, "but could you tell me—where are the Roccos staying now?"

"With me," she said, and moved on.

He could not figure out her sudden antagonism. Merely the petulance of age? He saw the name TONELLI on a marker at her walk. "Mrs. Tonelli?"

Again she turned only her head, not her body, pausing. "Do you expect them for lunch?"

"I will feed them if they come," she said.

"Thank you," he said. He felt as though he had been trying to sell her a magazine subscription.

He was sitting in the car, ill-tempered himself and trying to make up his mind what to do next, when he saw the two young people coming up the hill. Both of them were carrying boxes, which might well contain new clothes, and he remembered then having heard the bus stop. He got out of the car again and waited.

A great hulk of a lad was young Rocco. Bassett had seen him briefly the night before, trotting after him and Kearns when they left the fire. He was now sporting a splashy new orange sweater, the collar furled around his thick neck. The girl was quite something else: you would look twice at her, as Kearns had said.

"George?" he said when they came abreast of him. He tipped his hat to the girl.

"Yeah?"

"I'd like to speak to you for a moment—in the car here, if you don't mind. I'm a police officer."

The boy ran a pink tongue around his poutish lips. "What'd I do?"

Bassett suppressed the inclination to smile. It was the standard retort of the high school kid. "Nothing that I know of," he said pleasantly. He needed friends wherever he could find them in Hillside. "It's just a matter of what you may—or may not—have seen."

"Wait up for me, Jo."

"You don't need to, miss," the detective said. "He'll be along in a couple of minutes." He watched the boy's eyes as they followed his sister across the street, the round, wistful eyes of a youngster who has been left somewhere he hadn't wanted to go in the first place.

Bassett eased himself into the car and left the door open for Rocco to follow. The boy took up a lot of seat. "I got to eat lunch and get up to the football field," he said. "We got a big game this afternoon."

"I know. My son is on the Newport team."

"Yeah? What's he play? I'll try and not rough him up."

Bassett smiled and thought wryly that the youngster couldn't know how reassuring that was to the father of his opposition. "Left end. His name is Johnny Bassett."

"I'll look him up," Rocco said.

"What time did you get home last night, George?"

"You mean after the fire?"

"No, I mean before it. There wasn't much to get home to afterwards, was there?"

"No." The boy laughed nervously. "I guess nine-thirty, quarter to ten. The big game today and all. I mean—we may not beat your guys." Bassett waited him out, for he sounded as though he would run on. The detective tried to figure out why he was nervous. But then, in the lower economic strata, fear of the police was normal. Rocco added, "I don't know right on the button. But I was home by ten. I know that."

"Did you make a phone call in the booth outside the lunch room?"

"That's right. Yeah, I did just as I was starting home."

"Could it have been at a quarter to ten?"

The boy shook his head. "I don't think it was that late, Mr. Bassett. But maybe it was. I always hunch a little, telling Johanna when I get in. You know how it is."

"Whom did you call?"

"My girl friend . . ." The boy hesitated for a fraction of a second. Then he explained: "Sometimes I call my mother my girl friend. I was calling the hospital to see how she was. She's just had an operation, see. But that switchboard! Man, I'd hate to be dying and trying to get them on the line."

Rocco's girl friend had been in the *Crazy Cat* at closing time, so Morietti had said. Had the boy just caught himself in a lie: sometimes I call my mother my girl friend? Bassett decided not to push the matter at the moment. He was in no position himself yet to sift the lies from the truth of what anyone in Hillside told him.

He said, "Martin Scully says he wanted to use the phone at a quarter to ten—and that you got into the phone booth ahead of him."

Rocco said expansively, "Yeah. I saw old Martin looking down at me. Did he tell you I thumbed my nose at him?"

"No. I don't suppose he thought that a necessary detail," the detective said. "You can go now. Good luck this afternoon."

"Thanks," the boy said, and scrambled out of the car. He stuck his head back for a moment. "Good luck to you, too."

10

Georgie broke into a dogtrot crossing the street and kept to it all the way up the Tonelli walk. He could almost feel his skin letting go. While he'd been with the detective it had felt tight, like he was wearing new gloves only all over his body. And all the cop had wanted of him was to check up on old Martin! But that meant they knew now it wasn't a heart attack. They were looking—but not for him. Martin had given him, Georgie Rocco, as an alibi for a quarter to ten. That was all right. That's when he'd planned to say he started for home in the first place. He couldn't remember now what had made him say it was earlier. But in a way this was swell: most kids lied about when they got home if there was nobody to check up on them. Poor old Martin. They'd be giving him the works, everybody knowing how he felt about Mac-Andrews.

As Georgie ran, the change jangled in his pocket. He had folding money left too. What he had done was persuade Jo to open a charge account at the Teen Shop. She had a job. And he'd suggested Martin Scully for reference. Jo hadn't wanted to do it. Jo was great on the lay-away plan. You bought something neat but by the time you got it home you looked like last year's droop in it.

The minute he opened the door he smelled steak cooking, or at the very least hamburgers. He paused only long enough to comb his hair.

Mrs. Tonelli looked him over. "Well, that *is* a sweater."

"Cheerful, huh?" Georgie said. "I thought you'd like it. You don't mind if I start eating—on account of the game?"

"Better put your napkin around your neck—if you can find your neck under that collar."

Georgie grinned. "They call it a roll-away."

"I thought that was a bed," Mrs. Tonelli said. "What did the policeman want?"

"He was checking up on Martin—to see if he was telling the truth, I guess. You know, MacAndrews being murdered." Georgie got a real thrill out of saying the words, and then a funny feeling, like somebody else had said them, like he was away up high—in the balcony in a movie maybe—looking down. And he could see MacAndrews, just a little bit of a figure lying on the cement floor. It didn't seem to have much to do with Georgie Rocco, looking down from the balcony.

Mrs. Tonelli broke through his reverie, demanding: "Who told you that?"

The way she said it scared him a little. "I don't know. I heard it somewhere. I mean the cop asking questions and all."

"Eavesdropper!" she challenged. "You heard Mrs. Grey telling me this morning. Nobody else is talking about it."

"I didn't mean to listen," Georgie said, almost giddy with relief. Man, after this he'd do more listening and less talking.

Johanna said, "Why are they asking about Martin?"

"I don't know, sis. The police don't take me into their confidence."

Georgie filled his mouth with a great bite of the hamburger and bun. The juice spurted out of it. He had never tasted anything so delicious and said so.

"I will give your compliments to the cook," Mrs. Tonelli said. "Eat, Johanna."

"I'm not very hungry, thank you. I was thinking of Mr. MacAndrews' sister."

Oh brother, Georgie thought. "Yeah, the way she'd think about you if you were in her place. The Mafia. That's what she calls us. All Italians are Mafia."

"There was something to be said for the Mafia—in the old days, in the old country," Mrs. Tonelli said. "It was the only way poor people could get justice."

Georgie thought about that for a moment. He liked the

sound of it. "Yeah," he said, but affirmatively. The old girl had put her finger on the situation, on MacAndrews and what Georgie had done.

"I wish you wouldn't 'yah' like a goat."

"Yes, ma'am," Georgie said, and in one more bite finished his hamburger. Johanna had not yet touched hers.

She saw the look in his eyes. "Do you want it, Georgie?"

"You better eat it, Jo," he said, although the effort to say it almost made his eyes water.

Jo finally took a bite.

"Besides," Georgie said, "I ought to go light—on account of the game."

"You are excused, Georgie," Mrs. Tonelli said. "I do not like to see so much suffering at the luncheon table."

Georgie downed his milk and left the table. He was pretty sure the old lady was giving him the needle. But what the hell? If it made her feel good what did he care, as long as she was willing to pay for it in other ways? There was a time when it would have made him sore. But now he had bigger things on his mind. Just before he left the house he said, "Jo, don't forget—ma told you to call Mr. Mancuso."

Mrs. Tonelli waited for the door to bang as he went out, but there was no bang. Georgie was minding his manners. They were primitive, what he had of them, but he was minding them, and Mrs. Tonelli enjoyed whatever reverence she could exact from the young. She saw herself as a matriarch, but something had gone wrong early in her rule: her children had moved out of her sphere of influence.

"Johanna, you have not told me—how did the fire start last night?"

"I don't really know. Georgie says it may have been a cigaret I knocked out of his hand—accidentally."

"Football heroes should not smoke cigarets," Mrs. Tonelli observed. And she thought it interesting that Georgie had not yet proposed to smoke in her presence. "Will your mother come here? Did you ask her?"

"I think she'd rather we found a place of our own, Mrs. Tonelli. But she said to thank you very much."

"Did she?" the old lady remarked dryly. "Georgie would like to remain here."

"I know."

"And you?"

"Sometimes I would gladly give him away," Johanna said, a trace of a smile at the corners of her mouth.

The old lady gave a brief spate of laughter. But she was not to be diverted from the question. "You would like to live with your mother, Johanna?"

The girl lifted her head. She had a finely shaped head and a lovely neck. Just looking at her made the old woman ache with the memory of the mirrors of her youth.

"Oh, yes," Johanna said.

If she had not known the family better, the old lady would have believed her. "You are a good girl, Johanna," she said.

The girl looked at her sharply—and then away, a look, the old woman thought, in violent protest to such praise. The mea culpa of her father, all over again, as though his wife's infidelities were his fault.

"Your father always blamed himself. And he was wrong to do that. Don't you make the same mistake, Johanna."

"My father was a good man," the girl said without raising her eyes.

"In this world that is not enough. I am not sure it was enough in any world. The saint always stands alone. The rest of us live together—and we are the world, plain men and women. We keep each other warm. It is a terrible thing to have to beg—to be kept warm." She was thinking of Johanna's father again, saying that. "Virtue is a cold companion."

Johanna pressed her teeth against her lip. For all the girl's attempt to forestall it, the old woman had provoked again memory of the moment in the hallway. Father Walsh had held her for that moment. He had! She could still feel the hard ring of his arms about her.

Mrs. Tonelli said, "When will you and Martin marry?"

"I don't know."

The old woman had been trying—by way of warming herself—to fetch a confession of love from the girl: that was all.

Johanna's uncertainty gave off cold comfort. It put the old woman in a momentary pet. At her time of life she wanted the emotions simplified, and much as she thought herself interested in complicated people, age had robbed her piti-lessly of the concentration, which in her younger days would have held the strands of complication till she could see the pattern in them.

Johanna stared at her plate. The grease had congealed around the uneaten portion of her hamburger—the flesh within the bread—and all of it spoiled by her one solitary bite. She rose abruptly, taking her plate. "Excuse me. May I clear the table for Mrs. Grey?"

The old woman made no sign, simply scowling at her own thoughts.

Johanna returned. She had thrown off the sickening image. She felt sorry for the old woman, alone. "Don't you think there's such a thing as spiritual love, Mrs. Tonelli?"

"In church," she said, "but not in bed." Then she laughed. "You will find that out after you are married."

11

Both Newport and Hillside High Schools came to the game undefeated in four starts, and both schools were keyed up for the contest. The Hillsiders always prided themselves on being the underdog, even when they weren't, for they considered all the other schools in the county snobbish, class-conscious, and determined to keep Hillside in its place. And the fact was that the Hillside team did bring out the worst in its opponents; sportsmanship was never the feature of either win or loss. In every football game Hillside fought a little war and made, each boy of his opponent for its duration, a mortal enemy.

Bassett knew this from the moment of kickoff, Hillside to Newport, just listening to the howling exhortations from the stands. Newport was the faster team, Hillside the heavier, and when they hit, they hurt. They hurt, and he observed with some curiosity, they reveled in being hurt: their pride was in being able to take it quite as much as in dishing it out. Johnny Bassett was fleet of foot and lithe, much to his father's relief. Throughout the first quarter, he managed to dodge the bulldozers. But neither was he effective. He was outrunning his own passers, intent on outrunning the opposition. Bassett could imagine the invectives being snarled at him across the line. He dreaded the moment the boy's pride would take over—or worse, the moment the Newport coach would take him out of the lineup. And he realized that the latter dread made him quite as savage as any of the murderous baiters in the stands or on the field. He swore at himself for yielding to the instinct that made men kill, and wished to God he had never moved his family to so healthy an environment.

On the bench Georgie Rocco alternated his bellowed ad-

vice with prayers that he would himself soon get into the
game. Christ, Christ, Christ! With every player on the Hillside team that went down, he suffered exquisitely, and prayed
that the boy would not be able to get up. He wanted Hillside
to win, of course, but not as much as he wanted to win for
Hillside, he, Georgie Rocco. Fatso! He'd make them eat his
fat, by Christ. He kept saying "Please," to the coach, and
under his breath calling him all the foul names he could think
of, for he knew the bastard didn't like him. Christ, let me in
and I'll bury them, all the Catholic-hating, dago-hating,
mother-loving muck of them!

Pererro, the Hillside quarterback, had to take time out—
and for himself. He was bleeding at the mouth. Something—
a stone, a toe—had got through the chin-guard. The coach
wanted a big man in the secondary as well as on the line. He
cast his eye over his bench. Newport, running scared in the
open field, was going more and more to the line, throwing
in a fresh line every few minutes: they had the depth in men
that Hillside lacked, being numerically the smaller school.

"I know the signals," Georgie begged. "I know the plays.
Please, sir!"

"Shut up, Georgie," the boy next to him said. "You never
played quarterback."

"We don't need a quarterback! We need a brick wall,"
Georgie shouted.

And for his having hit it exactly on the nose, the coach
sent him in at a position he had never played before. Hillside
was leading 6 to 0, and the coach was willing to settle for
that score.

Georgie galloped onto the field, trying to concentrate on
his instructions. Only in his dreams had such an opportunity
ever come his way before. With every number he barked, his
heart sang, smash them, smash, smash, smash! Hillside held
and Georgie then began to pray for the spectacular, the hero's
chance.

Instead, he boneheaded, falling for a power decoy through
center. Johnny Bassett got loose around end and ran the distance. Newport converted the extra point and led, 7 to 6.

Georgie knew his chance for fame hung low. When he saw Pekarik running in from the sidelines he thought seriously of defying his own coach, of refusing to leave the field. Pekarik, of all people. Christ, he couldn't go out for him, not after last night. But Pekarik went into his regular position in the line, left end. The instructions were to hit hard, every man, and try for a fumble. The coach left the man in to carry out that particular strategy better than any other: Georgie Rocco. And in the last two minutes of play he had his chance: he hit the ball carrier himself, a shoulder block that lifted the Newport youngster three feet in the air and numbed him. The ball squirted from his arms, back toward his own goal, and Georgie, striving to keep his footing, simply deflected the ball with his hand, but by grace of whatever fortune shone on him that afternoon, he deflected it—ostensibly by his design—into the hands of Pekarik. Pekarik stood for a split second, and Georgie screamed at him, "Run, you bastard! That way!"

Pekarik ran, and Hillside won the game, 12 to 7.

The whole valley reverberated with the noise of automobile horns as the cavalcade of cars left the field and wound its brassy way back to the village. Shopkeepers came to their doors and waved, sharing in the great victory; the barber stood, razor in hand, and beside him on the step his bibbed, half-shaven customer, stripping the lather from his chin with his forefinger. The butcher's dog, the hungriest on the street, leaped to lap up the froth, no doubt confusing it with ice cream. Gerosa came out of his tailor shop and nodded happily as his daughter screamed, "Papa! Georgie won the game for us!" She was riding in the open car at the head of the parade, pointing to the hero. Gerosa shook his hands in the air, clasped in congratulations. It was the first time to his knowledge Georgie had won anything more than a can of peas at the firemen's raffle. Looking out from his second-floor window, Martin Scully counted the years since he had played for Hillside, and allowed himself a moment's self-pity—yesterday's hero. Beneath his window Billy Skillet was propelling himself along the sidewalk, cloppity-clop with his wooden discs, trying to keep up with the parade, and streaming the air with his oaths, not at his fate but at the interference by people with legs every time he got himself rolling.

"We did it! We did it again! Bravo, Rocco! Three cheers for Pekarik!"

The full length of the River Road the youngsters drove, shouting the news of victory, the score, waving pennants, sweaters, and in the front car—Tommy Lodini's convertible—Georgie's girl friend, Rosie, took off her wrap-around cheerleader's skirt and waved it like a bullfighter's cape. Her chubby buttocks, stuffed into red tights, were bouncing like twin balloons. Georgie, sitting in the back seat as might a politician on Decoration Day, got a nudge from Pekarik to look at Rosie's bottom. Pekarik was bug-eyed. Georgie lunged forward in his seat and slashed the girl's behind with his fingertips. She screamed with pain, and the pain ran up his own arm, a shock of it starting from the tips of his fingers.

"Put your skirt on, Rosie! You trying out for burlesque or something?"

Rosie sullenly obeyed him and sat down on the floor of the car at his feet. He wound his fingers through her hair and pulled it now and then, grinning and shouting and all the while waving with his free hand to the cavalcade behind him, urging more, more noise. The chain of cars U-turned under the bridge and snaked back toward the village. On the return trip Georgie glanced by accident at the MacAndrews house. Miss MacAndrews was standing on the porch, her arms folded. "Mafia!" Georgie shouted, though his voice was lost in the blast of horns. A wreath of flowers hung on the blackened door.

The cars edged, one after the other, into the Graham parking lot next to the *Crazy Cat*. Once inside, the whole gang, over Pete's gesticulated protests, writhed in what they called the Victory Twist, the jukebox going full blast. Georgie stood a round of Cokes for everybody in the house.

Bassett, his son beside him—it did not take the Newport team long to get out of the visitors' shower room that day—watched the Hillside celebration from his car where he had parked it in the alley next to the police station. Johnny was slumped down in the seat—not that anyone in Hillside was likely to recognize him if they saw him. "What squares," he said when the victory chain finally twisted into Pete's.

"But they won the game," Bassett said, irritated at Johnny's air of superiority. He realized when the words were out that at one stroke he had probably undone twelve years of liberal education. He did not even go into the stationhouse, but drove home intent on clearing his mind and spirit of Hillside for the rest of the weekend.

12

Georgie went up the hill to his supper at Mrs. Tonelli's confident that his fame had preceded him. If it had, there weren't any flags out or bands playing. He could smell meat roasting, but Mrs. Tonelli was sitting in her black dress—her whole wardrobe was a variety of blacks—reading the *County News* in the living room. Johanna had got herself another batch of wool and needles and had started knitting again. There was a clack-clack-clack in the room as Georgie listened outside the door, and you couldn't tell whether it was Jo's needles, the clock, or the old lady's false teeth. Man, talk about lively!

He tiptoed back to the mirror, touched up the crest of his hair, and then saw that he had spilled something down the front of his new orange sweater.

He thrust his shoulders back and marched into the room. "Hey, everybody! Haven't you heard the news?"

Mrs. Tonelli looked at him over the tops of her rimless glasses. "I have been reading it," she said. "What more has happened?"

"We won. Didn't you hear the cars?"

"I thought it was a wedding. With so much noise it should have been a wedding."

He looked at her, on the verge of asking, Are you kidding? Instead he turned to his sister. "Hey, Jo?"

She looked up. "I went to see Mr. Mancuso."

"All afternoon?"

"Most of it."

"How come?"

"I had to make out a list for him of everything that was in the house."

"Ha! That shouldn't've taken long. One word: junk."

96

"They do not pay very much for junk, Georgie," Mrs. Tonelli said, still looking over the tops of her glasses at him.

"Yeah," Georgie said. "That's right. They don't. Couldn't you've waited for me, Jo? I had some stuff in the basement that was pretty valuable."

"We can go over the list. I kept a copy of it," Johanna said.

"You will have time enough," the old lady said. "They will investigate."

She was needling him about something, Georgie thought. It was hard to dig old people, one minute giving you something and the next, sore because you took it. "Let 'em," he said. "It shouldn't take them long in that mess."

"You would be surprised at the things that don't get destroyed—even in a mess like that."

Georgie felt himself turning sick. Whatever she was talking about . . . He had meant to dig out the electrical tape from the bushes and get rid of it. He should have done it during the fire . . . But she couldn't mean that. It wouldn't mean anything to anybody but him anyway. He tried to be casual, crossing the room and sitting down beside her. It was like walking on wet sponge. But he said earnestly, and looking at her eye-to-eye so that she had to take off her glasses, "I don't understand what you mean, Mrs. Tonelli. Was there something in the house I didn't know about?"

"I'd be surprised at that," she snapped, telling him nothing.

But Johanna finally enlightened him. "It's just that they try to salvage the fuse box and certain things that might help determine what caused the fire," she explained.

The old witch, Georgie thought, trying to scare hell out of him just to see if she could get a reaction. "Well, we're just going to wait. That's all."

The old lady said, "Now. What about this great victory? You were a hero?"

She'd sure managed to take the polish off that, Georgie thought. "I played quarterback," he said.

"Only quarterback. You should play *full*back." She sat back and chortled at her own corn.

Man! "Anyway, we won," he said. "What's in the paper?"

"Not much. A man was murdered. An anti-gambling committee was organized. They will be raiding every place in the county soon. But nothing about the football game." She tossed the paper toward the table. It fell on the floor.

Wait till Monday, Georgie thought. He picked up the paper and read the account of MacAndrews' murder. He glanced now and then at the old lady who was just sitting, rubbing her rheumatic knuckles. He wasn't going to show himself eating up newspaper print in front of her. He could feel a tingle of excitement, nonetheless, reading of the discovery of the body . . . He made himself stop there and look at the old woman. She looked as though she was trying to crack one of her knuckles. If she did, he thought, his own nerves would snap. He finally got to the last line of the story and he liked that: *Police Chief Kearns and County Detective Bassett admitted that the motive of revenge could not be ruled out.*

"Hey," he said, "that Bassett is all right. Man, can his kid run! He got loose around our end today and I thought we were washed up."

The old lady made a clucking sound of mock sympathy.

Georgie started reading the gambling story. A lot of it was directed toward Hillside. You didn't have to read between the lines to get it either. The county committee was going to give the local authorities time to clean up. If, within a reasonable time . . .

"Johanna, tell me," the old lady said, "why do you knit?"

"I don't know," Jo said. "I like to—and I like to see the things I make afterwards."

"Don't you see them before you make them? I mean, in your mind's eye?"

"Oh, yes. But they never come out quite that beautifully."

"Most things don't," the old lady said and heaved a great sigh. She was bored, Georgie suddenly realized. That's all that was wrong. The poor old cluck was bored silly. He remembered now how glad she had been to have him and Jo come to her house, just for a piece of excitement. And there Jo sat. Knitting. She might as well be saying her rosary. And maybe she was . . . inside. Jo did a lot of things inside. And of course the old girl didn't understand football. He could remember hearing how she used to dance. In the old days. There used to be a fiesta in Hillside, the streets all hung with lanterns. He couldn't remember it, but he remembered his mother telling about when she was a girl. Everybody dancing on the street, a band. And wine. They made good wine once in Hillside. Now the grapes were puny and the vines half-withered. Like Grandma Tonelli. He wondered why all her kids had moved away.

"How come they don't have a fiesta any more?" he said.

He was right. The old lady's head shot up. "Ha! Lazy," she said. "Television. No conversation. The women sit and cry . . . over *Doctor Casey* . . . and *Man's Other Woman* . . . And the men . . ." She made a disparaging gesture with her hand, and Georgie noticed the jewels glittering on her fingers. "It is all in the paper there, dice and wheels, cards and the numbers racket . . . and things they don't put in the paper."

Georgie moistened his lips. An idea sprang almost full bloom into his mind. He knew what she meant about the things they didn't put in the paper: the Sunday morning cockfights behind the fence at the Graham plant. "Yeah," he said inadvertently.

"I wish you wouldn't 'yah' like a goat," she said.

"Yes, ma'am," Georgie said. "I'll try and remember."

Mrs. Tonelli reached across to the table at her side, picked up the bell there, and shook it vigorously.

A moment later Mrs. Grey came to the door.

"When?" Mrs. Tonelli demanded.

"Georgie can wash his hands," Mrs. Grey said and returned to the kitchen.

Brother! Whose mammy did she think she was? But he did wash his hands.

* * *

All through dinner his mind was charging itself like a battery. Still he managed to make himself pretty good company, by his own calculation. Mrs. Tonelli asked him if he would like to carve. He wasn't sure she meant it, but he wasn't going to do anything in front of her that he couldn't do well. "No, ma'am," he said earnestly. "I mean, I'd like to, but first I'd like to watch you for a few times."

She grunted satisfaction with his answer and tipped the garlic buds out of their pockets in the lamb with the edge of the knife. The easy way she slithered the knife through the meat made Georgie shiver. Lamb on Saturday night; what could they have on Sunday to top that? Breast of guinea hen under glass? His mother used to say that when he'd ask her what was for dinner. But he giggled at the merging of two thoughts in his mind.

Mrs. Tonelli looked at him. "Well?"

"I was just wondering how you'd carve one of Mayor Covello's birds," George said.

"I would like better to carve Mayor Covello," she said, and with a remarkably flexible snap of her wrist, she severed the crisp tail of the lamb and dropped it with disdain on the plate.

Georgie wanted to howl with laughter, but he didn't want to spoil the surprise he was planning for the old lady. He merely grinned appreciatively.

He was out of the house by eight o'clock. At eight-ten he picked up Mike Pekarik and headed for Daley's. Not until he had them both together and Daley's father had gone out for his usual Saturday night game did Georgie open up on his plans for the evening. "We're the Mafia, see? We take care of what's wrong in our own town. We clean it up." He was stretching even his interpretation of the Mafia. Nor did he realize that in this instance, neither of his two co-workers had much claim on an Italian brotherhood.

Pekarik said, "What d'you mean, clean it up? You gone crazy or something?"

"I mean we're going to organize a gambling raid tonight."

Both his companions looked at him, stunned. Daley got up and turned on another light. If he could see Rocco's face better he might have some chance of understanding him. But all that happened was that he saw his own living room better, the streaks on the wall, the cracked linoleum, his father's work shoes sitting where he had taken them off. He kicked them under the sofa.

"Let's go down to the joint," he said, meaning the *Crazy Cat*.

"I'm serious," Georgie said. He took the piece he had torn from the afternoon paper from his pocket. "Did you see this? They're going to be sending federal agents or somebody like that in here. I mean it. This guy Bassett is the D.A.'s stake-out . . ." He wasn't sure that was the right word, but it felt right.

Daley pointed to the column in the paper that was partly torn, next to the gambling story, the account of the murder at the Graham plant. "Did you see *that*?"

"So what?" Georgie said. "It was an act of God, him getting killed. I mean, it was an accident, but an act of God. There ain't nobody in this town who doesn't think old MacAndrews didn't have it coming to him. He was a one-man Gestapo."

Daley grinned a little at Rocco's saying that and the way he was setting himself up: the Mafia. He took a package of cigarets from his pocket and shook one out. "Okay, let's hear what you got in mind."

"Gimme one of them, huh?" Georgie said. He hadn't been smoking in front of the old lady. He lit his own and Daley's cigarets with fingers slightly a-tremble with excitement. "The way I figure it, we'll line up about ten other guys from around the joint, and we'll move in all at the same time, you know, simultaneous—just about midnight—on maybe four of the big games at once." He stuck the cigaret between his lips and smacked one hand into the palm of the other. "We'll just smash in, grab the money, and turn over the tables. They won't know what hit 'em, or who hit 'em—I'll get to that in a minute. And with this thing in the papers they'll be scared anyway. Man, we'll clean the whole damn town out in fifteen minutes. It's a natural.''

Pekarik said, "My old man'd wallop hell out of me."

"No, sir," Georgie said, "not if you give the money to your old lady, he won't. And that's what we're gonna do. Every cent we get goes to the women. We ain't doing this for personal gain. We're doing it for the good of our families. It's patriotic. We ain't going to wait for no strangers to come in here and make a haul and get all the newspaper headlines. Daley, you see it, don't you, man?"

Daley took a long pull at his cigaret and watched the ember crawl up toward his fingers. He was catching fire himself. "Moontown, too?"

"Why not?" Georgie said. "They're our responsibility."

"Going to do them in blackface?"

"No, sir. Democratic. I know a couple of guys over there who'd give anything to be in on a deal like this. I'll get them organized. Don't worry."

"Just see they work Moontown, huh, not moving up the hill with us, you understand?"

"What do you think I am? NAACP or something?"

Daley put out his cigaret in a broken cup. "Keep talking, Georgie. Maybe you got something."

"Got a pencil and paper?"

Georgie drew a crude map of the town and marked on it three places where he knew there would be a game in full swing by midnight. Daley added two more that Georgie hadn't known about. Georgie marked an X at the top of the hill, just down from the football field.

"What's that?" Daley said.

"That's Covello's chicken coop. The last thing I'm going to do tonight, turn loose every goddam hen and cock in the place."

Daley laughed. "You'll wake up the whole damn county."

"Man, that's just what I got in mind."

Pekarik moistened his lips. "We gonna wear the stockings again? I think I'd like to. I might funk out if I was to meet my old man face to face."

"Sure, we're going to wear them," Georgie said. "Nobody's going to recognize anybody. It's going to be fast and tough, and there's got to be so many of us we'll just swarm over 'em. That way they can't put the finger on anybody special afterwards. And by then we'll have the women on our side. Man, it's going to be as neat as if the cops was doing it—only no arrests, none of that jazz."

Pekarik said, "My old lady likes her cut out of what pa wins."

"And when he don't win?"

Pekarik shrugged. "That's his problem."

"She'll like it better this way," Georgie said. "Or do you want out?"

"Who said I wanted out?"

Daley leaned forward, unbuttoned his hip pocket and drew out a nylon stocking. He stretched it out and then let go, springing it like a snake.

Pekarik jumped. Daley laughed at him and put the stocking back in his pocket and rebuttoned it.

"I threw mine away," Pekarik said.

"Me, too," said Georgie. "I'll get us a couple some place. You don't mind if there's a run in yours, do you?"

Pekarik minced across the room mockingly. "I don't, sweetie, if you can't afford to buy me new ones," he said in a high falsetto.

"Any weapons this time, Rocco?" Daley said.

Georgie thought about it for a moment. "We ought to have something to scare the guts out of them. I mean something to show we mean business, but something we won't have to use. I mean, after all . . ."

Daley cut him off. "Broken bottles," he said easily. "The necks of bottles."

"Yeah," Georgie said, trying to keep the awe out of his voice. He turned it into a compliment to Daley. "Man, you're all right. You're real loose."

Daley said, "I'm glad you remembered that, Rocco. It was a good thing for you last night that I was."

"Did I say it wasn't? What's eating you, Daley?"

"Nothing. I just want you to know I'm not your stooge, Georgie. We're in this together, but just remember you're in deeper than Mike or me."

"Okay, okay, we'll call the whole thing off," George said, suddenly edgy under the cold, sharp eye of Daley.

"No, this is swell," Daley said. "It's a hell of a good cover-up for last night, and there ain't no calling off last night, is there?"

"Brother," Georgie said, "you're taking the whole fun out of tonight. I mean, this was an important thing we were going to do."

"We're going to do it," Daley said. "Just call your signals, Georgie. I'm ready when you are."

13

Johanna helped Mrs. Grey clear the dinner table and do the dishes. Mrs. Grey didn't really want her help; she liked to do things her own way, but she didn't want to hurt the girl's feelings. She was off Sundays, and she explained to Johanna what she had left for dinner, how long she was to leave the casserole in the oven, and how to prepare the sauce for the dessert.

At a few minutes after eight the phone rang. Mrs. Tonelli answered it in the living room. The little silver handbell tinkled.

"That means it's for you, Miss Jo," Mrs. Grey said. "Nobody's going to call me at this hour—I hope."

Johanna picked up the extension phone although she too would have preferred it not to be for her. It was Martin Scully. After all, he said, it was Saturday night.

"How are you, Martin?"

At that point she heard the loud click as Mrs. Tonelli hung up.

"Do you want to see me, Jo?"

"I can't tonight. I'm going up to church—and afterwards, I've promised Mrs. Tonelli . . . she isn't feeling very well." Johanna was not good at lying.

Mrs. Grey clattered the dishes in the sink.

Martin said, "She's never going to feel very well as long as she can get you to stay with her." Jo could have asked him to come up. It was his own grandmother's house. But he was not going to suggest it. "I'll see you then, Jo . . . around."

"Martin, tomorrow afternoon, maybe? Couldn't you come to dinner? I'm sure your grandmother would like it."

"I'm sure she would, too. Okay, Jo. I'll see you."

"Tomorrow?"

"I'm not counting on tomorrow these days. One day at a time, that's enough for me. So long, Jo." He hung up.

Johanna put the receiver gently in its cradle.

"You go along, Miss Johanna," Mrs. Grey said. "I got lots of time before the next bus. And there's plenty enough in that casserole if Mr. Scully comes tomorrow."

"I don't think he's coming," Jo said.

"He'll come. Men always do when they get hungry."

Johanna set out a few minutes later on the longest walk of her life. She had committed herself to herself, telling Martin that she was going to church, something she had been trying to do all day without success till then. But supposing Father de Gasso wasn't hearing confessions? Only Father Walsh. The older priest was not always there on Saturday night. In the afternoon he was sure to be hearing them: that was when the old people generally went, the very old people who told their sins in Italian, no matter what the language in which they had been committed. "Bless me, Father, for I have sinned. It has been two weeks since my last confession . . . I confess to Almighty God and to you, Father, that I have sinned . . ." How ever she was to go on from there, Jo did not know. She began to pray to the Virgin Mary, always her refuge—the gentle, the pure, the understanding—above all, the pure. She held fast to one image, then another, of the Mother of God: with the Child, the Flight into Egypt, at the foot of the Cross, with Magdalene at the tomb.

There was a smell in the church vestibule of the autumn dampness, of old cloth, and musty paper, and then the soft, warm smell of burning candles. Cigaret smoke mingled, too, clinging to the men who had taken a last deep drag before tossing the stub end away as they entered the church.

Johanna touched the stone bottom of the holy water font before dampening her fingers. It needed to be refilled. She blessed herself, and went to Father de Gasso's side of the church. Both priests were hearing. She must not think now, she told herself, or she would find an excuse to escape. Or she would just simply leave, fleeing the moment of confrontation to an agony of ever greater guilt. But suppose she could not bring herself, within the confessional, to tell the sin? Supposing Father de Gasso did not help her? Supposing she made a bad confession? Would it not be better not to go at all? To put off until she had found the words, the exact words . . . And was she truly sorry? He would ask that. And God knows what else he would ask in God's name. Why did God ask? God knew. More than she knew surely. "I loved Martin Scully until . . ." But that had nothing to do with it. That was not part of the sin. Martin: I've hurt him. That *was* part of the sin. Jesus, Mary, and Joseph . . . Mother Mary, help me to make a good confession. What other sins? What was a lie, a bit of gossip, anger with her brother? How many times? What matter?

She left her pew and took her place in line, and one by one the people before her told so quickly such little sins that they were in and out of the confessional almost like birds from a nest.

"Bless me, Father, for I have sinned . . ." She forgot even to mention how long it had been since her last confession. And somehow she whispered out the story; she would not remember the words ever in which she told of having been in a priest's arms. She could see the reflection of the streetlight on the old priest's white head as it was bent close to the screen. She heard him, even above the pounding of her own heartbeat, as he drew in a long, deep breath.

He said, "Have you made a date to meet this priest again?"

"Oh, no, Father." She was shocked at that suggestion.

"Did he ask you to meet him again?"

"No, Father, no."

"And you're truly sorry that it happened?"

"I am, Father. I don't mean it wasn't my fault, but I am sorry."

"Then put it out of your mind, child, as though it never happened, and so that you won't ever be tempted again. You'll do that?"

"Yes, Father."

"How long has it been since your last confession?"

"Two weeks, Father."

She could see the head nod slightly. "For your penance say ten Our Fathers and ten Hail Marys. Offer them up to the Holy Ghost for yourself and for the priest, and pray to the Holy Virgin, who is the mother of purity, that she will intercede for you with her Blessed Son. Now make a good act of contrition."

All the voices of Christmas and Easter combined, all the glorias in excelsis, the hosannas and hallelujahs were as nothing to the joyous thanksgiving Johanna sang in her heart. And when she went out from the church a few minutes later and met Father Walsh on the steps, she said, "Good evening, Father," and felt not a flicker of interruption to the serenity within her.

She walked to the village before going up the hill, and stood a moment on the street across from Martin's rooms. The lights were on, and once she saw his shadow pass in front of the drawn shade. That was all she asked. A gang of boys stormed out of the parking lot and into the *Crazy Cat*, noisy, jostling one another, and she thought how frightening they could be, any gang of them, moving together. Her brother was with them; in that wild orange sweater he shone in the night like a harvest moon. The din of music and adolescent voices rose and fell from the luncheonette with the opening and closing of the door. There were always moments of stillness in the village when the machinery of the Graham plant was off; otherwise the hum persisted like a ringing in the listener's ears. That night it was silent. Jo heard the monotone, statical voice on the police radio from within the station. A child began to cry, a forlorn crying that seemed to have been only suspended by a silence while she listened, for it was now persisting, a lonely child, perhaps comforting itself between lamentations with a rag of a doll. There was a clatter of beer cans into the garbage bucket somewhere down the street. A woman's loud, nagging voice shrilled after a husband, Jo supposed, for it was muffled mid-sentence by the banging of a door. She saw a man come out and walk determinedly down the street, clapping his hat on his head. A window was thrust open above him. "And you don't need to come back, even if you win, you stinking son of a bitch!"

The man answered with a two-word obscenity.

Somebody outside the *Green Dog Tavern* shouted encouragement to the man. Other windows opened. "Give him hell, Lizzie," a male voice urged the wife on.

Johanna went up the back way, following the tracks, so that she would not have to pass along the main village street. Joy was more quickly spent than tears, she thought, remembering the sudden rages of her mother with her father when he was alive, the cruel jibes at him because he made so little money and because he never went anywhere like other men. She remembered then, her father's records in the basement, and how he played them softly while he worked. *A Woman Is a Sometime Thing*: that was what made her think of it. He had loved Negro music. Georgie had used the record player. But it was gone now, too, as were all the records, Georgie's and her father's. Ashes to ashes, if records burned. Most things did.

Mrs. Tonelli had napped in her chair in Johanna's absence. She was alert and impatient for the girl's return. The "male calf" she did not expect till midnight. She had thought of odd chores for Johanna to do: more kindling for the fireplace, her jewel box—she wanted to show Johanna several pieces she had worn in her youth and to tell her of the occasions. She planned a hint or two of her intentions for their future disposition: she always gave jewelry to the brides of her family.

"Who was at church?" she demanded of Johanna.

It was a few seconds before Johanna could remember anyone she had seen—except Father de Gasso and Father Walsh. Then she remembered having seen Mr. and Mrs. Gerosa.

"Both of them? Hmph," the old woman said, "I think it's foolish, running to confession all the time. I like to save mine up for when Father Walsh comes so that I can make it worth his while." She laughed dryly. "I think he believes me a wicked old woman. I am always remembering something I might have forgotten to tell—years ago. He accuses me of making up. And I tell him the only thing I am making up is lost time. I like to see him blush. He is a very handsome man, don't you think?"

"Yes," Johanna said. "Is the kindling in the basement, Mrs. Tonelli?"

The old lady was looking at her with a sort of wicked merriment in her bright, dark eyes. "Ho, you are blushing too much. All the girls blush when I talk about Father Walsh. It's as well he is a priest. Otherwise he would have been gone long ago. I want to show you something, Johanna." She gave the girl a small gold key. "Go into my bedroom, to the top drawer of my dressing table, and bring me the jewel box."

Johanna did as she was bidden. She liked to be sent into the old lady's bedroom. It was scented with perfumes and powders. The huge bed was fitted in the daytime with a yellow silken counterpane that matched the draperies. Or, when it was turned down as it was then, Mrs. Grey having prepared it before leaving, she liked to see the pale green sheets and pillowcases and touch the elegant monograms. She had never seen anything so exquisite as the gold and mother-of-pearl brush, comb and mirror, and the cut-glass container that refracted light as it was said that diamonds did. Inside it were curled strands of hair, which Mrs. Tonelli had gathered from her brush and wound around her finger. Johanna did not covet any of the things; she merely liked to look at them, and sometimes to touch them, especially the sachets, for the scent lingered some time afterwards on her fingers.

She wondered, unlocking the drawer and taking from it the Florentine jewel box, at the ball of black tape that lay, filthy with grass and dirt, smudging the white paper lining of the drawer. But she would no more think of inquiring about it than she would about, say, the numerous medicines she had seen in the bathroom cabinet when sent to fetch something from there.

She half-listened and half-enjoyed the old lady's account of the various occasions on which she had worn these or those beads, an opal pendant. She liked the stories rather more than the jewels with which they were associated. That Hillside, having once been so gay and bright a place as Mrs. Tonelli described, was such now as she had seen and heard on the street that night was too terrible. If it weren't for Martin she would hate the town—sometimes. Listening to his grandmother, she knew now where his dreams of a better, happier living for his own people came from. And because Mrs. Tonelli was Martin's grandmother, Johanna listened with affection as well as politeness.

Toward midnight the old lady began to get peevish. She was bored with her own stories. What she had hoped for that night was that Martin would have come to see Johanna, that she might herself have insisted on going into her bedroom off the parlor, leaving them in privacy. How much of her life had been spent alone in the great, wide bed, listening in the darkness for any little rustle of courtship beyond the door. In the midst of the dark silence then she could put her hand to the emptiness beside her and remember the man who had lain there . . . and who had died there at the age of thirty-seven, leaving her a rich woman.

"Don't you worry when your brother stays out so late, Johanna?"

"Yes." The girl automatically reached for the knitting she had put by while the old lady was talking.

"Yes," Mrs. Tonelli mimicked. "Is that all?"

"No matter how much I worry, it doesn't change anything."

The old lady smacked her lips. Her mouth had gone dry with so much talking. "Do you think he is a good boy?"

"No," Johanna said after a moment, and then added with utter frankness, "but I try not to think about it very often. Is he worse than other boys his age? I don't know. And when I think what I was like at his age, it makes me ashamed on my own account, so I can't be too hard on Georgie. Adolescence is a terrible time really."

The old lady looked at her with a mixture of amusement and mockery. The girl was only two years older than her brother. "Oh, a terrible time," she said solemnly. "When will your mother be able to leave the hospital?"

"Soon. Early next week, they said."

"So soon. And such a serious operation."

Johanna suspected that Mrs. Tonelli was trying to fetch information. She rarely asked directly what she wanted to know most. The girl said nothing.

"*Why* doesn't that boy come home?"

"I'm sorry," Johanna said.

"Don't be sorry. I'm enjoying myself."

At a few minutes past twelve Georgie let himself in the side door and came directly to the parlor, for once not even stopping to comb his hair. He looked much as though he had just come off the football field, his plump cheeks flushed, the small eyes sparkling.

"I was afraid you'd gone to bed," he said. "Hi, Jo."

His sister nodded.

The old lady gave a little flourish with her head. "Hi, Georgie."

"I brought you something, Mrs. Tonelli," he said, and drew from within his sweater a brown, red and yellow feather. It was long and curved, almost a plume. She took it and turned it around in her fingers, her rings again glistening. Then she recognized it and burst out laughing. It was a tail feather from one of Mayor Covello's handsome cocks.

"Georgie Rocco, what have you been up to?" It was said with a glint of wicked understanding in her eye.

"What is it?" Jo said as Mrs. Tonelli laid the feather atop her jewel box.

Georgie knew then that he had been right: the old girl was with him. "Well, I'll tell you, Mrs. Tonelli, I don't think there's going to be any gambling raids in Hillside—not by outsiders, there isn't."

The old lady clacked her teeth, working her mouth excitedly. Her head quivered a little, nerves, impatience with her own infirmities. "Johanna," she said, "it is a long time since supper. Get us a sandwich. You would like that, Georgie? And some hot chocolate?"

"Man, would I!"

Johanna put down her knitting with great deliberation,

carefully arranging the needles to hold the stitches. She did not like to be sent from the room like a child, and she suspected that was what was happening.

"Thanks, Jo," her brother said when she finally got up.

"I haven't done anything yet," she said and left the room.

The old lady was leaning forward in her chair.

"Make a lap," Georgie said.

"What?"

He did not wait to explain. He took a fistful of dollar and five-dollar bills from his pocket. She made a lap as wide as a kite. He dumped the money in it. "You aren't to say anything," he said then. "I mean, we're all pledged. Nobody talks. What you're supposed to do with the money, you give it away, or save it up for something special. Sometimes maybe you can give me the price of . . ." he almost said cigarets, ". . . a haircut. But that's all I'm to have, see. That's part of the pledge."

"Whose pledge?"

"Me—and some other guys."

"What happened, Georgie?" she demanded.

"I can't tell you, Mrs. Tonelli. You'll see it in the papers maybe, only I don't think so. But I already told you more than I was supposed to. Can't you guess—from that feather and what I said?" Mentioning the feather, he observed the box on which she had laid it. He hadn't seen that before.

"Secrets," she said. "I am so full of secrets if I had a nickel for every one of them I would be a millionaire."

"Put the money away," he said. "I don't want to have to tell Jo. She's got no sense of humor." He plopped a fist into the fat of the other hand. "Man, you should have seen it!"

"If you aren't going to tell me everything, don't talk at all," the old lady said, folding the bills together. "Thirty dollars."

"Is that all?" Georgie blurted out.

"Do you want a certified accounting?"

"No, ma'am."

He had hoped she would put the money in the tooled leather box so that he might see what was in it, but she unsnapped her high collar and tucked it away in her bosom. "Am I the only beneficiary of tonight's—high jinks?"

"Certain other . . . ladies," Georgie said, immediately unsure of whether he had chosen the right word.

"Ladies?" she mocked. "There are all kinds of ladies."

"I mean the good kind," Georgie said.

She chortled. "Go and help your sister. She was worried about you. So was I."

"I'm sorry."

"I'm not. I enjoyed it."

Georgie grinned, but he sure couldn't dig this old girl. You couldn't be sure whether she was going to spit at you or wink at you. But one thing he liked about her, she wasn't always pawing him, the way some old people did. Even his mother. He didn't like to be touched, not by anybody, except maybe in a fight. His mind ran to Rosie. He'd given her a crack tonight for mauling him, poking her hand up under his sweater. He shouldn't have done that, but she shouldn't either. When he and the guys left the joint at eleven, she was sitting up on the stool, whimpering. Sitting there in her snug little skirt. How he hated flesh, his own, anybody's. That's why he liked the old lady, maybe. She was all bones in a skin bag.

"Give me your hand, Georgie." She pulled herself up. "Now, go and help your sister."

"Can't I help you?"

"No, thank you. I had to manage before you came, and I will have to manage after you go."

"I'm not going," Georgie said. "I mean, I'd rather stay here. You know what I mean."

"I think I do. Goodnight, Georgie. Tell Johanna to bring me a cup of chocolate to my room." Using her cane with one hand and taking the box under her arm, she didn't exactly skip from the room. But she could get around all right once she got started.

Georgie went to the kitchen door, lolled against the frame, and watched his sister take the pot from the stove when the milk came to a boil. "What'd you do all night, Jo?"

"What did *you* do?"

"I asked you first," Georgie said.

"We talked." With a nod of her head, she indicated Mrs. Tonelli. "Mostly about things she remembered in Hillside—dances and parties, and what people were like then."

"What's in the box?"

"Some old jewelry. Things she'd worn a long time ago."

"She ought to keep 'em in a bank," Georgie said.

A little uneasiness stirred in Johanna. Mrs. Tonelli *should* keep such things in a bank or somewhere safe, living alone as she did. Seeing the jewelry, she had supposed some of it valuable. She wondered now. She didn't like to think Georgie might be tempted—that way. But it passed through her mind. She knew quite a lot about temptation. He could be tempted without even knowing it at first. "I'll have my check Monday, Georgie, if you need some money."

"A couple of bucks maybe," he said. He went to the table where Jo had set out the cups and saucers. "The old lady wants me to bring her a cup of cocoa. She's going to bed."

"Don't call her the old lady," Johanna said in a low voice.

"Okay, okay. Don't fill it too full. I don't want to slop it in the saucer."

A moment later, he tapped at the bedroom door.

"Come!"

He opened the door. The old lady was sitting in front of her mirror, trying to put a great hunk of jewelry around her neck. The box was open.

"So! I have a new chambermaid. You are going to be more useful than I thought."

"Yes, ma'am," Georgie said, and by really concentrating, he managed to carry the hot chocolate across the room without spilling it. But by the time he reached her she had put away the pendant and closed the box.

14

Bassett, despite his intention of putting Hillside out of his mind for the weekend, spent Sunday afternoon going over the reports of the laboratory technicians. One particularly pertinent piece of evidence was the presence in the head wounds of the victim of a black, resinous, adhesive substance common to electrical tape. It would seem that the killer had taped his weapon. Why? Among the possibilities, Bassett reasoned, was that a familiar tool, say a wrench or a tire lever or even a large screwdriver could have been used and immediately returned to its place; the removal and destruction of the tape would banish all clues as to its deadly use. He made a note to have the plant tool shop searched immediately for the possible weapon. The removal of the tape would remove all prints, distinguishing the tool in that way.

Another possibility was that MacAndrews' assailant had taped his weapon to lessen its lethal potential, to make of it a sort of blackjack. He studied the photographs of the wound, and read the analyst's conjecture. One wound had been comparatively light, a second had crushed the skull: strong but inept, possibly scared killer. What had scared him? Having a weapon so doctored, he must have planned to use it. Bassett wondered if he would not have got some of the substance under his fingernails in removing the tape. There were a great many fingernails in Hillside and not a few of them could do with scraping—with or without police provocation.

He turned in the report of the two stockings found in the vicinity of the boxcar: nylon, not a pair, the brand name(s) worn away, variation in size and style. There were no dry skin flakes such as were usually present under the microscope when the hose had been immediately removed from a

woman's leg. There was a perfumed and slightly oily substance discernible in one of them, suggesting to the examiner
the possibility of sun lotion. This would account, too, for the
absence of dead skin tissue. Both stockings had been twisted
at approximately the knee area, suggesting that the stockings
had been rolled at the knee. And there were no marks of
supporters at the tops.

Bassett scowled. He did not like interpretations of evidence in such instances, preferring to make his own, fresh.
A woman, he reasoned, might wear an unmatched pair of
hose, but it was unlikely, even in Hillside. And rolled at the
knee? With skirts at their present height? Sun lotion in October? He doubted it. And on only one stocking? Hair dressing more likely. It had been in his mind from the beginning
that MacAndrews' assailants had used the stockings as disguises. This made possible the assumption that at least two
people were involved . . . one of them a killer.

For the first time he was sanguine of his and Kearns'
chances. A murderer could live with himself; a great many
of them did; there were not many Raskolnikovs in the world.
But the man who has seen murder, perhaps especially an
accessory, is a bad security risk to the murderer.

He drove over to see Kearns at the Hillside police station.
The chief had been at his desk for some time; the air in the
small room was pudding-thick with cigar smoke. Kearns
pulled continually at the lobe of his ear while the county
detective elaborated on his theory about the stockings. He
said finally, "A lot of kids in this town use pomade—or some
kind of guck on their hair."

Bassett thought for a moment. "That's interesting—what
you just said, Chief—a lot of *kids*. Do you think it was the
work of youngsters?"

Kearns grunted and rode a squeaking swivel chair back
from his desk. He lighted a fresh cigar. Bassett felt impacted
in the smoke. "I better tell you what happened here last
night," Kearns said. "I don't know just what to make of it
myself. I'll tell you this—there's some pretty damn sore men
biting their tongues this morning. A gang of our own kids

pulled off a gambling raid last night. Cleaned out every game in the town.''

Bassett's first impulse was to laugh. To cover himself he murmured, "I'll be damned." He remembered that just two nights before Kearns had said he didn't know of any specific gambling in Hillside. It had been obvious long since, however, that he had not wanted to know.

As though following Bassett's mind, he said, "Makes me look like a clout, don't it?"

Bassett wasn't going to moralize at this point. He shook his head and waited for the morose policeman to go on.

"They even cleared out Covello's cock-roost."

This time Bassett could not suppress a grin.

Kearns squinted at him through the smoke, a twist of grim humor on his own lips. "Yeah," he said, "think of all the poor bastards that'll be eating cock for their Sunday dinner."

Bassett laughed.

"Only it ain't funny," Kearns said. "The kids went in armed with broken bottles—and wearing stockings over their faces for masks."

Bassett sobered. "How many of them?"

"Maybe twenty. They hit five places at once."

"Twenty," Bassett said disconsolately. Then he added, "Well, it's not two hundred anyway. I think we'd be on the right track looking for our killer among them. Don't you?"

Kearns pulled at his cigar and shot the smoke toward the ceiling. "The trouble is, nobody's talking. Ask any teenager where he was last night and he'll shrug and say, 'Around.' Even kids who weren't in on it. I asked my own boy at lunchtime where he was last night, knowing for a fact he was in a movie with the wife and his sister. But what does he say to me? 'Around.' I wanted to smack him across the face, but it wouldn't do any good. And that's how it is around the whole damn town."

"The Vigilantes," Bassett said after a moment, "the children's crusade. No chance, I suppose, of finding out who organized it?"

"Not from inside the organization," Kearns said.

"You think there's an organization?"

"It ran last night like one—like the Democratic primaries."

"Mind if I ask you a touchy question, Kearns?"

"The answer is yes," Kearns said bluntly. "I see no goddamn harm in a Saturday night poker game. I was eighteen dollars ahead when the stinking little punks moved in on us."

"All right," Bassett said. "How did it happen? Give me every detail. I wish to God I'd been in one of them."

"I wish you'd been, too, because you ain't going to understand this, not being there. It was a stiff game—four of us sticking it out. The fifth man was the dealer, and he was concentrating just as hard as the rest of us. It was me finally called. So did the guy next to me, and the guy next to him. The minute we showed cards, one of the young punks said, 'Keep your hands on the table and nobody'll get hurt.' I could feel the jagged end of a bottle in my back. I didn't know what it was till later, but I knew it was something sharp. 'Push all your money in the middle.' You couldn't see a thing—you know, we had one big light hanging over the table, a lot of smoke, and all you could see was shapes—and those stocking heads, one behind each man at the table. One of them scooped up the money—just the paper money— tipped over the table and they were gone. The guy who'd been dealer said, 'Let 'em go. They got raw glass. Somebody could get hurt bad.' "

"You didn't recognize even one of them, for Christ's sake? His shape, his voice, something?"

"Not so's I could swear to it, Bassett."

Bassett thumped his hands on his knees in frustration. He rubbed his palms against the rough tweed. After a moment he said without enthusiasm, "I suppose we can ask Morietti to post us on the free spenders in the next few days."

"There won't be any," Kearns said. "Every jack-nipping kid of them took his cut of the swag home to mother. Let me tell you, it'll be a rainy day before any of that money comes out in the open. And do you think the women are going to talk? I don't. No, sir."

"But one of those kids is a killer."

Kearns set the stub of the cigar in the crowded ashtray. Mercifully it had gone out. He said, without looking at the detective, "If you'd felt the naked edge of glass in your back, Mr. Bassett, you'd've got the feeling that maybe all of them were."

15

The first period on Monday mornings was left open at Hillside High School for religious instruction. Those who did not attend Father Walsh's class went to study hall, a small group, primarily Negro who were Baptist, with a smattering of the children of the middle class residents of Hillside, the people who lived north of the village, along the river, and who commuted to the city to their work. Most of the latter youngsters did not stay to complete high school locally: it had been their parents' intention that they should, enrolling them; for the most part they believed in public school education and they believed in the democratic leveling—theoretically. But most of them got qualms at the first sound of the Hillside accent in their children's speech, and very soon all sorts of doubts set in about the whole school system, and not long after that, a way was found in such homes to send the children to private schools or other public schools in the county of better scholastic record.

Men like Father Walsh worked hard among this middle class to persuade them not to transfer their children, to join with him and other local leaders in trying to improve Hillside. They were sympathetic. They liked the young priest. So did their children. While Father Walsh taught only religious instruction, he sometimes dropped in on the other classes and gave what the youngsters called a pep talk. He could even rally a class in mathematics. "Well," he'd say, after a few minutes' observation. "I'd better go now. I don't want to learn too much that's new in one day. Not at my age. But you . . ." He would tap the head of a youngster in passing, ". . . you've got lots of room left up there. Fill it up."

Georgie, trying to cram that week's assignment in Chris-

tian Doctrine into his head in the last five minutes before the
first bell, decided that on account of all that had happened
to him—his mother sick, his house burning down—he could
get away with saying he didn't have time to do his homework.
Only the funny thing was, he didn't want to have to say that.
No more excuses for Georgie Rocco. Georgie could do anything he wanted to do. *A mortal sin is committed by one who
sins against God, 1, in an important matter, 2, with clear
knowledge, 3, with full consent.* He closed the book, holding
the place with his finger, and recited the words to himself.

Tommy Lodini went by. "Hey, Georgie!" Lodini clasped
his hands in the air and shook them. A lot of the guys did
that—not saying anything, but congratulating him on the raid
Saturday night. The girls were still making happy talk over
the football game. Somebody had chalked the score on all
the school steps, on the walls, all over. Georgie himself had
almost forgotten about the game, it seemed so long ago,
with the raid and all. Man, this was how to live, one bang
after another!

A mortal sin . . . one, an important matter, two . . . He
had to look it up. When you can't remember something, Father Walsh always said, try to think of what it means. That's
all that counts. Words are simply the tools you put something
together with. Something important. When you came right
down to it, Georgie thought, important things were done by
important people, good things, bad things. So only important people could commit mortal sins. Man, he had something there, Georgie decided, something to try on old Padre
Walsh that would get him talking most of the period maybe.
Some of the guys did that, got a teacher started on a subject
he was hipped on so the first thing he knew the bell rang
without half the class being called on at all. Georgie had
always wanted to pull something like that, but he hadn't been
smart enough. Anything he'd ever tried turned out to be silly.
Even guys dopier than him would join in the ha-ha's. It always
made him feel like a creep. Only Georgie Rocco wasn't
creeping any more, not for any man.

"Father . . ." Georgie raised his hand.

"Yes, Georgie?"

"For a mortal sin . . . I mean, to commit a mortal sin, just an ordinary person couldn't do it, could they?"

"I think they *could*," the priest said, "but I think quite a number of people go through life without ever committing a mortal sin, if that's what you mean. They obey the commandments of God, and the Church, they try to control their passions . . ."

"That's what I mean," Georgie interrupted, for he knew that once old Walsh got going, it wasn't going to be Georgie's question any more. And Georgie liked his question. "I mean, an ordinary little guy doesn't have passions, does he?"

Georgie Rocco, the metaphysician. The priest looked at him. "We are each of us responsible before God to the limit of our understanding. A man does not have to be a king or a bank president or a lawyer to commit a serious sin . . ."

"I know, but, Father . . ." Georgie tried to interrupt.

This time the priest went on: "Our Lord Himself seems to have made a point of being an ordinary little man, but there was nothing ordinary about His capacity for love and suffering."

"I didn't mean that kind of passion," Georgie said.

"Ah," Father Walsh said, an exaggerated sound of sudden understanding, "you mean the Elvis Presley kind, or the television bang, smash, boom kind, that kind of passion."

One of the girls in the class tittered.

"A lot of ordinary people seem to understand that kind," the priest said. "I'm not sure I do."

The hell you don't, Georgie thought.

"But I try. Let's take a look at this word 'passion.' What is it? It's excess. An excess of hatred, of love, of anger, of any of the emotions that make up the human being. When they are controlled by a man's will, they are forces for good. Let go—they are the forces for evil in the world. Now I don't think your ordinary little guy could do as much evil as Hitler did, but somebody killed a man in this town last Friday night, cruelly struck him in the back of the head and killed him. It wasn't Hitler that did that, but the man's dead. The Fifth

Commandment says 'Thou shalt not kill.' It doesn't say thou shalt not kill one, or six, or six million. It says simply thou shalt not kill. And the commandments of God were given to all men, rulers, and laborers.''

He knows, Georgie though. Or he thinks he knows. Why would he harp on murder if he didn't? Twisting a question like that. Georgie wished now that he had not opened his mouth. But having opened it—no retreat. That was Georgie's code now: no retreat.

''Now then, to come back to your question, George—you remember it, don't you?''

''Yes, Father, but I wasn't sure you did.''

A little shivering sound of shock ran through the class.

Father Walsh got that hard, tight smile on his mouth that made many a wise guy squirm. ''I was wondering when you asked the question, George, if you were making a pitch for the ordinary man—or for mortal sin?''

''I was just asking a question,'' Georgie said sullenly.

''Somehow, I got the feeling it was a loaded question,'' the priest said. ''But I'm a suspicious man on Monday mornings.'' His tone grew lighter. He was getting himself out of a spot, Georgie thought. And sure enough, Walsh fired his question: ''How many things are necessary to make a sin mortal, George?''

''What I meant, Father,'' Georgie persisted, ''it'd be easier for a priest to commit a mortal sin than somebody ordinary, like me.''

''I thought I answered that part of your question, George. We are, each of us, responsible before God to the degree of our understanding of what we do. Since a priest's understanding of the nature of sin—and of the danger of temptation to sin—is greater than most laymen's—so would his responsibility be greater, and his sin graver. As for the word 'easier,' I've always said to you that words are tools. It's the meaning that counts. Some men get their job done by using the tools backwards—as you've just done. And in those terms, yes, it is easier for a priest to commit a mortal sin.'' The priest addressed the class: ''Who will tell me the three things necessary to make a sin mortal?''

Christ! What did that mean, using his tools backwards? It couldn't mean what Georgie thought of, the screwdriver handle he had used on old MacAndrews. It was just one of those tricks that happened. Coincidence. When people threw words around like Padre Walsh, some of them were going to hit home. Walsh couldn't know . . . unless Pekarik or Daley told him. Daley wasn't even a practicing Catholic. Pekarik . . . no, Georgie was sure of it. Pekarik was getting to be like Georgie Rocco's shadow. He'd never had it so good— scoring the touchdown, thirty bucks for his old lady . . . Georgie listened dully while Rosie Gerosa told the priest the three things that made a sin mortal. But Georgie had learned one thing: he was a man of action—no more philosophic ping-pong for him.

And if Padre Walsh thought he knew something, okay. What the hell? Georgie Rocco knew something, too. And he *knew* he knew it. And Padre Walsh knew he knew it. The nerve of him, talking about sin like the price of eggs. And after what Georgie had seen. Talk about cool! Georgie had learned something else: you couldn't tell what was inside a man by looking at his face—or listening to him preach—or watching him play football—or seeing him tape the handle of a screwdriver. He'd never gone back to dig out the tape: that was a funny thing about himself, Georgie thought. He was always going to look for it when he couldn't do it. Then when he could, he put it out of his mind on purpose. No retreat, Georgie said to himself, explaining something inside him that was close to fear. No retreat!

''Now, George.'' The priest returned to him suddenly, having ranged the class and the subject of sin, mortal and venial, and all the circumstances necessary to make a sin mortal. ''To go back for just a minute, before winding up, to who commits what kind of sin. It was the soldiers and the rabble who crucified Christ, it was one of His own beloved disciples who denied Him, and one of them who betrayed Him, but on the Cross, with His dying words, Christ made no distinction when He said, 'Father, forgive them, for they know not what they do.' We must look into our own hearts for the gravity of our sins, not into the hearts of others. And beyond that lies the mercy and understanding of God. Class dismissed.''

After class, on the way to study hall, Georgie said to Pekarik, "How about that? I made him sweat, didn't I?"

"Yeah," Mike said with a sort of giggle, "but, man, you gave me the sh-sh-shakes!"

16

The mourners at James MacAndrews' funeral were not numerous, Bassett observed from where he sat in his parked car across the street from the funeral home: a member or two from the church in which MacAndrews had been an elder; he would say three friends of sister Grace's, who had an almost professional air about them as though attending funerals was their business; lodge brothers, Bassett supposed of the four men who stood near the steps smoking till the last minute, congenial among themselves, eager to assist. That the warmest personal support Grace MacAndrews found in her hour of bereavement was the arm of Alden Royce, the Graham Company executive, was an irony too painful, in Bassett's view, for a person given to the ordinary human sentiments to contemplate. She walked from the limousine, stiff and proud and tearless. Mourning becomes Electra, he thought, for those who saw her stood in awed respect until she passed, the lodge brothers concealing their cigarets behind their backs.

The one person whose presence stirred the detective's curiosity was Martin Scully. He would not have said from what he knew of the young man that conscience would have sent him here. Nor was he a hypocrite. Curious. Bassett waited out the service, and when afterwards Scully, an obvious stranger among the mourners, moved quickly to the nearest bus stop, Bassett turned his car around and offered him a ride home.

Scully accepted. He took for granted that Bassett knew where he had been, asking, "Were you at the funeral?"

"I was curious to see who would show up," Bassett said. "You never know."

Scully was silent for a minute. "Did you notice the big man with Miss MacAndrews? You'd have thought he was bosom family, wouldn't you?"

Bassett said, "I shouldn't think there was much bosom in that family."

Scully grinned.

"Fact is, I met the man Saturday," Bassett said. "Alden Royce, vice president of Graham—in charge of the southern hospitality division among his other duties."

"Did he try that on you? Clean up the mess quick, or we move south?"

"It set me to wondering," Bassett said, "if they use the same line down there: Keep these boys in line or we'll move the whole operation up north."

"Maybe," Scully said. "Maybe they do. Wouldn't that just serve us damn right—if it was all bluff? I keep telling the fellows, you've got to play it that way—call their bluff."

"Like a poker game," Bassett said, rather too pointedly. But he caught the quick glance Scully gave him out of the corner of his eye. "I don't suppose you were sitting in on a game Saturday night?"

"Saturday night I was getting as drunk as I'm ever likely to," Scully said, "at Luke's Tavern. I heard about it."

"What did you hear?"

"That a bunch of juvenile delinquents broke up the games. It's crazy, isn't it?"

"Wild," Bassett said dryly. "Of course, I don't know Hillside like a native."

"I guess I'm what you'd call a native, but it's crazy to me, too. What I'm trying to figure out is how I've been caught up in it."

"Are you?" the detective asked.

Scully stretched his neck, maneuvering free of his topcoat collar, and rubbed the back of his head. "It's not like a dream exactly. Everything's familiar, but I just can't get hold of things. I mean, at their beginning. Halfway through I'm suddenly involved and I don't know how it started. Do you know what I mean?"

"Not exactly," Bassett said.

"Well, if I'd had a fight with my girl, for one thing, I'd understand it. I mean, that's part of it, too. That's why I got drunk Saturday night. I don't drink. But Jo and I . . ." He shook his head and laughed a little at his own predicament. "That's *my* problem."

Bassett chanced a direct question. "What happened?"

"Nothing. Nothing I can think of—between us, I mean. But she doesn't want to see me. I always thought Jo and I were different, what we wanted, and hanging on in Hillside to make it come out of ourselves, our own people. Everybody's swinging out for himself, you know? Take my grandmother—where Jo and her brother's staying now—I've got six uncles and they're all gone—New York, Jersey, and their kids, scattered all over the country. And now, that night after the fire, Jo wanted to go away, too. It's crazy." Again he shook his head in bewilderment.

"It's in the times," Bassett said, trying not to seem portentous. "No roots. Nobody wants roots. They're afraid they'll get hurt, afraid they'd get excavated when we start building fall-out shelters. Stay loose: that's what the kids say these days, isn't it?"

"Yeah," Scully said doubtfully.

Bassett put his next question carefully: "Are you on good terms with your girl's—what's her name, Johanna?—with her brother?"

Scully thought about it. "On as good terms as you can get with a kid like that. Football, the *Crazy Cat*, mooching quarters from me. You wouldn't know him and Jo were brother and sister, I'll tell you that."

Bassett pulled the car off the road below the high school. Far out on the river a freighter was moving toward Albany. A vast span of quiet water was otherwise deserted, the pleasure craft out of the river for the winter. "Let's talk here for a few minutes," the detective said. "What you were saying a minute ago—about the breaking up of families. Jo would have absorbed some of your feeling about that, wouldn't she?

What I'm suggesting, Scully, couldn't she be torn in her loyalty between you and her own family?''

Scully said after a moment, ''Her mother's got a funny attitude toward me, I'll say that.''

''And her brother?''

''I'm a square as far as he's concerned. I guess that's how Mrs. Rocco feels too. She'd like Jo to marry a businessman.''

Bassett did not want to get into a discussion of the Roccos' mother, having heard what he had about her. But the whole case seemed to have waves within waves. ''I suppose the boy is the mother's pet,'' he said.

''She likes boys, I'll say that,'' Scully said unguardedly. The color rose instantly to his face. ''I'd better get on home, Mr. Bassett. I've done my duty to the men. Now I've got to do it to myself.'' He explained: ''The men at the plant elected me to represent them at the funeral.''

''Ah, I see,'' Bassett said. ''I wondered why you were there.''

''Now I've got to go up to the office and give Mr. Royce my final answer to his crummy offer.''

A series of waves sloshed against the cribbing, the backwash of the freighter reaching the shore. Waves within waves.

''He offered you MacAndrews' job?''

Scully nodded. ''The oldest trick of management—buy off the opposition.''

''How do the men feel about it?''

''I didn't ask them,'' Scully said. ''But I know: they'd like me to take it.''

''Who'll get it if you don't?''

Scully shrugged. ''They'll probably bring somebody in from the outside. Like MacAndrews—they brought him in twenty years ago.''

''You can't blame the men, in a way,'' Bassett ventured.

''Maybe you can't,'' Scully said, and his jaw went rigid for a second. ''But I hope they bring in a real Simon Legree. Then maybe we'll get somewhere.''

Bassett turned on the ignition. ''It's such an old-fashioned problem to be fighting out in this day and age. The issue seems so clean, if you know what I mean. I was about to say that I was on your side—but I can't imagine anyone not being on your side.''

"That's Hillside,'' Scully said.

Bassett waited for a beverage truck to pass and then pulled into the road behind it. "There's something I want you to think about, Martin, till we get to your place: do you think young Rocco was part of the gang putting on the gambling raid?''

"I'm sure of it,'' he said, "which doesn't mean I could prove it. But he'd be in on anything like that if he didn't have to go it alone.''

"And MacAndrews' murder?'' Bassett shot the question at him.

This time Scully was slow to answer. "Do you think there's a connection, sir?''

"I do.''

"Oh, my God,'' Scully said quietly, and then repeated, "Oh, my God.'' He did not speak again until Bassett stopped the car to let him out. "What about the fire at the Roccos'?''

Bassett said, "It seems a remarkable coincidence, doesn't it?''

Scully made no move to leave the car. "Something Father Walsh said to me once—he's our assistant pastor—'Martin,' he said, 'you're working with the wrong generation. Leave the old men to the likes of me. Get youth on your side. Old men follow young men when you kick the past out from under them.' It was Father Walsh who got me coaching the kids in track and baseball . . . But off the field, I've got no relationship with them . . . Funny. Like my cause or whatever you'd call it, I'm old-fashioned, too. No rapport with my own times.''

"What about football?'' Bassett said. "Do you do any of the coaching there?''

Scully shook his head. "They've got a pro for that.'' Then he looked at the detective. "Georgie was Saturday's hero, wasn't he?''

Bassett nodded. "It was a brutal game. I saw it. My youngster was on the other team, and I found myself wishing one minute he'd stop running away, and the next thanking God that he did. But it gave me a chance to watch young Rocco play quarterback.''

"Quarterback? That takes brains," Scully said in undisguised sarcasm. "I wonder where he found them."

"You seem to have underestimated your future brother-in-law," the detective said with a purposeful touch of sarcasm of his own.

"Have you talked to him?"

"But not to his sister," Bassett said in his way of sometimes skipping a direct answer. "Not yet," he added.

"And you're going to have to, I suppose?"

"Yes."

Scully started to say something, changed his mind and got out of the car. There he changed it again. "Tell her . . ." He faltered.

"Better tell her yourself, Martin. I don't always get messages straight. Good luck, boy."

Driving away, Bassett saw a worried young man staring after him. As he drove across the tracks, he caught a last glimpse of Scully, his head back, crossing the street toward the gate of the Graham plant.

The detective doubled back and checked in at the Hillside police station. A thorough search of the Graham machine shop had failed to turn up even a possible murder weapon.

Kearns said that he was glad of that.

"Why?"

The police chief shrugged. "The men are edgy—scared maybe of what's going to happen at the plant. I feel as though we're sitting on a dynamite charge myself."

Bassett felt like asking him why he didn't get the hell off it then. But that was an easy thing to say to a man who didn't know which way to jump.

"You were up at the fire Friday night—after sending MacAndrews to the mortuary. Was there any suspicion of arson?"

Kearns thought for a moment. "I wouldn't say that. I know

Lodini was puzzled as to how it could get such a good start—with both kids in the house—before the alarm was put in.''

"It's a certain fact that both the kids were in the house?" Bassett said.

"We can go over to the station and check Lodini's report. He'd have made out a record, you know, in case there was an insurance investigation."

"Why don't you do it alone? I'd be conspicuous. A routine sort of check, that's all."

"What got you onto this, mind telling me?"

Bassett said easily, "It just seems to me now that we ought to check into every unusual happening in the town from that night on."

"Fires happen in this town fairly regular," Kearns said, "specially around early in the heating season. But I guess you're right. We ought to check."

"I'll wait here," Bassett said.

Kearns was nettled at having to do something at once, but he started out, having instructed Bassett on the operation of the phone board. At the last minute Bassett gave him a cigar. "It ought to be a pretty good one," the detective said. "My neighbor became a father this morning—first time."

"They're generally the best," Kearns said, presumably of the cigar, for he put it to his nose and nodded confirmation. "Thanks."

Bassett, sitting in the police office, gradually became aware while he was waiting, of an increase in traffic overhead. The station was on the first floor of the brick building that also housed the town hall. Something was going on. Odd, he thought, that a meeting should convene in the middle of the afternoon. He popped his head out the door in time to see the mayor of the village go upstairs. He heard the scraping of chairs across the floor. Then he was occupied for some moments with the area police checkouts. A bad accident had occurred between a bus and a trailer truck on the highway five miles north. They could manage without Hillside's help, he decided.

Kearns returned. He handed Bassett a page from a loose-leaf notebook, the handwriting neat and round: a careful entry. "Read it for yourself," the chief said. "Wasn't anybody around so I borrowed it."

You could borrow almost anything in Hillside, Bassett thought, with the possible exception of money. He read:

"Fire reported from telephone number Hillside 6-2724 at 11:33. Second report from alarm box No. 3 at 11:35. First truck on scene 11:40. Fire centered in living room, first floor . . . Quick spread through flues . . ."

Bassett skipped to the paragraph starting with the word COMMENTS printed in block letters, and what followed:

"J. Rocco, age 19, upstairs in bedroom when first smelled smoke. G. Rocco, age 17, in basement. G. Rocco says fire might have started from cigaret sister knocked out of his hand in fight. Estimates time at 10:30 o'clock.

"House wooden frame, built 1912, electrified 1920. No record subsequent wiring. Oil heat to furnace in basement. Underground tank sealed off by fireman M. Scully immed. on reaching scene.

CONCLUSIONS:

The report ended without the fire chief having yet filled in any conclusions.

Bassett studied the fairly terse report: several things provoked his curiosity in light of his present information, the fight between brother and sister, for example. Free swinging quarrels no doubt occurred frequently in most families, even in his own which was far less volatile than the majority of Hillside's. But in view of Martin Scully's subsequent difficulty with the sister, it warranted exploration.

He picked up the phone on Kearns' desk and asked the operator to find out for him whose phone Hillside 6-2724 was. Before he got the information he remembered the old lady's telling him that she had called the fire department. He asked Kearns, "Has anyone talked to old Mrs. Tonelli?"

"About what?"

It was a good question: to talk to her the interrogator would need to know what he was about. From his own brief encounter with her, Bassett suspected she would tell what she thought suited the occasion, truth or half-truth or, if she thought it appropriate, telling a lie would not faze her. She had the aged crone's contempt for fact, trusting rather to her own intuition. And having taken the two Rocco children to her lonely hearth, she was likely to be fiercely protective of them. "I just thought she might be the community sage," he said, "the matriarch to whom younger people might go when they needed advice."

Kearns grunted. Obviously he did not think much of the idea. Nor did he try for subtlety in his next remark, an association with another of Bassett's bright ideas that had failed to come to anything: "I got to go over and reopen the laundromat. Some people got pretty sore about that."

The laboratory reports on the contents of the various machines had been negative.

"They ought to be pretty sore about some rather more important things," Bassett said. He tossed the report across the table. "That can go back any time." He put on his topcoat. "Johanna Rocco works at the post office, doesn't she?"

Kearns took the half-smoked cigar from his mouth, looked at it, and threw it into the bucket in the corner. "Why don't you leave the girl alone? She's got her hands full—mother sick, no house to bring her home to. Grill the brother, if that's what you're after. I'd even say that was a pretty good idea. But Jo's a real nice girl and I don't want us making trouble for her."

Chivalry wasn't dead in Hillside, Bassett thought. He asked, "Is that an order, Chief?"

"Hell, no. That's a recommendation, and I don't guess you'll be any more likely to take that than you would orders from me."

"I promise you, I'll be as gentle as a father with her," Bassett said.

Kearns snorted at what he knew of parental gentleness. Then he said, "Her old man was one of the best, God rest him. They don't make 'em that way any more."

17

Johanna had waited all day Sunday, hoping that Martin would call or come. He had not attended the nine o'clock Mass where it was their custom to meet and then go back to her house for breakfast. But Martin had not called. On Sunday afternoon she had gone alone to see her mother, Georgie begging off to do his homework. After all, he'd lost most of his books in the fire and had to borrow Rosie Gerosa's when she wasn't using them. Her mother had behaved strangely even for her whose moods were always unpredictable. She had been out of bed, dressed, and tossing her head in derision of the nurses who, she said, wanted to get rid of her. Johanna had proposed that she come to Mrs. Tonelli's for a few days. And that had sent her mother into a fury. "A son who doesn't care what happens to me and a daughter licking stamps in a post office. Look at you, Johanna!" And then, suddenly and inexplicably, she had become tender. "My little girl, my beautiful little girl. Don't waste your life like your mother. Marry a man as good as yourself. The insurance money, take it and go away. Be somebody!"

Money, Johanna thought, counting the pennies in the post office cash drawer. In Hillside people bought one stamp at a time. Martin was right—if money was everything, life was worthless.

"Miss Rocco?"

She glanced at the man outside the window grating and tried to remember where she had seen him before. He had a nice face, and he took off his hat when he spoke to her.

"I'm Ray Bassett, a detective, and I think I can call myself a friend of Martin Scully's."

"Has something happened to Martin?"

"No. I'm sorry if I frightened you that way. I didn't mean to. When I told him I was coming to see you, he proposed to send you a message, but I thought he had better save it until he could bring it in person. I wondered if we could talk for a few minutes, perhaps in the postmaster's office?"

"Mr. Jacobi is in there now himself." Johanna remembered now having seen the detective when he was waiting to talk to Georgie Saturday. He had wanted to talk to Georgie about Martin; so her brother had said. Now her. Johanna became even more guarded than was her ordinary way with strangers. But Mr. Bassett knocked on the door marked POSTMASTER, and now Mr. Jacobi came from his office through the inside door and jerked his head at her that she should go in.

"How is your mother?" Bassett asked, indicating the extra chair in the tiny room. He had drawn Mr. Jacobi's chair from behind the desk and sat down beside her.

"She's much better, thank you," Johanna said. She sat very straight, her hands tightly clasped in her lap.

"I'll tell you what I'm trying to do," the detective said quietly, almost soothingly. She knew he had noticed her hands, the way she was holding them, as though by keeping them quiet, she could also slow the beating of her heart. "I'm helping in the investigation of the murder at the plant Friday night. At this point, I'm having to go at it backwards, you might say. I'm trying to eliminate one after another of persons who might possibly have been involved."

"Martin isn't a murderer."

Bassett smiled a little. "I'm as convinced of that, Miss Rocco, as you are." He looked away from her, the quick relief in her dark eyes too painful. Whatever the trouble between her and Scully, she was still in love with the young man. Which made the detective's job at once simpler and more difficult. But who ever said a cop's job was easy? "Certain things have been happening in Hillside—perhaps you heard of the gambling raid Saturday night?" He watched her carefully, putting that question.

"No."

He would swear that she had answered him truthfully. Odd, the Vigilantes reportedly having taken home the money to their womenfolk. But Georgie would be saving his for his mother, of course. "A number of the boys of the town of, say, your brother's age, took it upon themselves to clean out the card games. They did it with a show of violence—and certain other characteristics that worry the police. I want to ask you: what time did your brother get home Friday night?"

"Saturday night. You said Saturday night." Johanna did not realize herself the urgency with which she corrected him. Bassett was well aware of it.

"We want to start with Friday night," he said as though oblivious to her reaction. "That's because, well, all our troubles seem to have started from then."

She did not look at him as she answered. "He's supposed to be home at ten."

"And was he?"

"I didn't look at the clock," she said, grateful that that much was the truth. In her heart, Johanna tried to pray: "Lord, help me not to have to lie. Please, Lord."

"I understand you and your brother had a quarrel. Do you mind telling me what that was about?"

"We often quarrel," she said, glancing furtively at him and then away. Then she forced herself to meet his eyes. "I'm responsible for him in a way if he's done something wrong. He hasn't really had the supervision a boy his age needs. And my mother . . . but you know that. You asked about her. I'm not trying to make excuses for Georgie. Or for myself." She paused and took a deep breath. "What has he done, Mr. Bassett?"

"He doesn't take you into his confidence?"

"Only when it suits him," she said.

"But you are reasonably sure he was home by ten o'clock Friday night?"

It was after ten, she knew, when Father Walsh had come, for she was already looking then for Georgie and wondering what she would do if he didn't come by midnight as had often been the case since her mother had gone to the hospital.

"Miss Rocco?"

"I was trying to remember," she said, and in that she knew at once that she had lied, for she was trying to forget. But Father de Gasso had told her in confession to forget, to put it out of her mind as though it had never happened. And Georgie had said, "Remember, sis, I was home at ten. That way, I didn't see a thing." *Put it out of your mind, child, as though it never happened.*

The detective let it go. "Did he call the hospital after he got home?"

The girl was surprised. "I don't think so, sir. But I went upstairs. I guess he could have."

"Is he in the habit of calling your mother?"

"No, sir." Then, by way of justifying her brother, she added, "Mother doesn't have a telephone in the room."

"Is your brother on an allowance?"

Johanna thought then that she understood. Perhaps some money had been stolen, and she knew Georgie had been spending freely. "I give him a dollar a week," she said, "but after the fire, Mrs. Tonelli—we're staying with her for a few days—she gave him some money to buy things we might need. I don't think Georgie needed everything he's been buying. But that's where he got the money, Mr. Bassett. He doesn't really get enough for himself. Or he doesn't think so."

"Most youngsters think they have that problem," the detective said. "And if they don't, they have a worse one."

She smiled, for the first time freely. It was a charming smile and it made Bassett ache a little. He would have wished her and Martin Scully free and clear of this mess. But he was deeply afraid that they were far from free of it. And he would have preferred not to have to ask his next question; yet he put it with all the deceptive cunning that his job demanded. "This may seem like a crazy question, but I'm asking it of all the girls: have you been missing any stockings lately?"

"Isn't that funny?" she said. "I got a new pair Saturday, and when I went to put them on Sunday morning, there was only one stocking in the box."

Whatever it was, it wasn't funny. "And before that, had you missed any?"

"Last week . . . I wasn't sure. I could have dropped it in the bathroom. Behind the tub, you see, there was a space. I forgot about it. It must have been Thursday. And then, after what happened Friday, the fire, I mean, a stocking didn't seem very important."

Not very important, Bassett thought. God in heaven! He was about to go back and force the issue of Georgie's ten o'clock alibi. The postmaster opened the door without knocking.

"You've got to take over out here, Jo. I'm going up to the village hall. The night shift's just been locked out of the plant."

Johanna looked at the detective. Her eyes pleaded for release.

"We can talk further at another time," Bassett said.

18

From where he stood in the doorway of the police station, Bassett could tell the temper of the men treading heavily upstairs. Nor was there any sort of recognition of him in the cold, dark eyes of those who measured him in passing. He'd have been more welcome in a New York dope pad than he was at that minute in the village hall of Hillside. He watched the legless man lift himself up the first step. Two men came up behind him and without a word, lifted him, each taking an elbow, and carried him cursing up the stairs.

Bassett turned back to where the chief of police was sitting morosely behind his cigar. "Just like that," Bassett said, "they can lay off two hundred men."

" 'Temporary suspension,' " Kearns quoted the official notice posted on the plant gate. "The stinking thing about it is, the men themselves have to decide how to split up the work—who'll go on the day shift next week."

"So that's what they've got a union for," Bassett said sarcastically.

Kearns threw him a sour look. "It don't take much of a brain to figure out the company's real motive. This time they're going to squeeze Scully out all the way. Started by offering him MacAndrews' job."

"I know," Bassett said.

"He should've taken it," Kearns said. "A lot of people depended on him there."

"If Graham wants him out so badly, why not fire him? They don't seem to have to show cause to anybody."

"That way they'd make a martyr out of him," Kearns said. "And you never just know what that might kick up."

"And this way, they'll let his own people crucify him."

141

"That's about it."

Bassett didn't say anything more. He watched from the window as others drove up and parked. Martin Scully came out on the stoop of his building, took a stick of gum from his pocket, unwrapped it and stuck it in his mouth. He wadded the wrapper, stepped to the empty waste container and dropped it in. He wore only his jacket, his shirt open at the throat. Bassett realized that the boy was steeling himself for an ordeal. Scully crossed the street and met trouble head-on before he reached the top of the stairs.

"Boy, you got a hell of a nerve coming here."

"Nobody's got any better right," Scully said. "Get out of the way."

"No, sir. We could've been going on work right now if you'd taken the job."

"If I'd turned myself into a rotten fink! You'd 've liked that, wouldn't you? Twenty more years slave labor, part-time, no pensions. And me checking the timeclock. No, sir, by God, I'll see 'em in hell before they get that kind of cooperation out of me. You want the job? Apply for it. I'll give you a recommendation. Joe Strego, company man."

"Don't be so goddam free with your recommendations. I can make some of my own. For example . . ." The man raised his voice over a murmuring chorus. While Bassett could not see what was happening beyond the turn in the staircase, he could see the shadows converging on the wall, a grotesque melee. "For example," the preface was repeated, "Mac's death played right into your hand, didn't it? Let me tell you, Scully, I know a thing or two about Red tactics. I know how they work. I been reading a series in the *Journal American*, and by Christ, if you didn't write the book for 'em, you could've. I want to tell you, man, come the revolution, it ain't going to come in Hillside."

An affirmative refrain echoed from those less articulate than Scully's attacker.

"What's your recommendation?" Scully said. "You said you had a recommendation. What is it?"

"That you get the hell out of town before Kearns gets off

his ass down there and finds out what really happened Friday night.''

The next phase, Bassett thought, if something didn't happen to forestall it: suspicion of the murder cast on Scully. It was a danger he had known to be latent in the situation from the beginning. He turned back to Kearns where he was sulking in a tent of cigar smoke. "How many kids have you questioned, Chief?"

"Ten or twelve. I might as well be whistling *Dixie*. None of them know from nothing since Saturday night. One of them had the nerve to say it to my face: 'I can't remember anything happening around here before Saturday night.' 'What happened Saturday night?' I says to him. And he just stood there, grinning, his hands in pockets jingling his change. Tell me the truth, Bassett, do you think it would do any good if I resigned and let them get somebody in here who could do the job? Me getting caught in that poker game just about washed me up.''

That was the trouble, Bassett knew, authority in Hillside was hamstrung, and the knots accumulating. Old Mrs. Tonelli, for example: he knew she wouldn't talk to him, a stranger. She had proved that on their one brief meeting. The Rocco kid would swear he was home by ten o'clock the night of the murder and maybe he was; just maybe he was. Bassett couldn't prove otherwise. He needed time and he needed help. Kearns was all but useless. He realized that he had been counting on Martin Scully. But what was happening on the stairs right now was no encouragement. Everything was getting more rigid. He decided to make a move before it was too late.

He went into the hall and up the stairs a few steps. "Scully!" he called out. "Will you come down here for a minute?"

The men looked down at him, those near the railing. One of them said, "Need some more aspirin, mac?"

Bassett remembered his first meeting with some of these men at the bar in the fire station. "A tranquilizer," he said, "like everybody else around here."

He closed the station door after Scully and motioned him onto the bench that served in lieu of extra chairs. "I'm going to ask something of you, Scully. It will go against the grain with you, but I'm hoping you'll see some merit in it. I need time. And I need more time than I would if I was getting cooperation. The screws are getting tighter all the time—and this business isn't helping." He jerked his head to indicate the activity in the upper hall.

Scully was listening, but there was a cold look in his blue eyes that was scarcely less discouraging than the black stares he'd been getting from the rest of the natives.

But Bassett went on. "Why don't you take the job at the plant for the time being? Get the men back to work till we get the murder solved. A few days on the side of management won't kill you. You might even learn something useful."

Scully was shaking his head. "After that nobody'd trust me."

"Who trusts you now?" Bassett said.

Scully thumbed his own breast. "*I* trust me."

All Bassett's persuasions availed him nothing. There was no compromise in Scully, and for all that the detective admired it in him, he saw in the inflexibility part of the reason Scully had got no further in unionizing the plant.

Kearns spoke for the first time. "Goddamn it, Martin, in this world we all got to make compromises."

"Not with the devil," Scully said.

Kearns got up and stalked to the door, muttering an obscenity. When he opened the door a young priest was standing just outside it as though uncertain whether or not to knock before opening it.

"Afternoon, Father," the chief said.

"I'm looking for Scully," the priest said.

Kearns said, "Help yourself," and went out.

"Well, Martin, I hear you're embattled," the priest said. It was not said lightly, but neither was it ponderous. He looked curiously at Bassett who then introduced himself. The two men shook hands. Bassett wondered then why he hadn't thought of the priest before. Young, open-faced and vigorous, he must be on good terms with the majority of his parishioners. There were disadvantages to being anti-clerical, the detective thought of himself; to being too much anti-anything.

"Mr. Bassett has been trying to persuade me to take MacAndrews' job at the plant," Scully said.

"And you're standing like Horatio at the bridge."

"I'm not sure what Horatio did at the bridge, Father."

The priest grinned and sidled his thigh up on Kearns' desk. "Matter of fact, I'm not either." He looked at the detective. "I'm afraid I'm on Martin's side, Mr. Bassett."

"So am I, but I've got a murder to solve and all these sideshows aren't making the job any easier." Bassett thought he was beginning to sound a little hysterical himself. "Take that gambling business Saturday night; all the kids who were in on it wore stockings over their faces. I'm pretty sure MacAndrews' killers did too. Coincidence? I don't think so. But can I get anybody to talk freely with me? No."

"Did you see Johanna?" Martin asked.

"Yes. She talked—up to a point. Then she had a bad memory—or maybe too good a memory."

"Why Johanna?" the priest asked.

Martin answered him, Bassett hesitating. "In my book, her brother qualifies as a fine prospect for juvenile delinquency."

"I see." The priest wasn't smiling. "That gambling business was nasty, wasn't it?" He addressed himself to the detective.

"Vicious," Bassett said. He would have liked to know when and how the priest had heard about it.

"I've just been to call on one of its beneficiaries," Father Walsh said. "Her husband asked me to. He owes somebody money who's putting the pressure on him, and he can't raise a cent, not even from his own wife. I didn't get any further with her than he did. She just sat and rocked and shook her head and said of her seventeen-year-old hero, 'My son is a good boy.' It would be funny if it weren't tragic."

If the priest couldn't get any place, Bassett thought, what chance had he?

"I'd better go upstairs if I'm going," Martin said. "They don't want me, but they're going to get me."

"Martin, wait a minute and I'll go with you," the priest said. "Those of the men laid off can go on unemployment insurance, can't they?" Scully nodded.

"I was talking to somebody who wants to build a ceramics factory in the county—cheap reproductions in quantity. God knows why people would want them. But they do. This whole expansion of light industry—why don't we get some of it into Hillside? Give Graham a run for the labor market. It can't happen overnight. But let's call this blind man's bluff of theirs."

"I think it's a hell of a good idea," Bassett said, "if you don't mind an outsider's opinion."

"What we need is to bring in a few more outside opinions," the priest said.

Scully said, "That'll be the day."

"You're wrong, Martin," Father Walsh said. "*This*'ll be the day. Bassett?"

"Yes, Father?"

"Are you coming up?" The priest got to his feet.

"Yes. Why not?"

No one barred their way but even the priest's reception in the men's midst could not have been called more than polite. And when Mayor Covello asked him if he wanted to say a few words to the men, and the priest launched into a spirited presentation of his idea for breaking the Graham tyranny, he might as well have been preaching a Sunday sermon—a dull one at that. They heard him out, and Bassett thought, if he had passed the collection plate at that point, he might have collected the few pennies left in the men's pockets. But no one else in the room, including Martin Scully, Bassett suspected, had either vision or wish to see beyond the Graham smokestack.

Suddenly the priest was angry, his face ruddy with wrath. He took off his Roman collar and threw it on the table. The eyes of the men standing near focused on it for a moment, then on him. Bassett felt his own heartbeat quicken.

"So what are you going to do, gentlemen? Draw lots to see which of your families eat and which go begging? That's *real* gambling, isn't it? That's a game of chance worthy of real men." His sarcasm was scathing. "After that's decided, you'll be masters in your own homes again, won't you? How in the name of God will you look yourselves in the eye, much less your sons and your sons' mothers after that?"

Now, Bassett thought, he was getting through to them. The shuffling feet, the downcast eyes. Give 'em hell, Father! he thought.

"Don't you see that you can't escape tyranny by obedience to it? You all want your jobs, don't you?"

A murmur of assents.

"Then stop laying one another off! That's what it amounts to. Either all of you go back to work! Or none of you go back to work. The answer to half a lock-out is a whole strike. Do you think for a minute that if they wanted to close this plant they'd take your vote on it? You know as well as I do—in one week they'd dismantle and ship the machinery out of here— the very machinery half of you are going to keep warm for them till they've got all of you where they want you—hungry and servile. They're thirty years late with these tactics. For the love of God and one another let's turn our clocks up in this town."

The men were staring at him now. They were not with him, but not against him either. When the priest waited for their response, Martin Scully said quietly, but clearly: "It sounds wonderful, Father. But it won't work. Not *this* time. We can draw unemployment compensation during a lay-off, but not during a strike. They know the position we're in. But next time . . . If we start getting ready for it now there might not even be a next time . . . if we start a strike fund: something every week. And that's what we *can* vote today."

"To be paid out of what if half of you aren't working?" the priest said.

Scully drew a deep breath. He looked at Bassett. Then he

said, "If we vote a strike fund today and elect a man in charge of it, I'll take their goddamn night manager's job."

There was no cheering, only the sounds men made beginning to see hope, a sort of change in their breathing.

The priest said, "They don't want you, Martin. That's what this is all about. They knew you wouldn't take the job when they offered it."

"Then they knew wrong," Scully said.

"And if they won't take you now?"

Scully looked to the plant workers.

One of them shook his fist in the air. "Then we strike, fund or no fund."

This time the assents rang loud enough to be heard round the hall.

One could only hope, Bassett thought, that if Scully won it would not turn out to be a Pyrrhic victory.

19

Georgie waited at the *Crazy Cat* for Johanna to meet him as soon as she got off work. By reminding Pete of how much money he had spent there after the football game Saturday, he persuaded the old gentleman to trust him for a Coke until his sister got there. This knighthood bit was rugged, giving all that dough to the old lady. He'd have been willing to bet half the guys sneaked a buck or two for themselves. Maybe not. Pete was groaning about how awful business was.

"Hey, Pete! Where is everybody?"

"Eh?" Pete turned his good ear.

"Nobody's around," Georgie said.

"Good," Pete said, whatever the hell that meant.

Johanna arrived no more than a minute before the bus was due. Georgie started out to meet her.

Pete called to him, "Hey, big shot!" By the rubbing of his fingers he reminded Georgie of the short-term credit.

"Sis, give me a dime. Nobody trusts nobody in this dump." He plopped the dime on the counter while Johanna got more money from her purse for the bus. "Keep the change, Pete."

Johanna was silent in the bus, her mind turned in on her own thoughts. She was trying not to think of the detective, or of her brother: she didn't like Georgie, really, but she had never allowed herself to admit that before, feeling rather strongly that even if it were so, it was a sin to admit it. She didn't even like the way Georgie sprawled his legs so that, fat as they were, the one next to her rubbed against her own. Involuntarily she drew away.

"Excuse me," Georgie said, and got up and moved to another seat.

Johanna followed him. "I'm sorry, Georgie."

"Too bad I ain't a priest." Johanna pulled herself into her shell. "C'mon, sis, I didn't mean that. It was you made me sore first. What if ma wants to come home?"

Johanna forced herself to tell her plans. "I've put up a notice in the post office asking if anybody has a small furnished apartment—cheap."

"You'll get us another firetrap," Georgie said. "Why can't we stay with the old lady? Mrs. T. wants us. She's begging us to stay."

"I don't want to," Johanna said, "but if you can get mother to say yes I won't say anything against it."

" 'Atta girl. See, I'll do some work around the place for Mrs. T., you know, repairs, things like that, and it won't be as if we weren't paying our way. Besides . . . I already gave her some money."

"Where did you get it, Georgie?" His sister looked round at him, sharp as a woodpecker.

He shouldn't have said anything, he realized. "A guy owed me some money. It wasn't a fortune. You don't have to worry."

"But I do worry. That Mr. Bassett, the detective, came to see me in the post office."

"What for?"

"He wanted to know about when you came home—Friday night."

Georgie's heart began to pound. "You told him, didn't you? That I was home around ten o'clock? You told him about Father Walsh being there? I don't mean you and him. I wouldn't ever tell that to anybody. You know that, Jo. I mean, I tease you, but I wouldn't tell anybody else."

"I didn't tell him about Father Walsh. I just said I thought you were home when you said you'd be."

"You got to tell the truth, Jo. It don't pay to lie to these guys. I was poking around in the basement, waiting for the padre to leave. Then I thought he was gone when I went outside and he wasn't sitting in the living room with you any

more. I didn't mean to spy, Jo. I couldn't help what *you* did.
Could I?''

Johanna had thought the whole picture was gone forever
from her mind. But after penitence came penance: ten Our
Fathers and ten Hail Marys had not been enough. She prayed
now within herself—to the Holy Ghost, as Father de Gasso
had counseled, but the Holy Ghost was a stranger and she
couldn't get a picture of Him. She commended her trouble
to the Sacred Heart.

Georgie was trying to figure ways of bolstering his own
defense. "You could get old Martin in trouble that way, Jo.
I mean, I don't want to scare you or nothing, but the reason
they keep asking about me—Martin and MacAndrews, you
know, the guy that got killed? They were enemies—and the
only way they can be sure Martin was in his room when he
said he was is because I said so.''

"*You* said so?''

"Sure. He was trying to get the phone, watching from the
window—you know the way he does?—wanting to phone
you. And I seen him. I could tell them he was there, see? I
saw him on my way home.''

"But he didn't phone me," Johanna said.

"What difference does that make? Sometimes you can be
awful stupid, Jo, even for a girl.''

There were times when this would have angered Johanna,
but now she just sat, silently hugging her own fears and
doubts.

They had to ask at the hospital desk for special permission
to visit their mother, the visiting hours already past. Johanna
explained that she had not been able to get off work until
four-thirty.

"What ward is she in?" the nurse asked.

Johanna told her. The nurse picked up the phone and made
inquiries the girl could not hear. When she hung up, she said,
"Mrs. Rocco was discharged this afternoon.''

Johanna and Georgie looked at each other.

"You mean she's gone?" Georgie said to the nurse.

"That's what I mean, young man.''

"But she didn't have any money," he blurted out. He knew that much of hospitals, that until you made arrangements for paying, you were stuck.

"Why don't you speak to the cashier?" The nurse nodded at the caged window across the hall.

Johanna lingered at the reception desk while Georgie lunged toward the cashier's window and, since no one was on duty, began to pound the handbell that had been placed there. "Please," Jo said, "isn't there someone who could tell me how she left? I mean, did someone come and get her?" Premonition was already nauseating her.

The white-clad receptionist said, but not unkindly, "I can't give out that kind of information, dear, even if I knew. But I wasn't on duty."

Johanna lifted her head. "I wouldn't want my brother to know—if it was—someone."

"I tell you what you do," the woman said. "I'm just a nurse's aid. But when you get home, you call your mother's doctor. He'd be more likely to know than anybody else."

"Thank you," Johanna said, and went to get her brother. "Come on, Georgie. Maybe mama's already home, at Mrs. Tonelli's."

"I was there at four o'clock," Georgie said. "There wasn't nobody home, not even the old lady. She's getting me the information." He nodded toward the cashier, who was riffling the card file on her desk.

The cashier looked up, holding one card above the others. "The bill was paid in full."

Georgie was quick and bold as Johanna could never have been. "Who paid it?" he said, and then qualified at once in a tone calculated to take the sting out of his directness: "I mean, if it was a check, the hospital'd want to be sure it didn't bounce, wouldn't they?"

The woman looked at her record. "Mrs. Teresa Tonelli."

"Yeah?" Georgie said, feeling foolish. He recovered. "Thank you, lady. You don't need to worry about that check, no, sir."

To Johanna on the way out he said, "Don't that beat everything? Don't that just beat everything? Man, do I admire the old lady. What she wants, she gets. No arguments, no horsing around. She probably kidnapped ma. I wouldn't put it past her, Jo.''

''But mama didn't want to go there.''

''Jo, you know as well as I do, mama doesn't know what she wants.''

Johanna was ashamed of her own first if unnamed fears. In truth, there wasn't anything she liked about herself lately. Even her prayers, she thought, were like bedsheets she pulled over her head in the dark. You couldn't pray and not be honest; that wasn't prayer at all. And then even more unaccountably in her reckoning of herself, she said aloud, ''I do hope she's there.''

''Man,'' Georgie said, ''you ought to *really* have something to worry about.''

But they reached home to find Mrs. Tonelli alone with her housekeeper, giving the last instructions for dinner to Mrs. Grey.

''Where's ma?'' Georgie burst out.

Mrs. Tonelli looked at him coldly. She did not like to be interrupted. Nor did she like to have Mrs. Grey ignored, a tendency of Georgie's unless he wanted something from her. ''Go into the living room and wait for me,'' she said.

Georgie followed his sister, stumbling over his own feet in the carpeted hall. Johanna ran as though she were expecting to find her mother waiting there to surprise them.

The room was lighted, but empty, so neat with all its well-upholstered chairs and shining little tables, its tall lamps and silk draperies, it looked like a magazine advertisement you were supposed to imagine yourself walking into.

Johanna found her knitting basket in the window seat and took it to a chair with a lamp beside it.

''I wish you wouldn't knit, Jo. It makes me nervous.''

''That's why I want to knit.'' But she put the basket away.

Georgie lighted a cigaret, his first in Mrs. Tonelli's house, and having lighted it, he couldn't find an ashtray. He threw the dead match into the fireplace.

The first thing Mrs. Tonelli said, coming into the room, was, "Who is smoking?"

"I'll put it out," Georgie said.

"It is not good for football heroes." She caned her way to the chair she always sat in and let herself down carefully. "I am tired," she said, and then, looking from one of them to the other, "So, your mother has gone away. You can both stay with me now."

"Where'd she go to?" "Why did she go away?" Brother and sister spoke simultaneously.

"Sit down," Mrs. Tonelli said. The children obeyed her. "I made it possible for her to do exactly what she wanted to do. I assured her both of you would be taken care of. She sent you her love."

"I'll bet!" Georgie said, for everything that Johanna had told him about his mother's operation came back to him, a flood of color like blood in his eyes. Dr. Tag: he made it possible. Not Mrs. T.—Dr. Tagliaferro.

Johanna said nothing, stunned. She had been right in the first place.

Mrs. Tonelli looked at Georgie. "So. Already you are a judge. You are not out of high school, but you are a judge."

"Poor mama," Johanna said at last.

Mrs. Tonelli grunted. "I agree, Johanna. But there is nothing you can say to a woman like that."

Johanna drew herself up in the chair. "Georgie, I wish to speak to Mrs. Tonelli alone. Will you please go upstairs? I'll come up in a few minutes."

"What kind of corny crap is that? I'm no kid. I know she's been sleeping with some guy for months, for years maybe. What'd she need an operation for?"

"Be quiet!" Johanna commanded.

The old lady looked at him with contempt. "Loud waters run muddy. You will make me regret my invitation to you, George Rocco."

Georgie's recovery was almost complete and the more remarkable for what he had to hide of a sudden—raw hatred for the doctor involved. "You mean you still want Jo and me to live with you? I mean, even knowing that about our mother? What are people going to say? I mean, it wouldn't be right for Jo and me to do that to you . . .''

"Shut up, Georgie.'' The old woman laid her head back. "People were talking about *me* before your mother was even born. And I tell you, I cannot even remember whether or not it was true. That's how important it was in my life. Georgie, if I ask you to leave it will not be on account of your mother. So do not be a hypocrite for my benefit. You are a smart boy. Don't be too smart.'' She took a deep breath and raised her head. "Johanna, Martin called you. He will come to see you tonight.''

Thank God, Johanna thought, thank God.

Mrs. Tonelli said, "Now go and dress up your hair, young Mr. Rocco. You have shaken it up like a mop. Dinner will be ready in five minutes.''

Georgie got out of the room with the best grace he could manage. When he was gone, Johanna said, "Do you know where she is, Mrs. Tonelli?''

"No. I only know I went up to offer her the hospitality of my house. I knew from Dr. Tagliaferro she was ready to be released. She said, 'You want my children to stay with you, don't you?' I said yes, because it is true and because I knew she wanted me to say it.''

"She did it because of us,'' Johanna said, "for our good.''

"Child, do you believe that?''

"Yes, I do!'' Her eyes flashed defiance at anyone who thought otherwise.

"I envy her her daughter. Help me up, Johanna.'' On her feet she was unsteady. "I think I had better have my dinner on a tray in my bedroom. Please send Mrs. Grey in to me.''

Throughout dinner Georgie occupied his mind with a number of wild schemes for revenge, though he was by no means sure for what he proposed to be revenged. This way he got what he wanted, to stay in the luxury—to him—of the Tonelli house. But even that was losing some of its flavor. The old lady was getting beyond his savvy, bugging him all the time. He wasn't sure she didn't fatten people up the better to eat them. After all, old Martin had cleared out, and he was close kin. All he'd have had to do was stick around and collect her insurance and everything else once she kicked off. Insurance . . . He was about to ask his sister what was holding it up. But she wouldn't know. She'd wait till doomsday and say it took time. She always made excuses for everybody but him. He should have gone to see the agent with her, but he couldn't do everything, could he?

"Jeez, Jo, this meat is tough."

"Not when you chew it," Jo said.

He could have expected that. How was he going to know it was tough if he hadn't chewed it? He took a mouthful of green beans. He hadn't had a bite of pasta since moving in. Funny, he'd thought he'd never want to eat another string of spaghetti as long as he lived. Now he'd settle for a dish of it in plain oil and garlic.

"Know what, Jo? The old lady and Der Tag, they've trapped us like a couple of mice they're playing with. With ma here it'd been different. We'd 've been a family, you know?"

"I'm going to find her, Georgie. I've made up my mind."

"What for? She doesn't want us."

"I think she does."

"You got a funny way of believing what you want to believe, Jo. Look, why couldn't we put the heat on old Mancuso to get us our insurance money? Then you and me could clear out, you know, maybe go and live in New York or some place. I could go to a good school for a change. I ain't learning anything in Hillside, Jo. You know that yourself. You're always saying I could if I applied myself, but if I really applied myself, first thing you know I'd know more than most of them teachers we got."

Johanna laughed, and laughing, enjoyed it. She and Martin used to laugh a great deal. It was strange—Friday night she had asked Martin to take her away from Hillside, and now here was Georgie proposing to do it. She lost the feeling of laughter.

Georgie saw her eyes go dead on him. "Oh," he said, "I forgot about old Martin."

"This is our home," Johanna said.

"That ash-pile across the street?"

"We'll find a place and bring mother back."

"What'll people say? I got to grow up in this town. God-damn old Doctor Tag!"

"Will you stop blaming him, Georgie!"

"Why? He's an abortionist. All the guys say he is. I heard 'em talking at the firehouse. That's why they call him Der Tag."

"*Der Tag* means 'the day.' I took German in high school."

"*Der* means German and German means Nazi and Nazi means killer. That's where it comes from, and I'd be ashamed to admit I took German if I was you."

Holy Mary, Mother mild, Johanna said under her breath. "Are you through with your supper?" She got up from the table and took their plates.

"Why don't you ring the bell? That's what it's on the table for."

"For the same reason I took German!" she all but screamed at him and backed her way into the kitchen through the swinging door.

Georgie did not wait for dessert. Having said the word "abortionist" he had suddenly hit upon a scheme of proving it of Doctor Tagliaferro. It was going to take some doing, but if he could pull it off it would be sensational. And like the gambling raid, it'd be for the good of everybody, cleaning up Hillside. The Mafia strikes again!

Rosie Gerosa met him in the grade school playground. She'd come running when he called her, but the first thing she said was, "I can't stay out very long. I've got homework to do."

"Me too. I'll do it with you," Georgie said.

"I was beginning to think you didn't like me any more."

Georgie couldn't see her face clearly, but he could hear the pout in her voice. "I been busy."

Rosie giggled. "I know."

"You don't know from nothing," Georgie said warningly.

"I don't mean I'm saying I know. I just mean I'm knowing I know."

Georgie kicked a beer can from under one of the swings and sat down, wedging his bottom in. "I want to ask a big favor of you, Rosie. What I really mean, I want to make you a partner."

"For life?" Rosie said, giggling again.

Life, Georgie thought, Life! She was already popping out of her brassiere. Next thing, she'd be like her old lady, always hooking her thumb into her girdle to get what was overflowing tucked back in.

"I was only kidding, Georgie."

"No. I was thinking serious," he said. "I figure what I got to do is important, and if you help me out, well, we're kind of engaged."

"You didn't even ask *me*," Rosie said, and gave herself a start on the swing next to his.

"I'm asking you now, ain't I?" Georgie said. "Sit still."

Rosie dragged her feet till she came to a stop, but she said, "I don't think I'd like to be married to someone who told me to sit still and then didn't do anything."

How the hell had he got into this? He wanted to kiss Rosie just now like he wanted a bellyache, but he pulled her swing close to his and kissed her cheek.

"The great lover," Rosie said sarcastically.

"Listen, are you going partners or not?"

"Maybe," Rosie said, and he realized he was going to have to make her feel it was for keeps between them. He got off the swing and began turning her around, knotting the chain so as to raise the swing higher and higher. It got harder all the time. She was no midget. Finally he got it to where he could bend a little and kiss her the way she wanted. The taste of her lipstick made him want to throw up. But Rosie tried to squiggle off the swing and doing it, caused his hand to be pinched in the links of the chain.

"Christ!" Georgie cried, "you've busted my hand."

"My poor darling baby, let me see it," Rosie said, and began crawling all over him.

"It's bleeding," Georgie said though he thought himself that the red might be lipstick.

"I'll have to take him to see Doctor Tagliaferro," Rosie persisted motheringly.

"Cut it out," Georgie said, and put his wounded hand under his sweater where he hoped she wouldn't go after it. "I want you to go see Dr. Tag."

"Me?"

"Rosie, he does terrible things, like taking women's insides out, you know, their sex organs, and things. I mean, this is a secret between you and me, and I wouldn't even talk about it to a girl if I didn't have to."

He told her then, with his own embellishments, some of the things he had overheard, eavesdropping at the back of the fire station. "That kind of doctor, Rosie, shouldn't be allowed in Hillside. Shouldn't be allowed, period."

Rosie was a little sick with the combination of shock and pleasure that Georgie would tell her such things. "I better sit down for a minute," she said.

"Better keep walking," Georgie said. "I know how you feel. I felt that way too when I first heard about it." He felt it was safe to start them down the deserted path toward the street on which Tagliaferro had his office. "What we're going to do is trap him and then make an exposé, like they do in the newspapers."

Rosie didn't say anything, but she took Georgie's arm and clung to it.

"I figure it's our duty," Georgie went on. "Don't you?"

"I guess so."

Georgie began then, pouring it on about how good-looking she was, that there wasn't a boy in town wouldn't want to call her his girl. Rosie revived under that treatment. "Man, would I go around telling everybody you were my girl if you wasn't something special? And I don't mean just that way. I idealize you."

Rosie said a very humble "Thank you, Georgie."

"What we're going to do—I'll wait outside and you go in and see Doc Tagliaferro. Maybe if you could look as if you was going to bust out crying any minute, you know, scared? You'll tell him you think maybe you're going to have a baby."

"Georgie!"

"It happens all the time. I mean, you know girls yourself, don't you?"

"I know of somebody," she admitted.

"It's just to see what happens, Rosie, to see what he says."

"What if he calls my mother?"

"I guarantee you on my word of honor he won't. I'll bet he asks you if you told her, and when you say no, that's what I want to find out—what he says then. You got to tell him you've got some money . . ."

"I don't, Georgie."

"You don't have a baby, either, do you, stupid? I got money, Rosie. At least I got some coming to me soon. I'll have enough money we could get married on, Rosie, if we wanted to."

"Gee," she said, tempted. "I got to think about it, Georgie. I mean about what you want me to do."

"No. When you think you get mixed up. It's tonight or we're quits with each other. I got things to do, Rosie, important things, and if I'm going to have a partner, it's got to be now."

The girl agreed reluctantly. Georgie thought that if she acted as scared in Tag's office as she did of going in at all, it would go over fine with him. And what he didn't tell Rosie, building her up about how good-looking she was, one all-around look at Rosie and it wasn't going to be hard to believe that maybe she was in trouble.

Georgie watched two women come from the doctor's office, waiting in the shadows, and fed his fantasy on what Der Tag had done and said to them. Georgie moved cautiously to the window of the waiting room. Empty. Rosie would be in with him now. What if she broke down and told him? Tag had a way of getting around women, making them confide in him. They'd tell him what they wouldn't tell their own husbands. He'd heard the guys say that at the station, too. But suppose Rosie did tell him it was all put up? She wouldn't do that. She'd be almost as scared of doing that. It wasn't nice of him even to have thought about it. If you couldn't trust your girl, who could you trust?

Rosie came out of the inside office, Dr. Tag following her. He even had his big hammy hand on her shoulder. Rosie was dabbing at her eyes as if she was crying. Maybe she was. She could cry a bucketful at some corny movie. Georgie retreated down the walk and waited behind the trunk of the dead elm tree. Rosie came out of the office and behind her, Dr. Tag turned off the lights. The better to watch, Georgie thought, keeping himself well concealed. Rosie bumped her way down the steps, looking now one way, then another. Man, did she look guilty!

"Keep on walking," Georgie said when she passed the tree. "I'll catch up with you by the playground." He waited until he saw the lights go on in Tagliaferro's living room.

Rosie was still sniveling when he joined her. The tears were for real. Then she really let go. Somebody listening could've heard her wailing for two blocks. "Oh, Georgie, I'm so scared."

"What's to be scared of? Wasn't I right out there watching all the time?"

"He wants me to go to New York, to a hospital there for tests."

"Man! Did he say anything about an operation?"

Rosie sobbed and shook her head. "He said . . . he said something about being able to make arrangements."

"Man!" Georgie said again. "Did he ask you about money?"

"I said you could get some."

"*Me!*"

"I didn't say you by name, I said, 'The boy said he could get some money.' "

"Rosie, you're cool, real cool." It was Georgie's highest praise and he kissed her salty cheek by way of proving it. "When does he want you to go to New York?"

"Georgie, I don't have to go, do I?"

"Sure you have to go. We're partners, ain't we?"

"But I don't want to take any tests—like that. I'm scared, Georgie. No! You can't ask me to, you can't make me . . . Please, Georgie." She gave a great hiccough. She was going to get hysterical on him if he didn't do something.

"What are you scared of—if you ain't pregnant?"

"I'm not," Rosie cried. "Georgie!"

"How do I know if you don't prove it to me? I'm not the only guy in Hillside . . . feeling that way about you." He made himself say the words.

"But I love you, Georgie," Rosie wailed.

"Okay, okay. Me too—I mean *you*, I love you, but . . ."

"Do you, Georgie?" She forced him into a clinch right there and then, and right under a street light.

Georgie did what he felt he had to do. She was sticky with tears and something sweet, the damn lipstick again. He must've eaten a ton of it. But it calmed her down one way. Man, it wouldn't take much to get her pregnant for a fact. He broke away from her finally and wiped his mouth on the inside of his sleeve. "When'd he say he wanted to see you?"

"Tomorrow afternoon or Thursday," Rosie said. "Tuesdays and Thursdays he's there."

"Where?"

"That hospital . . . in New York."

"We'll skip our last two classes," Georgie said, "just disappear—like we'd eloped." That last, he thought, was real inspiration. "I tell you what, we'll take the noon bus, and I'll buy you lunch in a New York restaurant."

"Gee," Rosie said, and tried to put her arms around him again.

Georgie managed to hook his arm behind her back and get her started walking up the hill.

Rosie said, "The last time I was in New York was when the whole class went by bus to the Metropolitan Museum of Art. There's the cutest restaurant there, Georgie, with little stone cherubs sprinkling water, you know?"

"It sounds dirty," Georgie said.

"I don't mean *that* way. It's like they were spitting."

"Where you're eating lunch?" Georgie said incredulously.

Rosie sighed. "It's kind of hard to explain, but it's real pretty."

"Man!"

Georgie decided he didn't want to have to talk to Rosie's mother just now. She'd be asking all kinds of questions about his mother, and the insurance. He had the feeling she was always adding up things for Rosie's future. And the old man hadn't much use for Georgie. That was all right with Georgie, a man who could spend his life making over dead people's suits to fit live people! Besides, he had to raise ten bucks before tomorrow noon. He wondered if Pekarik would lend him the car. He ought to. After all, Georgie had pitched him the winning touchdown in Saturday's game. The damn fool had almost run the wrong way with it. But ten bucks. Then he remembered: he'd tell Jo he needed it to buy new books. His had been lost in the fire. He didn't have to tell her he'd been given a permanent library loan of most of them for the rest of the semester. He walked Rosie to her back gate.

She hung onto his hand. "I love you, Georgie."

"Me, too," he said, and got away.

Georgie got a bad shock, walking into the living room. He had heard Martin's voice and remembered Mrs. T. saying that he was coming. But what he hadn't expected was to find the county detective sitting there like a friend of the family.

"Excuse me," Georgie said and tried to back out of the room.

"It's all right, young man. I've been waiting for you," Bassett said, getting up and coming at Georgie like he was going to walk right through him. "Your sister says we can go up to your room and talk without disturbing anyone."

"I got to do my homework," Georgie said. "I mean, I'll be glad to talk to you, but I ain't got much time."

"I understand."

Georgie clumped up the stairs. The light was already on in his room. It looked like somebody'd been there, maybe looking for something. What? He didn't have anything, not even any spare clothes. "Man," he said, "can your kid play football! I mean!"

"You play a pretty rugged game yourself," Bassett said mildly.

"He didn't get hurt or anything?" Georgie tried to sound concerned.

"Not beyond mending. Sit down, Georgie." The detective gave him no choice but the chair under the lamp, and the bastard then tilted the lampshade so the light would shine in Georgie's eyes.

"I don't know what I can tell you that I ain't already told you, Mr. Bassett," Georgie said, wanting to get the first word in, but immediately unsure that it was a good idea. "Course, I don't even know what you want to know."

The detective straddled a straight chair, sitting where he could look directly into the boy's face. "If I told you what I wanted to know, would you tell me?"

"If I could, sure."

"Who killed James MacAndrews?"

Georgie could feel his mouth twitch as he tried to smile. "If I'd knew that, I'd 've told you."

The detective nodded. "I'd hoped you would." He took a nylon stocking from his pocket, stretched it and let it spring together. "Your sister tells me she's lost two of these lately."

Georgie felt his mouth going dry. He wasn't sure he could say anything if he wanted to. He shrugged.

"It seems to have become the fashion in Hillside to wear them on heads instead of legs. Or did you know that?"

Again Georgie shrugged. He wasn't going to say yes or no; a lot of guys wore stockings the night of the raid, and they were sworn not to say anything, no matter who asked the questions. Just thinking about that, Georgie regained a little confidence. But Jo blabbing that. He didn't even know she'd missed them. She couldn't very well not miss the last one though, buying only one pair Saturday morning. He'd tried to get her to buy two pairs as long as he had the money.

Bassett balled the hose and tossed it to the boy. "Smell that."

Georgie sniffed. He couldn't smell anything, but he knew now what the detective was after. He kept his eyes tight in front of him, but his mind was on the new bottle of hair dressing he'd left in his top drawer. "Smells like perfume," Georgie said.

"Does a little, doesn't it?" the cop said. He went to the dresser drawer and got Georgie's bottle of hair dressing, uncorked it and held it under the boy's nose. "There's a strong resemblance, wouldn't you say?"

"No, sir. I ain't got that good a smeller." It was now or never for Georgie. He knew Bassett had been up to his room in his absence. "You got a search warrant, Mr. Bassett?"

"No, something better—permission." He put the bottle back.

"Lots of guys wear that stuff. I recommended it myself."

"To whom?"

"Lots of guys. I don't remember."

"It would be very helpful to me if you could give me their names."

"I can't do that. We got a pact, sir."

"Not to tell the name of your hair dressing?" Bassett said, smiling.

Brother, he could sneak through on you like his skinny-assed kid between guard and tackle. "Something like that," Georgie muttered.

"The secret order of the Mafia," Bassett said.

Somebody had squealed, Georgie thought. Maybe not. He had an idea everything Bassett said he was putting out like a feeler. "That's what they say about us dagos all the time," Georgie said. And man, he'd caught him between the eyes with that one. He could tell by just looking at him, he was as soft as his kid! A cop!

Bassett got astride the chair again. "Now, Rocco, I want you to tell me what you were doing on Friday night, where, whom you were with, and how you traveled—from eight o'clock on."

"I don't know if I can tell you all the whoms," Georgie said. "There were a lot of kids in the *Crazy Cat*."

"Try," Bassett said, and took out a notebook and pencil.

Georgie gave him the names of the kids who usually hung out at Pete's. Maybe he was adding a few. Hell, the more the better. He wasn't even sure Bassett was writing their names, scratching some kind of shorthand. "Who'd I say there?" Georgie tried him once.

Bassett repeated the name.

"Yeah," Georgie said, "I think he was there. Then, maybe nine-thirty, quarter to ten, I remembered I was going to call the hospital about my mother."

"Were you in the habit of doing that?"

"I guess I must've done it three or four times while she was in the hospital. I mean, I don't know if you could call that a habit."

"From a public phone?"

"Yes, sir. You see, I was worried about her. I don't exactly trust Dr. Tagliaferro. I mean, he's all right for some things. And I didn't want to scare Jo—my sister, that is, calling from home all the time."

"I see. Then at a quarter to ten you called the hospital?"

"Yes, sir. And that's when I looked up and saw Martin. He was in his room, all right. I'd swear to that."

"Wouldn't you swear to the other things you've told me?"

"Sure. I mean, I wouldn't swear to all those names I gave you. I don't have a photographic memory or anything like that."

"After the telephone call," Bassett prompted.

"I went home. I'd told Jo I'd be home about ten. She's a worrier, like I told you before."

"Did you see anyone on the way home?"

Georgie thought carefully about this one. Did he dare mention Daley? He thought not. If Daley was being asked these questions he might say Georgie and him left the *Crazy Cat* at the same time, then he'd say he went on home with Pekarik to play gin. He tried to remember the main street of Hillside that night. He hadn't actually seen old Martin. Then he remembered something: "Yeah, I remember Big Molly coming out for Billy Skillet. He's the guy without any legs, you know?"

"Was there anyone else around there? Any men?"

"I don't remember seeing anybody else in particular. But generally there is, a lot of guys . . . around Molly's." He hoped Bassett would ask him to explain that.

Bassett said, "Get on with your journey home."

"I took the short cut up through the high school grounds, and nobody's ever around them at night."

"How long do you estimate it took you to get home?"

"Couldn't 've been more than ten minutes. Then I seen Jo and Father Walsh sitting in the living room, and I figured maybe it was something I'd done they were talking about, so I wasn't going to walk in on that, no sir. I went down to the basement and got banging things round down there so they'd know I was home."

"Why did you want them to know you were home?"

"Jo always accuses me of listening at the ventilator. I guess maybe sometimes I used to. I mean, it's natural, a kid of my age, and her entertaining her boy friend. Martin, I mean!" What a slip that almost was! Georgie moistened his lips. "After a while I got bored down there. I figured they must be talking about her and Martin getting married or something like that. I mean, it was pretty conceited of me, thinking they were talking about me." All the time, the detective was just looking at him, kind of a faraway look on his face like he was damned bored, too. "So, after a while I just went round and in the house. I said, 'Good evening, Father,' and went up to my room."

"In other words," the detective said, "no one actually saw you arrive home at ten o'clock."

"But they'd 've known. Jo knew I was downstairs. That's what we had a fight about afterwards," he improvised, feeling he had said something wrong, but not sure what it was. "I mean, me eavesdropping and spying and things like that. Jo likes things private, you know?"

"Are you always that careful about being home before ten o'clock?"

Georgie knew then what was wrong: he'd been making the ten o'clock pitch too hard. He'd been advertising his alibi. "No, sir," he said earnestly, "I'm not usually. Only since ma was in the hospital, I've been trying to be more careful."

The detective drew a line beneath his notes and said, so abruptly that he took Georgie completely off balance, "Thank you very much, Rocco. That's all." He got up and put the chair back against the wall, straightened the lamp shade.

"That's all right," Georgie said. "I'll fix them. I wish I could've been some help to you, Mr. Bassett."

"What makes you think you weren't?" Bassett said, but did not wait for an answer.

20

When Detective Bassett and Georgie went upstairs, Johanna and Martin were left alone for the first time since the night of the fire, and utterly miserable in each other's company. Too much of evil foreboding hung between them for words to bridge. Johanna had expected Martin to come alone to see her; instead, he had brought the detective. Both of them felt the presence of the old lady although when Martin had visited her bedside she had made a deliberate point of saying to close her door tightly. Martin knew of old that her taking to her bed portended a crisis to which she had contributed. Johanna sat listening to the echo of Georgie's heavy footfalls long after the sound of them had faded. Her eyes and Martin's met, but still they could not speak, not to reprove, to commiserate, nor to encourage, though the impulse for all pressed agonizingly in on each of them.

Finally Martin thrust himself up from the chair and cried out, "It's like a roomful of spiderwebs, Jo!"

"Yes!"

He held out his hand to her and said one word: "Come."

Johanna leaped up and took his hand, allowing him to lead her out of the room. At the hall door she paused, looking up the stairs.

"Georgie can take care of himself," Martin said. "He knows how. By Christ, he knows how." He took his grandmother's black shawl from the hook by the door and flung it around Johanna's shoulders.

The night was sharply cold, the damp smell of the river mixing with the acid dankness of burnt leaves and wood and an occasional waft of scorched mattress. Whenever the wind came from the east Johanna was reminded of Friday's holocaust. She tried now not to look at the ruin as they passed it. "Where are we going, Martin?"

"To my place where we can have some privacy, and be-damned to what people say." He was unaware of the contra-diction in his words.

"It doesn't matter any more," she agreed. "There are more important things."

He paused and looked into her face under the one street lamp within the block. "What's the most important thing, Jo?"

"You and me."

"That's all I wanted to hear," he said and, putting his arm about her, he kissed her gently at the temple. It was like falling in love all over again, just the first, tentative, fleeting moment of it. "I want to help you, Jo. We've got to help each other."

"I know what I must do, Martin. I want to find my mother and bring her home. You know . . ."

"I know," he said. He had heard it at the fire station, having gone there after the meeting of the locked-out plant employees. The news of Catherine Rocco's precipitate flight from the county hospital had reached Hillside with the return of the ambulance team from a call there.

"Do you know . . . him?"

"No, I don't," Martin said quickly, for it was a lie, a cowardly lie after saying he wanted to help her.

"Father Walsh knows, I'm sure," the girl said.

Martin was relieved. A priest would better know how to deal with such things. Still, he was ashamed of himself until he realized that it was for Johanna's sake he had kept silence, that she not be embarrassed by his knowledge. He did not know how far she was beyond a false decorum.

"Jo, do you want my place? It isn't much but you could fix it up, and it wouldn't kill me to move back in with Grandma Tonelli."

"Thank you, Martin. For the time being, that would be fine." Johanna had reached the determination to take what help she had to have without false pride or idle protest.

"It's clean," Martin said when he unlocked the door and threw it open for her. He lighted the lamp hanging over his desk. "You can't say much more for it."

Johanna viewed the wall sweep of books. "I think it's beautiful."

"Thanks," he said, and then because he was embarrassed, he went on: "I'll have a phone put in in the morning. I've always needed one."

"I don't like telephones very much," Johanna said. "They don't really help."

"Well, they're not as good as people," he said slyly, making her smile. And when she smiled he opened his arms to her. They held each other for a long time, an embrace of sustenence, not of passion: that would follow, they knew, and were secure in the knowledge.

"I'll see Father Walsh in the morning—about mama," Johanna said.

"There are enough dishes," Martin said, "and that bed opens out, and I know where I can get an extra cot for—when you need it." He could not bring himself to say Georgie's name. Yet that was the one thing he felt he had to talk with her about. Bassett was no fool. He was a man who made his moves, Martin was sure, only when he had eliminated all other possibilities. Johanna had to be prepared for the worst—if it came to the worst.

"I wonder if we'll need it," Johanna said in a way that set an icepick stabbing at him.

"Jo . . ."

"I must plan for mother," she said, forestalling him, and sat down in a straight chair, herself as straight and steadier by far than the chair.

Goddamn mother, Martin thought, but he said nothing. He listened to her tell in her deliberate fashion what she felt had to be done. That Georgie was not mentioned he knew to be deliberate. He yielded to Johanna's way, knowing it to be stronger and, perhaps, wiser than his own. She would always do what had to be done.

When Martin left her no more than an hour later back at

the door of Mrs. Tonelli's, Jo went in to find her brother sitting at the old lady's bedside. They seemed to be in the best of humor, both of them, as though they had been exchanging jokes. There was a kind of guiltiness to their suspended mirth when Johanna came into the room. She tried to remember where she had seen a picture they resembled—the chubby, red-cheeked youth and the old lace-nightcapped woman staring round at her, half-laughing. She tried to remember, because if she couldn't she felt that she must be near madness—or they were. They did look mad, their eyes wild, insane!

"Your brother has been telling me, Johanna—this Mr. Bassett—is that his name?" Georgie wagged his head in affirmation. "Mr. Bassett is investigating the places of ill repute in Hillside."

Johanna simply did not know what she was talking about, not in that night's context.

Georgie said, "He was asking me about Big Molly's." He shrugged and opened his hands, looking at Mrs. Tonelli. "Jo wouldn't know." To his sister he said, "He was asking me about Billy Skillet and Big Molly, that's all. When I'd seen them, if there was any men around. Imagine him asking a kid like me something like that."

"In my day," the old lady said, "Molly was a girl in pigtails, which the boys dipped into inkwells. But there was not a boy in the neighborhood she did not beat up at some time or other."

"Man," Georgie said, "how people do change!"

Johanna left them, having not spoken a word, and ran upstairs. She turned the key in her bedroom door, not because she was physically afraid, but because she felt the need for as much isolation as it was possible to have.

Downstairs the old lady said from her bed, "Bring me my pocketbook, Georgie. It is in the lefthand drawer on the top." She watched him. He was about to open the other drawer whether by design or stupidity. "The other drawer!"

"I used to be lefthanded," he said. "It makes me opposite."

"Opposite to what?" the old lady said, taking the purse from his hands.

He shrugged. "Opposite to what I should be, I guess."

"Ten dollars is a great deal of money, young Mr. Rocco."

"I know. I swear I'll pay it back to you, Mrs. T."

"Do not swear. Just pay it back."

And after he'd given her thirty bucks Saturday night, Georgie thought.

21

Johanna went to early Mass in the morning and afterwards waited at the sacristy door for Father Walsh. She watched his shadow against the wall where the light of the early sun was bright and multi-colored, filtered through the stained glass window. She saw him remove his stole and kiss it. She went outdoors then until he came. He took off his biretta, speaking with her.

"Father, do you know the name of the man my mother has gone to?"

The priest took her into the rectory parlor to talk. "Yes, I know who he is, Johanna."

"Is he married, I mean to someone else?"

"Yes."

"Someone in Hillside?"

"I don't think you need to know that, Johanna."

"But everyone else must know it," the girl said. "I can tell. That's why they make allowances for Georgie . . . and me."

"As I said to you the other night," Father Walsh said, "people are sometimes merciful."

"I want to go to my mother wherever she is, Father. She's not bad, not like some people."

"Nobody is altogether bad," the priest said.

"I don't know about that, Father, but I know my mother isn't. My father loved her."

The priest merely looked at his hands. "How can I help you?"

"Tell me where she is."

"I don't know that."

"Then tell me who the man is. If you don't, Father, I'll

find out." The girl thrust her head up. "I'll go from door to door and ask it if I have to. Someone will tell me. I'm sure someone will be glad to tell me! I might even ask his wife, and wouldn't that be funny?"

"Give me a day or two," the priest said. "I'll do what I can."

"But you've already tried, haven't you, Father?" He did not say anything. "Isn't that really why you came to the house the other night?" Still he did not answer. "People always talk about telling the truth, and then they find all kinds of ways not to tell it," the girl said.

"Christ spoke in parables," he said quietly.

"But not to hide the truth, surely."

"You are right, Johanna. You're quite right. Will you give me a day or two to try and find her?"

"And will you find her?"

"I think so."

"Tell her that I need her . . . desperately."

The priest nodded. The girl got up and opened her purse. Father Walsh held up his hand and shook his head. He neither needed nor wanted money. "I'll pray for you, Johanna."

"Thank you, Father. I'll pray for you, too."

He smiled a little, taking her to the rectory door. If he had been an ancient mystic he might have taken this visitation as divinely prompted. Perhaps it was. God is eternal. The customs of men change, and priests, in the end, are only men.

And, as though by way of proof, the housekeeper came from the dining room, a great maiden Irish lady whose mission in life was the care and feeding of the clergy. "Will you come in now to your breakfast, Father, before your eggs have skirts on them?"

22

Sitting in his parked car a few doors up from the church, Bassett saw the girl go into the rectory with Father Walsh and come out again so soon. He had stopped on his way to Hillside, parking as was his habit a distance away from his destination. But was the rectory his destination? He was of two minds on the matter of talking with the priest. It was a ticklish business, even for a heathen like himself, perhaps especially for a man who called himself a heathen. In answering his questions, Johanna Rocco had omitted mention of the priest's presence when her brother arrived home Friday night. He could not believe that to have been accidental. That her brother had embroidered it into his story was not accidental either, Bassett was sure. That a slob of a boy should have a quicksilver mind did not amaze him. But it made it almost impossible to pin down his testimony, to sort fact from fantasy.

Without collaborating testimony he was not going to be able to make a case against the boy. And whether the boy was the actual killer or merely part of a gang, possibly its leader, he did not know. The only physical evidence was the two stockings, and they had been found near a railway car used for cockfighting! For all he knew the gang might have been in action before MacAndrews' murder. Kearns did not think so. But Kearns was not the most reliable chronicler of Hillside delinquency. Piece by piece, he was going to have to sort, compare, and put together as close an approximation as he could come to the truth.

Bassett decided against seeing Father Walsh for the time being. He did not want to call so quickly in the wake of the Rocco girl's visit. He liked the young priest, after what he

176

had started yesterday. How that would come out he didn't know. Nobody in Hillside knew. But the men had voted to start their strike fund.

The detective started his car and drove up the hill by way of the nearest side street in order to avoid passing the girl.

And what kind of work do you do, Mr. Bassett? one of his son's teachers had asked him at a recent P.T.A. meeting. "Well, you might say, I do piece work," he had answered, and then explained his office. But that was as large a mouthful of truth as ever a man was likely to say in jest.

He watched the Tonelli house from the distance of a block away and saw Georgie start out with an armful of books. He wondered what he did with the books besides cart them between house and school, but then he often wondered that of his own children: ten pounds of books out of which they seemingly did ten minutes of work. The boy, unaware that he was observed, stopped for a moment at the ruin of his house; he just stood and looked, kicked then at a piece of rubbish or two, and shook his head. Even from where he watched, Bassett could see him heave a great sigh before going on his way. That lad never let himself off-stage, the detective thought. He didn't need a mirror to see himself. He saw himself wherever he looked.

When Georgie had disappeared through the school gate, Bassett proceeded to the Tonelli house. The old matriarch had refused to see him the night before, pleading her exhaustion to Martin while Bassett had waited with Johanna in the living room.

"Get her in the morning when she's fresh," Scully had suggested. And that he intended to do right now.

Mrs. Grey opened the door to him. "Thank you," he said, and stepped into the hall before she could close the door against him if that were her instructions. "I've come to see Mrs. Tonelli. Bassett is my name." He had caught a flicker of movement in the living room and followed the housekeeper down the hall. She turned and looked at him over her shoulder, as much as to say she had expected him to wait. He merely smiled and nodded for her to proceed. She would

know his business. In her part of town they watched policemen as sparrows watch a cat.

"Mr. Bassett to see you, Mrs. Tonelli."

"Leave the door open so I can call you, Mrs. Grey," the
old woman said. She sat in a high-backed chair, a shawl over
her knees although the room was already hot, the fire glow-
ing in the grate. Her eyes were as bright.

"I have the feeling you've been trying to avoid seeing me,
Mrs. Tonelli. Perhaps I'm wrong. May I sit down?"

"That's what the chairs are for," she said. "Bassett: what
kind of a name is that? Did you change it from Basso?"

"No, if it was changed it was done before my time. It goes
back to England somewhere along the line." He selected a
chair he could move a little closer to hers. "Do you remember, when we met on the street Saturday morning, you told
me that you had called the fire department Friday night?"

"I remember," she said, aloof as a stone tower.

"I was wondering how you happened to see it. I assume
you are in the habit of retiring early?"

"Do not assume, Mr. Bassett. I am not a prisoner of habit.
I go to bed when it suits me."

Bassett smiled a little. He could believe that. "Do you
mind telling me what first caught your attention?"

"You want to know if I am a busybody, if I watch constantly out of my window. Is that not so?"

"Busybodies—your word, not mine, Mrs. Tonelli—are
sometimes a policeman's best friend. They can also be his
worst enemy. They often see things that don't even happen.
I don't think you are a busybody."

"Thank you," she said. "Now I will tell you how I happened to be looking out of the window." She spoke with a
slight accent, he observed, but her English was by far the
best he had heard in Hillside. "You will maybe decide I am
a busybody after all. Father Walsh came to see me that night.
I like to confess to him. It amuses me to tell him certain
things in my past. I like to make him blush. He reproves me
for enjoying it. I have become repetitious with him. But I

say, 'then you have something new for which to give me absolution, Father.' But you are not a Catholic. I can see.''

"I think I get the point, however," Bassett said. He had certainly got the picture—the old vixen tormenting a young priest, his having to see her face to face without the shield of the confessional screen.

"He was later than usual Friday night and after he had gone I turned on the radio, but I had already missed the ten o'clock news." She paused and with the ball of her thumb pressed her upper teeth. It was fairly delicately achieved, the making firm of the dental plate on gums that were shriveling in old age, and it gave Bassett the pause in which to take his notebook from his pocket and say,

"I'm going to take note of what you're saying, Mrs. Tonelli, so that I won't have to ask you to go over it again." He made his point without distracting or causing her suspicion.

She smacked her lips, a punctuation to her settling of the teeth, and said, "Do not put in the part about my teasing Father Walsh."

"Of course not," he said, and then prompted, "You had missed the ten o'clock news."

"I decided therefore to stay up and wait for the eleven o'clock on the television. I said my rosary . . ." She pointed to where the black beads lay now on the table beside the silver bell. "And then I went to turn on the television. While it was getting warm I looked out the window and was surprised to see Father Walsh's car still parked in front of my house. I thought he might not have been able to start it. I looked out once or twice afterwards. It was still there. Then I watched to see what the movie would be after the news. A dreadful thing, nothing but gangsters. I turned off the television and looked out again. That was when I saw the flames going 'whoof' at the windows of the Rocco house."

Quickly, for he had memorized such as he knew of them, Bassett correlated the time elements. Father Walsh had been at the plant very shortly after the ambulance arrived. He had undoubtedly been on his way from the Rocco house when he saw or heard the ambulance.

"What station do you generally get for the ten o'clock news, Mrs. Tonelli?"

She named the station. "I like to listen to the commentator afterwards. He's such a fool."

Bassett could not allow himself the luxury of being amused. "And you'd missed him, too?"

"Yes."

Bassett avoided asking a direct question about the priest. Instead he sought his information by saying, "Then you were alone here after ten-fifteen?"

"Ten-thirty. I went into the bedroom to get my watch . . ."

Young Rocco's alibi was cracked. By his own testimony, the priest had been in the living room with his sister when he came up from the village—at ten o'clock. But the priest had not left Mrs. Tonelli's until almost ten-thirty. Unless . . . Father Walsh had stopped first at the Rocco's, then here, and after confessing Mrs. Tonelli had gone somewhere else in the neighborhood, leaving his car still where it was.

Bassett could feel the raw edges of his own nerves. "How long would you say Father Walsh was here, Mrs. Tonelli?" He had to ask it that way; he could think of no other.

And all it invoked from the witness he had thought his triumph was a petulant question in return: "How long does it take an old woman to tell her sins? I don't know, Mr. Bassett." She began wagging her head. "I don't know. I don't like clocks."

"But if he hadn't been here by then, you would have listened to the ten o'clock news?"

"*If* I remembered," she said, compounding the imprecision of testimony he had thought his most precise.

Ashes everywhere, Bassett thought, glancing down at ruin as he left the Tonelli house. His own mouth was full of them.

He had no choice but to query the priest on his schedule of that night's calls. But when he reached the rectory, Father Walsh had already gone out of town, probably for the day.

23

By paying Pekarik four dollars Georgie got the loan of his car. The old crate wasn't worth four dollars wholesale, Georgie thought. Besides, he was afraid to drive in New York City so they were going to have to park it somewhere and take a bus as well. And maybe a taxi if they got lost. And lunch. And Rosie sat there beside him wearing gloves and her Sunday coat as though he was her private chauffeur.

"You got any money?" he asked.

"What?"

"Are you dreaming or something? Have you got any money with you?"

"Fifty cents," she said.

"Big deal."

They were approaching a roadside restaurant, a sign outside it advertising curb service: frankfurters, hamburgers, ice cream. Georgie slammed on his brakes and turned sharply off the road; a trailer truck that had been trying to nudge him out of the middle of the road for the previous mile, swerved and very nearly jackknifed. Georgie grinned, thinking of what the guy driving it was saying just then.

"What's the matter?" Rosie said, suddenly coming to.

"We're going to have a hotdog. I don't trust them city restaurants. You could get poisoned and never know it."

"I don't like hotdogs," Rosie said, pouting.

"All right, you can have a hamburger. But no French fries. You're getting fat."

Rosie giggled. "You sound like papa," she said.

"For Christ sake," Georgie said, and blasted the car horn for service.

Rosie crawled over closer to him. "Georgie, I wouldn't really mind."

"Mind what?"

"Having a baby. I was thinking all last night how nice it'd be, keeping house for you and it, making things to fit it. Papa's got all kinds of odds and ends. When I was a little girl I used to sit in his shop and make clothes for my dolls. He'd cut them out for me and help me sew them." She sighed. "I wish I *was* having a baby."

"Man!" Georgie cried, and gave three long blasts to the horn.

A customer coming out of the restaurant with a toothpick between his teeth stopped at the car. "You can blow all day out here and just raise your own sweat, sonny. They only got curb service in the summertime."

"Why 'nt they take the sign down then?"

The man shrugged and got into his own car.

Georgie opened the car door. "I'll bring us something out to the car," he said.

"Are you ashamed of me? I don't look pregnant."

Christ! What had he got into? She'd been making believe she was going to have something. That's how she'd still been willing to go this morning, faking to herself it was all for real. He glanced at her before slamming the door. She was sitting spread out like a fat cat. The hell she didn't look pregnant! He opened the car door again. "If you was, you'd be in *real* trouble. You ain't married to me, you know."

"But you promised, Georgie."

He slammed the door and lumbered into the restaurant.

Rosie didn't eat much of her hamburger and for once, Georgie wasn't hungry either. He wrapped what was left of the sandwiches in a napkin and put them on the back seat for later. Then he undertook to get some of the facts of their expedition across to his companion.

"The reason we're doing this at all, Rosie," he said with careful logic, "supposing you were going to have a baby, and supposing you wanted it . . ."

"But I do!" Rosie interrupted.

"Will you listen to me! If that's how it was, we wouldn't be going to New York at all. I told you about Doctor Tag, what he does, didn't I? That's what we got to find out. It's a sin! It's a crime what he does. All I'm asking you to do, Rosie, is when he starts giving you these tests, you look up at him with those great big eyes and say to him, 'Doctor, if I *am* pregnant, can you help me?' That's all you got to do, Rosie. And find out what he says then. Okay?"

"Okay, Georgie."

He started the car. "I'll tell you the truth, you're making me sick to my stomach making me talk so much about it."

"It was your idea. It's you got me all worked up over it."

"It was the only way I could think of—to get even with him," Georgie said in a moment of unguarded truth. He started the car.

"Georgie . . ."

"I don't want to hear another word out of you till we get to that hospital. I got to concentrate."

"You've made me scared again," Rosie said.

Georgie, having got the car back on the highway, put his arm around her. "We're partners, aren't we?" He gave her a hug. "Aren't we?"

The grey stone hospital building on New York's East Side was small, which Georgie found to be some consolation. It was not nearly as large as the county hospital where his mother had been. It smelled of medicine, but it wasn't even clean, he thought, the green walls specked with fly dirt. Rosie was looking pale. In fact, she looked like she was going to pass out any minute. Georgie squeezed her arm. One elderly woman sat at a telephone behind a glass window. Four plain, straight chairs were the only accommodation of the waiting room, the windows of it so high he'd have had to stand on one of the chairs to look out.

"Ask her for Dr. Tagliaferro." Georgie indicated the woman. "Tell her he knows you're coming." Georgie had not intended to come into the building himself, but he knew Rosie would never have made it this far without him.

The woman slid the panel open. "Yes?"

"Doctor Tagliaferro," Rosie said scarcely above a whisper.

"What's your name, please?"

"Rosalie Gerosa."

"Does the doctor expect you?"

The girl nodded.

"Please have a chair in the waiting room."

Rosie sat down like the chair was wet. Georgie gave her a quick kiss on the cheek. "Okay?"

She only nodded.

"I'll be across the street watching for you." It took him all his will power to keep from running. He'd never seen such a creepy place. What kind of a hospital didn't have customers rolling in and out? He didn't dare look back at Rosie for fear she'd follow him.

Georgie waited and waited and waited. How he hated New York! You couldn't see any place for all the buildings. Dogs. A million dogs on leashes, and all of them with people standing around watching them crap. And all of them constipated, hunching up one place, then another, dancing around the spot like something in a circus. Man, in Hillside, a dog just dropped it when he felt like it and went about his business.

In the street, splurge after splurge of cars went by, crowding up between traffic lights. He began to count the cars and trucks backed up every time between the change of lights. What if Rosie never came out? If that was a real hospital, he'd eat his hat. He'd heard of things like that: girls just disappearing. What a story that would make! DOCTOR CHARGED BY BOY FRIEND IN GIRL'S DISAPPEARANCE. Man, that was better than anything they were going to get on old Tag. But Georgie, the realist, began to plan what he was going to do if Der Tag did what Georgie expected, if he suggested an operation. He hadn't told Rosie that part of it, but he had it all doped out in his own mind. He'd just go into Papa Gerosa's shop and tell him the story: Rosie wasn't feeling very good so Georgie advised her to go and see Dr. Tagliaferro. After all, Dr. Tag was his mother's doctor. And what happened then . . . Well, Georgie Rocco felt it was his man-to-man duty to tell Rosie's father, Dr. Tag making Rosie think she was pregnant. He was dead sure he could count on Papa Gerosa's reaction: he wasn't going to listen to Rosie's story, or Der Tag's or anybody else's, not after hearing what Georgie had to say to him. Zoom! A bomb wouldn't blow any faster.

Rosie came out the door at a gallop and, seeing Georgie, didn't stop till he caught her in his arms. Her eyes were puffed up with crying, her whole face looked like a blob of strawberry ice cream. Georgie wondered if she had any clothes on underneath, the way she was clutching her coat around her.

"Hey!" he said, "take it easy. People are looking at us."

"I don't care . . . after what he did to me."

Georgie took her by the arms and shook her. "What'd he do? Tell me, what'd he do to you, Rosie?"

Rosie managed to wail through her sobs, "He looked at me . . . there."

"The dirty bastard!" Georgie cried and clenched his fists.

By then people *were* looking at them. Georgie took her arm. "We got to get out of here. We got to get out of this stinking town."

Rosie pulled away from him to blow her nose. "He said he'd take us home if we wanted to wait an hour for him."

"I'll bet," Georgie said, and pulled her along toward the opening of the cave at the end of the block. The wind was colder there. It was warm and cold by turns, the sun going in and out of the clouds. But there weren't so many people. "Now what happened? Tell me exactly."

"It was all right at first," Rosie said. "He explained to me how he wanted to examine me, and how the nurse was going to stay in the room all the time . . . And then she gave me a sheet and told me to lie down."

"Man!" Georgie cried.

"He didn't do anything but look, Georgie. But it was awful. I mean, it didn't exactly hurt or anything."

"What'd he say? That's the thing. What'd he say?"

"He said . . ." Rosie drew in a great gulp of breath. "He said, 'My dear, you're still a virgin. What made you think you were pregnant?' "

Georgie was stunned, momentarily speechless. "What'd you let him examine you for? He could've hurt you bad. For life, maybe."

"But he didn't . . ."

"How do you know? They've got all these anesthetics. You didn't feel anything, did you?"

Rosie shook her head.

"You're a minor," Georgie started again. "He shouldn't 've examined you. I'll bet that's illegal. I'll bet it is. What'd he say? Did you ask him the question I told you to? Did you, Rosie? Or did you just go in there and start bawling?"

"I did ask him, Georgie, and all he said was, 'We'll talk about that after the examination.' "

"Man, I should've known. Der Tag's smarter than both of us—he thinks."

"I didn't tell him anything, Georgie. Honest I didn't."

"Like what didn't you tell him?"

"Who my boy friend was."

"What's it his business? Did he ask you?"

"I said, 'nobody special.' I wasn't going steady."

"Good girl," Georgie said.

"But I think he knows. He said, 'A nice girl like you shouldn't go with a boy that's got trouble at home. You should go with somebody from a good family.' "

"So Der Tag said that, did he?" Georgie said. It hurt him so much it felt good. He tried to lay his head back against his collar, forgetting that he wasn't wearing the orange sweater. He had on his old pea jacket that he'd been wearing the night of the fire. "Okay, Doctor Tag," he said quietly, "der war is on."

Georgie flagged down a taxi and asked the driver how much it would cost to take them to the George Washington Bridge. He had enough money. It was the first time either of them had ever been in a taxi. Georgie leaned back and closed his eyes and let the hate unroll his fantasies. Rosie was fas-

cinated with the taxi meter. She told him every time another
nickel was added to their fare. When the bridge came into
sight, Rosie calling his attention to it, Georgie sat up and
combed his hair, trying to see himself in the driver's rear
view mirror.

"Can I use your comb, Georgie?"

"No. I don't want to catch something."

"Look who's talking," Rosie cried, the nastiest retort she
could think of on the spur of the moment, and for emphasis
added, in Georgie's fashion: "I mean!"

"Yeah," Georgie said coldly, squinting at her sidewise,
"a kid with a whore for a mother, you could, couldn't you?"

Rosie was so shocked she couldn't say anything.

"Like Der Tag said, Rosie, better get yourself a new boy
friend."

Rosie sat as deep in the corner of the cab as she could. "I
don't want to see another boy as long as I live," she said.

"Ditto with me for girls. I hate every mucking bitch of
them."

When they reached Hillside late in the afternoon, Georgie
let the girl out before he crossed the tracks. She could walk
home from there the back way. Georgie himself went directly
to Papa Gerosa's tailor shop.

24

County Detective Bassett waited with Mrs. Gerosa in her kitchen. He had come in with his nose ahead of him, for Mrs. Gerosa did her own baking. It was a much better way than merely trying to get his foot in the door. In any case, this plump, voluble woman was far more hospitable to a stranger than anyone else he had met in Hillside. Possibly, he thought wryly, he was becoming less of a stranger than he felt. Then, too, Mrs. Gerosa did not have a son. It was the mothers of sons that bore him the greatest suspicion. Rosalie, a late-born and unexpected child, was both the joy and the trial of her parents' life.

"Her father," Mrs. Gerosa said with an ample gesture, "to him, nothing she does is wrong. Rosie, I say, has a good heart. She loves excitement. And bad company—it makes the most excitement."

Amen, Bassett thought. He had explained his call as part of interviewing all the youngsters who had been in the *Crazy Cat* on the night of the murder. He knew Rosie, however, to be Rocco's girl friend. He also knew both of them to have been absent from afternoon classes at the high school.

That the girl's mother was not aware of it was obvious: she kept saying that her daughter would be home any minute. Bassett watched her closely for the little signs of apprehension. She was more apprehensive, when it was getting on toward five o'clock, of her husband's calling than of her daughter's failure to call. "He does not understand young people—and such a temper, Mr. Basso . . ."

By then Bassett had decided there must be a family in the town named Basso, the mistake had become so common.

"He always says I don't see what he sees. But I see. Only

188

different. You know what I mean? He sees everything from here." She tapped her bosom. "Everything don't go that deep."

At five minutes to five Rosie came into the house by the front door. Her mother cocked her head at the sound and called out, "Rosie?"

"Yes, ma."

"Why you go that way? Come in here. Somebody wants to talk to you."

It was a deeply troubled girl who stood in the doorway: both Bassett and her mother saw it at once.

"What's the matter?" Her mother looked from her to Bassett, and at him for the first time with suspicion.

"Nothing," Rosie said. "I had to stay late." An evasion of the truth: plainly she had had to stay somewhere late.

"You know who this man is?" Mrs. Gerosa said.

Rosie shook her head.

"He is the county detective, and he wants to talk to you . . . about your boy friends." The last words were said in heavy sarcasm.

Bassett bade the girl sit opposite him at the round kitchen table. She took off her coat, her motions slow as though her arms were heavy. A pretty face—without much character, he thought, the ordinary pretty girl whose ambition it would be to, perhaps, open a beauty shop or be somebody's secretary until marriage but above all, to marry. He would have given a great deal to know what had happened between her and Georgie Rocco that afternoon. Whatever had happened, she was not bursting with happiness over it, and for his grim purpose that was good.

"I want to talk with you about George Rocco."

The girl's mouth trembled, her eyes almost wild, rolling from him to her mother when Mrs. Gerosa said contemptuously, "Him!"

"Don't you approve of him, Mrs. Gerosa?" Bassett said blandly.

"A show-off, a bag of wind."

If that were only all, Bassett thought.

Mrs. Gerosa said, "I try to get her to go with some nice boy, some nice family boy."

Rosie said her first words in her own defense: "I don't go with any boy. I won't ever."

If he had not been there, Bassett thought, she would have let go then, throwing herself and her misery into her mother's arms. "But that's a fairly recent development, isn't it, Rosie? Up until maybe this afternoon, you did go steady with him?"

The girl did not answer.

"After a party—or a date of any kind, he always brought you home, didn't he?"

"I guess so," Rosie said.

"Always they stand and boo and coo outside the door there." Mrs. Gerosa gestured broadly toward the back steps. All her gestures were round, like herself.

"Why didn't he bring you home Friday night? You were both at the *Crazy Cat*, weren't you?"

"We didn't really have a date," Rosie said. "We just both were there."

"What time did you come home?" the detective asked, his tone still quite casual.

Her mother answered for her: "Weekends, ten past eleven. As soon as the *Crazy Cat* closes. Her father sits and watches. She don't have to come in the house, Mr. Basso, but she's got to be where he can hear her."

"I'm curious why Georgie would not have brought you home. You lived only two blocks apart."

"He wasn't coming home," the girl said. "He was going to play poker."

"With whom?" Bassett's voice and eyes were steady.

The girl shrugged.

"Tell him!" her mother commanded her.

"Phil Daley—and that crowd, I guess."

Bassett had got the information he wanted, if that, too, didn't explode in his face. Georgie's pious protests of early homecoming did not jibe with the story he had given Rosie. The girl sat, biting a pale lower lip, and he remembered her for a moment as she was on Saturday afternoon, rosy Rosie,

the noisy, cheering, pennant-waving girl friend of the football hero, riding at the head of the victory cavalcade.

"I thought the young men of Hillside were opposed to
gambling," he said.

Neither mother nor daughter answered him.

Bassett stopped at the police station to talk with Kearns
before setting out to find Phil Daley. Whatever the police
chief's shortcomings, he had a pretty good line on the origins
and habits of most of the people in the town. He was standing
at the stationhouse window when Bassett drove up, and was
still there when the detective went inside. He motioned Bassett to join him, and pointed down the street. Georgie Rocco
was getting into an old Dodge coupe.

"Where did he get that?" Bassett asked as Georgie drove
off.

"Mike Pekarik's. One of his pals. It's Mike's father's, but
the old man doesn't drive it. Won't get glasses. Rocco's just
been in seeing his prospective father-in-law. Look."

The two men watched Gerosa come out of his shop, trying
to put on his coat and lock the shop door at the same time.

"He's in a hurry," Bassett said.

"And he's mad. I wouldn't want to get in his way right
now." The chief turned from the window. "What can I do
for you?"

Bassett hesitated, watching Gerosa half-run, half-walk to
the corner where he turned up the hill. A domestic crisis—
to which, he had no doubt, young Rocco was the chief con-
tributor. Suddenly he had too many leads to follow at once.

"Phil Daley. What do you know about him, Chief?"

Kearns rooted among the cigar butts in the ashtray and
selected the largest of them. "Not much. Always been a cold
fish, even as a kid. Lives alone with his father. Old man
works at the plant. The kid does odd jobs around the docks.
Quit school early. Good fireman, one of the best on the truck.
Hunts a lot . . . I don't know what else. No money. A cold
kid. Nobody ever seems to get next to him. I don't know how
else to put it."

"Doesn't seem like the kind to pal around with Georgie Rocco," Bassett commented.

Kearns thought about that. "You can't just tell. If you were going to put a couple of different types together, they'd make a pretty good team."

Bassett grunted. "Where does he live?"

The detective found Phil Daley oiling his rifle at the kitchen table. His father was preparing the evening meal, using the crowded sinkboard as his base of operations. Bassett, for reasons that he had not undertaken to examine, had throughout the day been thinking of the odd Biblical phrase—sometimes in, sometimes out of context—in Hillside the children were father to the men.

Bassett identified himself to young Daley. His father had not acknowledged the detective's presence. In any case, he and the boy had met before—at the firehouse bar after the Rocco fire on Friday night. Bassett asked him what he had been doing up to the time of the fire.

"Playing gin with my friend, Pekarik. After I left the hangout, that is, till the old man here got home. Then we sat around jawing about MacAndrews."

Pekarik owned the car Bassett had just seen young Rocco driving, the detective remembered.

He asked, "Any of you have ideas then how he'd got killed?"

"Pa said it was a heart attack."

Whoever had killed MacAndrews, Bassett thought, must have gotten quick relief from their anxiety with Kearns' prognosis. "What time did you leave the *Crazy Cat*?"

"Quarter to ten, something like that." Daley looked down the sight line of his gun.

"What made young Rocco back out of the game?" the detective asked.

Daley made some adjustment in the gun, shrugging the while. He never looked at you directly, just a glance that slid off without ever having made contact. "Football. Homework. I don't know. Maybe he didn't have any money."

"But he had planned to sit in on your game?" Bassett said.

Again Daley shrugged. This was a town of shrugs. "Lots of guys plan. If they show up, swell. If not, the hell with them."

"But I asked you about Rocco—if he had planned to play cards with you."

"Seems like."

"You left the *Crazy Cat* together, didn't you?"

"I wouldn't say together. Same time, maybe."

His eyes weren't the only thing that slipped away ahead of direct contact with his interrogator.

"Where was Pekarik then?"

"How should I know? I started home and he came along and gave me a lift."

"And you decided to have a game of gin."

"We'd already made up to play cards. He just happened to come along in time to give me a lift."

Bassett nodded. Neat. Everything seemed so neat. He said, "I want you to come down to the station with me now. Tell it to Chief Kearns. I think he'd be interested."

"Anything to oblige." Daley put the gun barrel on the table. "Don't mess around here, pa."

His father said, "When are you going to eat?"

"I'll eat."

Bassett's only purpose in taking Daley down was to be sure he was not in contact with Pekarik before the detective could get to him.

But his visit to Pekarik yielded no further information. Pekarik was a scared boy, Bassett thought, but either he was telling the truth or what he told had been drilled into him by a mighty tough drillmaster. That, the detective surmised, was Daley. Rocco was too mercurial. He might lead a flamboyant charge, but Bassett doubted he could organize a retreat. He remembered the merest chance by which Rocco had led the Hillside football team to victory. Good God! He was back to that again.

After he left Pekarik, Bassett returned to the police station.

Daley and the police chief both went home to their supper. There wasn't anything to keep either of them from it, Bassett thought grimly. He crossed the street and climbed the flight of stairs to Martin Scully's apartment. Scully, his sleeves rolled up, had just given the place a good cleaning.

"Something's different," Bassett said, looking around.

"Telephone," Scully said with a touch of pride. "I finally had one put in . . . for Johanna in case they move in here. Jo didn't have enough trouble. Now her mother's gone off with the boy friend."

"I see . . . and they're all going to move in here?"

Scully laughed bitterly. "Not quite. Just the Roccos—if Jo and Father Walsh can break up the romance."

Bassett understood then the girl's close liaison with the priest.

"I don't know. It's crazy," Scully said. "The night of the fire Jo wanted me to take her away—to get out of here. Now I wish to God I had. Her mother means trouble, Mr. Bassett. She always has."

"To say nothing of her brother," Bassett said. Scully looked at him, waiting. The detective sat down heavily. "No proof," he said.

Scully, in spite of himself, drew a deep breath of relief. He said: "I hate to discourage you, Mr. Bassett, but there are things buried in this town that aren't ever going to be dug out, even murder."

"And that's how it's going to be with MacAndrews?"

"I didn't say that. But there are things everybody knows and nobody tells."

Bassett just sat for a moment. "Any word from the Graham office?"

Scully shook his head. "The status is still quo."

Bassett got up. "What are you doing for dinner?"

"I generally go down to the diner."

"Is that the best place in town?"

"No. That'd be the *Halfway Inn*."

"Come on," Bassett said. "I'll stake you to dinner there."

Scully grinned. "Don't you have a home either?"

"It's funny, stranger that I am in this town, I feel more at home here just now than in my own house."

"Couldn't be you're getting to like it here," Scully said.

Bassett shook his head. "But there's something. There's something."

They were going out the door when the phone rang. Scully grinned at his new possession, and went back to answer it. Bassett waited downstairs.

"I should have had that put in long ago," Martin said rather too heartily when he rejoined the detective. "It just appointed me night manger of Graham Manufacturing."

"Congratulations," Bassett said with measured enthusiasm.

"I start training with the day man tomorrow. Seven A.M."

"And the night shift?"

"Back on next week."

"I guess it's better than never."

"Sure," Scully said.

When they reached the *Halfway Inn* a number of cars were parked alongside the building. Scully said, "Rotary night."

"Good. That's an aspect of Hillside I haven't been exposed to."

The *Halfway Inn* had been, in the nineteenth century, the stopping place for the railway travelers from the north and west who chose to rest before finishing by water their journey to New York. From the outside the clapboard building looked much the same as it had in the old days, but the inside was modern: chrome and red artificial leather. A fiberglass partition separated the dimly lighted bar room from the dining room, and this being the night of the Rotary meeting, tables for diners who were not associated with the club were provided on the bar room side of the partition.

Bassett, facing the door, recognized a number of the men arriving for the meeting: Mayor Covello, Lodini, the fire chief who also ran the Triple-X garage, the postmaster, Gerosa, the tailor. Being there, Gerosa had apparently settled whatever domestic crisis had sent him scurrying home. He still looked dour. Kearns arrived, out of uniform and wearing a fresh cigar. The owner of the inn, tending bar himself, hailed one and another of the men. Their response was terse: not a gay crowd. Gerosa had not even answered him.

Bassett took a sip of his scotch and soda. "Are they usually this glum?" Scarcely a murmur of conversation could be heard from the other side of the partition although the tinkle of glassware and silver was clearly audible.

"No. It's usually pretty noisy," Scully said.

"Maybe they think I'm spying."

"I don't think anybody noticed you."

Bassett said, "You mean I'm beginning to blend in?"

"We're all beginning to blend in," Scully said, and Bassett knew he was brooding over the new job.

"How long do you think you'll stick it out, Martin?"

"I don't know. Long enough to justify the men anyway. They've got a good man heading up their strike fund—the young fellow who said they'd go out, fund or no fund, remember?" Bassett nodded. "He's going to represent power some day, and that's what they need. I never had it. I didn't want it: that's the truth. I can see that now myself."

"A voice crying in the wilderness," Bassett said.

"That's right," Scully said. "That's exactly right . . . a voice preparing the way."

The two men talked, over a second drink and the shrimp cocktail, of matters not concerning the Hillside of that day— the origins of the town, first as a rail terminal, then as the site of the Graham plant. They talked of themselves, their families. Bassett was particularly interested in Martin's grandmother: she had left Italy as the very young bride of a man who had worked for her family, and she in turn had been no more able to dominate her children than her parents had succeeded in holding her to their traditions. Not even money had been able to hold the clan together, and the old lady had quite a lot of it. "Three of my uncles are teachers," Martin said.

"And everybody knows teachers don't need money."

"The funny thing about my grandmother," Scully said, "she'll give you petty cash maybe, but when it comes down to a solid amount, she won't give it to you for what you want. That way you might think she was trying to buy your affections."

"Will she give it for what you *don't* want?"

"Yes," Scully said speculatively. "At least she'll offer it for what you don't want. Me, for example, she offered to put me through pharmacy school. But law school, no, sir."

"Suppose you'd taken her up on the pharmacy school?"

Scully said, after a moment's thought, "I think she'd have had nothing but contempt for me."

In a way, Bassett thought, that perverse independence ran through the whole town. In their day the Tonellis had made their mark on it.

In the dining room, a hum of conversation had finally risen.

A large, heavy-jowled man came into the inn. Taking off his topcoat, he called to the bartender, "How are you, Joe? Good crowd tonight?"

"Hello, Doc."

"I'm late," the man said, hanging up his coat, smoothing his hair with the palms of his hands.

"Who's that?" Bassett asked as the man nodded at them and started toward the dinner-meeting.

"Doctor Tagliaferro."

The minute the doctor passed beyond the partition, silence again prevailed in the dining room. A sound ensued that caused Bassett and Scully to look at one another questioningly. It was a few seconds before Bassett said, startled, "They're hissing him."

Somebody rapped on a glass with his fork, but the hissing persisted, merging then with a chorus of boos.

Scully put his napkin on the table. "Something's up."

The bartender was hurrying around the bar. In the dining room men were shouting, others loudly placating. Bassett heard one phrase: "Sit down, Gerosa."

"Let's see what this is all about," Bassett said. He got up and watched from the end of the partition. Tagliaferro was standing a few feet from the long table, his hands on his hips. Two men were trying to hold onto Gerosa, a little man who,

Bassett thought, wanted his hands free for gesticulation more than anything else.

"Let me go!" Gerosa wrenched his arms free. He shook his fist at the doctor. "Here he comes—in a crowd. To me he isn't home. He knows! I'll put him like another sputnik in the sky!"

"Aha!" the doctor said. He had a great, booming voice that would carry over a hall. "Do you want to hear my side of the story?" He moved in to stand in front of one of the unoccupied places at the table.

"I'll kill him," Gerosa said. "I spit at him. Abortionist!"

Covello rapped on the table with the handle of his knife. "Gerosa, you're out of order!"

That, Bassett thought, was putting it mildly.

"Please," Gerosa said, "I am a father. You are a father. Let me talk."

"All right, shut up and talk!" somebody shouted.

Covello said, "Sit down, Doc. Sit down, Gerosa. Then talk."

Gerosa talked, but his voice was quivering almost to the point of incoherence. "That man—he took my daughter to that New York place of his. He examined her in such a way . . . my daughter, sixteen years old . . . and he tells her she is pregnant . . ."

The doctor's face turned purple. Bassett thought it looked as though it were going to burst the skin, his eyes bulging.

"That's a goddamned lie!" the doctor shouted.

Other diners were crowding in behind Bassett and Scully to see what was happening. The bartender tried to herd them back to their places.

"This is George Rocco's doing," Bassett said to Scully. "He was with Gerosa this afternoon."

"Then why do you take her in to the hospital, then, what for, eh?" Gerosa challenged. And to this all the men on Gerosa's side of the table responded, reinforcing his point.

"I didn't take her! She came in. She was dragged in by a rotten little blackmailer of a kid." The doctor had a temper of his own. "I examined her—yes! In my nurse's presence.

Tests could prove whether or not she was pregnant. But by examination I could tell she was a virgin. There's a difference, you know, in being not pregnant and being a virgin!"

"*What* difference?"

Tagliaferro threw up his hands. Then he drew a deep breath and reached for a glass of water. But his hand was trembling so much that he did not try to pick up the glass. "I suspected a trap, that she was being used to get me into trouble. I swear to God, Gerosa, I did only what any doctor would do to protect himself, found out the truth from her. Then I talked to her like a father. That boy Rocco, I told her, she should not go with him. She is an innocent child. He is—I don't know what he is . . . a monster."

"He is a good boy," Gerosa shouted. "He came to me, her father. He told me everything. You said if anything was wrong, in New York you can take care of it."

"That's a lie! Did you ask your daughter?"

"I ask her—and I beat her! Yes, it kills me, but I beat her, and I ask her, and she says yes, Georgie is telling the truth."

Tagliaferro stared at the man; then he looked from one hostile face to another. "You believe him? All of you?"

It was Lodini who said, "Why the New York hospital, Doc?"

Scully, touching Bassett's elbow and indicating that he wanted to quit the scene, said, "That's the question, all right."

Tagliaferro shook his heavy jowls. "A doctor must use what facilities are made available to him. All my life I've worked in this town. For this?"

Bassett followed Scully through the people who had closed in on them. The remains of their dinner was cold. "Let's have coffee at the diner," Scully said. "Okay with you?"

"He's quite a lad, Georgie, isn't he?" Bassett said when they were outdoors.

"Tag operated on his mother," Martin said. "And the truth is, he's very quick on the knife, especially with women."

"Hysterectomy, you mean?"

"That's his specialty," Scully said.

"The remarkable thing about this Rocco boy," Bassett said, "he has an uncanny instinct for finding out men's weaknesses—and using them. He's found something in every one of us to play on—even me and my son who were virtual strangers to him. He has a natural instinct toward evil, that boy has. And I'm beginning to think it's going to take the whole town to stop him—or nobody will."

"Johanna's brother," Scully said. "Christ have mercy on us!"

25

"Jo! Telephone call for you." The postmaster came out of his office. "Take it in there if you want to."

Johanna finished making change, a penny from a nickel, and said "Excuse me," to the customer.

"My stamp!" the man called after her. "You forgot my stamp."

"Take it easy," the postmaster said. "I know where they are."

Johanna prayed her way to the telephone.

"Johanna?" It was her mother's voice.

"Yes, mama." She tried to hold back her tears. "Are you all right, mama?"

"Do you want me to come home, Johanna?"

"Yes! Please, mama, soon. Right now. I have a place, an apartment. It's small but it's nice . . ." She was afraid to say that it was Martin's place. She could never tell how her mother would react to anything about Martin.

"I am so tired, Jo."

"I know, mama."

"And I'm sorry . . . I made a big mistake."

"It's all right. You don't have to say anything. Just come home. Have you any money? I could get somebody with a car maybe . . ."

"Father Walsh will come for me this afternoon."

"Oh, mama, I'm so glad."

Only a sound like a great sigh came from the other end of the line.

"Mama, don't cry!" She could no longer keep from crying herself. "Everybody will be glad to see you."

"Everybody," the woman repeated and her voice broke

on the word. "Thank you, Johanna," she managed and hung up.

Johanna tried to compose herself, putting the phone in its cradle. But she did not care. Really, she did not care. She walked proudly from the office and announced to the postmaster and the other clerk on duty: "My mother's coming home today."

"That's swell, Jo," her boss said. "That's just swell." And he meant it.

When Mrs. Mancuso came in, Johanna told her. The woman's eyes welled up with tears. "I'm so glad," she said and caught the girl's hand. "I'm so glad."

Johanna worked until noon. When Martin came in, as he did regularly for his mail and a word with her, she told him of her mother's call. The quickness of her joy very nearly lifted his own sense of foreboding in the matter.

"Want me to tell my grandmother?"

"No, I want to tell her myself. She's been very kind to Georgie and me."

The old lady took the news without a word. The girl's eyes were sparkling, and it made her sad to think how long it had been since she had reached that deeply into the soul of anyone.

"You understand, don't you, Mrs. Tonelli?"

"Too well," the old lady said. "Too well."

The doorbell rang. Johanna reached it before Mrs. Grey could come from the kitchen. It was Mrs. Lodini. "Is it true, Johanna?" Behind her were Mrs. Gerosa and Mrs. Mancuso.

"Yes! My mother's coming home. We're going to live at Martin's for a while . . ."

"When is she coming?"

"This afternoon. Father Walsh says four o'clock maybe."

"You will come to supper at our house," Mrs. Lodini said. "It is big and everyone can come. She must know her friends welcome her home."

The other women nodded. Mrs. Mancuso plunged her hand within her ample bosom and drew to the surface a small

fold of dollar bills just far enough to show their presence.
She tucked them out of sight again: found money to celebrate
the return of one they had thought lost.

Johanna laughed and hugged their spokeswoman.

"So," Mrs. Mancuso said, "In this game everybody wins.
Every hand a winner!"

Georgie, arriving home from school, was met at the door
by his sister. "Mama's coming home today. We're going to
move into Martin's."

"Who says?"

Johanna retreated a few steps into the house, for he pushed
in and stood over her, a glowering hulk.

"Georgie!" The girl was shocked by the sullen rage in his
eyes.

"What's she coming back here for?"

Johanna stood her ground, from where she would move
no more. "I asked her to. I begged her."

"I ain't moving into that dump of Martin's. Not me, sis.
You asked her. You live with her. Down there with all them
whores? Big Molly's down the street just. What'll people say,
ma living there after what she's did? Christ, sis, not me. I
got a future and it ain't going to be like that. No, man!"

Johanna brought her full strength into one vicious slash of
her hand across his face. Georgie shook it off; he wiped his
nose with the back of his hand, in the manner of a boxer.
"Okay, Jo. If that's how you want it, have it your way."

"Georgie, you don't have to come with us. Sometimes I
don't even think you're my brother."

"That's something you better ask ma. Maybe you're
right," he said, trying to hurt her.

But Johanna turned her back on him and went into the
kitchen. Mrs. Grey was baking a cake for the party at Lodinis'.

Georgie went to the living room door, knocked and opened
it. The old lady was nodding in her chair. She came suddenly
awake to see him standing, his feet spread, in front of her.

"I'm going to stay with you, Mrs. T. Okay?"

She clacked her tongue around her teeth, sucking moisture into her mouth where it had gone dry while she slept.

"I want to go to the party," she said.

"I'll take you," he said although he didn't know what party she was talking about.

She began to grope for her cane which had fallen to the floor. Georgie bent down to pick it up for her. She stretched out her bony hand and raked it through his hair. "Then get a haircut," she said.

He jerked his head away, but smiled. "Okay. For you I'll do that. For you, anything."

"For me," she said, and her voice dropped to a whisper, "nothing."

26

Bassett watched the homecoming, or such as he could see of it from the police station window, Kearns beside him. Theirs were not the only faces crowding windows on the street. And Billy Skillet did not bother disguising his curiosity. He rolled himself along the sidewalk from his usual station at the corner as soon as he saw the flutter of curtains at the second-floor windows.

Father Walsh got out of the car and went around to help his passenger out. Martin and Johanna came down the steps. As the woman got slowly from the car it occurred to Bassett that her lover, whoever, wherever he was, might well be enjoying relief instead of grief at the moment: an ailing mistress sobered many a cavalier. He turned away from the window at the meeting of mother and daughter.

"No Georgie," Kearns said.

Bassett looked back in time to see Martin Scully shyly kiss the cheek Johanna's mother turned to him. She took his face in her hands then and kissed his cheek in turn.

"She ain't the looker she used to be," Kearns said.

"Who of us is?"

Slowly the family moved indoors, all of them having thanked the priest profusely.

"There's going to be a big shindig tonight at the Lodinis'," Kearns said. "The gals are doing some free-spending."

Bassett grinned. "Enjoy, enjoy."

Kearns looked at him and allowed himself a sour smile. Then he said, "I'm not in that crowd. They're kind of on their own up there on the hill. I don't mean if I showed up I

205

wouldn't be welcome. Even you'd be welcome tonight. That's how they are. Italians, you know.''

"I think we'd better keep a watch up there tonight, you and I," Bassett said. "Will Tagliaferro be there?"

"I wouldn't think so. He got a bad scare last night. He'll watch himself for a while, but hell, the town needs him. He's the only doctor we got.''

"Do you think he'd perform an illegal operation if it came right down to it?"

Kearns went back to his desk for a cigar.

"That's a question just as well unanswered," Bassett said. "Forget I asked it."

"I'd just as soon," the police chief said.

"What time's the party?"

"It'll start rolling early," Kearns said. "The men'll be wanting to get their money's worth.''

Georgie could understand a party to which they'd invite his mother maybe as long as she was around. But even that, he couldn't really understand. And a party made especially for her . . . Man, this town was sick. They really needed a Mafia. He wondered how many of the guys would be there. Daley would. His mother had been Italian, Rosie's mother's sister. His old man used to work for the railroad. When he was laid off in Hillside he just stayed there. Man, come to Hillside and die. If ever he'd seen a walking corpse it was old man Daley. Georgie put on the clean shirt Mrs. Tonelli had bought him, then the corduroy jacket. She'd sent Mrs. Grey up on the bus to buy them. They weren't bad, he had to admit. And the tie was way out. He brushed his hair, pomaded it, and built up the folds to crests on either side of his head. Tomorrow he'd promised to have his hair cut. The old bag would hold him to it, too. Greater love hath no man, Georgie thought.

Mrs. Tonelli called up the stairs for him. When he went down she said, "I have never had to wait for a man before in my life."

Georgie grinned. "Look at me, Mrs. T."

"I don't have to. I can smell you."

"You look swell," he said. What she was wearing looked swell, anyway: the crown jewels. It made his eyes blink, just trying to look at her.

As soon as Georgie reached the Lodini house he was faced with a dilemma: everybody would be watching to see how he acted toward his mother. Christ! He didn't recognize her at first. She looked all sunk in, eyes, chest. He crossed the room, self-conscious. It was like getting up in front of class when you didn't even know what the assignment was.

"Hello, mother."

"Mother," she repeated, a funny look in her eyes.

Georgie's face reddened. He'd never called her mother before.

"I thought maybe you'd say Mrs. Rocco," she derided.

"Hi, sis," Georgie said to Johanna.

She did not even answer him. He looked at her as hard as he could, trying to warn her he wasn't going to take anything from her—or her mother. Who the hell did they think they were?

"If looks could kill, Georgie." His mother made a deprecating gesture with the back of her hand to him. "Go away."

Mrs. Tonelli made her way carefully across the glossy floor. Mrs. Lodini had waxed it to mirror brightness. "Well, Catherine, it did not work out the way we thought." She gave a dry laugh and glanced at Johanna. "A split decision, as they say on the radio." She drew in a deep breath and let it out. "I thought it was for everybody's good . . . But mostly for my own."

The latter admission made Johanna and her mother smile.

"I want some wine," the old lady said. "I want quite a lot of wine."

"I'll bring you some, Mrs. T.," Georgie said.

"Bring us all some wine."

"Yes, ma'am."

Her glass in hand a few minutes later, the old lady toasted: "To the prodigal returned."

It was the signal for the night's revelry to start. Everyone drank and laughed and talked, and soon forgot the occasion in its bounty. There were antipastos of every sort, roasted meats, lasagna, fruits, salads. And there was music. The trio that played at the *Halfway Inn* on Saturday nights had been hired by the Ladies' Auxiliary of the fire department. As Mayor Covello said, they ought to do this every night this week, as long as the men were off work and the women loaded with money. There were men making love to their own wives where most of them had hardly spoken since Saturday night.

Georgie finally made himself speak to Rosie. She'd been hanging round Phil Daley and Tom Lodini all night. To hell with her. But he finally spoke to her: "Hi."

Rosie stuck her nose in the air.

"What's eating you?"

"Leave her alone," Daley said.

He'd been drinking, Georgie noticed. Man, what a Mafia he made.

"You all make me sick," Georgie said, and turned his back.

Rosie giggled. That goddamned giggle of hers. Georgie didn't know what to do with himself. Nobody was paying any attention to him. There wouldn't have been any party if it wasn't for him. He knew where the money for it came from, and it was his idea to give it to the women! What he'd give a woman from now on you could count on Billy Skillet's legs. Christ! He had to talk to someone. He went in search of Mrs. Tonelli. She'd got herself an audience, a circle of the people he'd like never to see again in his life: Papa Gerosa, his mother and Jo, cow-eyed Martin, the padre. He'd even taken off his Roman collar. And the old lady had him by the hand. And wasn't it typical, Georgie thought, the old parish priest, Father de Gasso, had fallen asleep in his chair.

"How I like to tease him," Mrs. Tonelli said of the young priest. "He has an Italian heart, but an Irish conscience." Suddenly she cocked her head around and looked up at the glowering Georgie. "Ho! Look who's jealous!"

"Of him?" The words were out before Georgie knew it.

The priest slowly withdrew his hand from the old lady's. Johanna half-rose from her chair.

"What I know," Georgie said, "God ought to send a thunderbolt and burn up this whole damn town."

The laughter and the music subsided even in other parts of the house.

"That's enough, George," the priest said. "You're not God's messenger."

"Somebody's got to be," Georgie shouted. He looked around at all the gawking, dumbstruck faces. "No wonder our house burned down, what was going on in there Friday night. If I was to tell . . ."

Georgie paused and moistened his lips. The priest and Johanna exchanged one long look, their heads up in the air, just waiting. But what got Georgie was the looks on the faces of the rest of the people: like *he'd* done something dirty. Him! the innocent bystander who'd just been trying to sneak into his own house. He brushed his nose with the back of his hand, again the gesture of the wary boxer. "All right," he said. "All right. When I got home that night the two of them, my sister and him," he pointed at Father Walsh, "they were standing together in the hall hugging one another. I mean, I thought at first it was Martin and her. But the priest! Man, I didn't know what to do, seeing them in a clinch like that."

Georgie looked from one shocked face to another. Some of the women looked as though they were going to throw up. He went on desperately, "I mean, that's what Jo and I was fighting about afterwards. Ask her. Go on, somebody, ask her if you don't believe me."

Only silence.

Then Mr. Lodini said quietly, disdainfully, "Get out of here, Georgie. Get out of my house and don't come here any more."

Georgie wanted to go, but he didn't seem to be able to lift his feet.

Mr. Gerosa was moving in on him, crossing the room like he was walking on tiptoes. "You, you rotten kid!" he said,

and shook his fist in the boy's face. Georgie fended him off
with his elbow. "Liar!" Gerosa addressed himself to the
entire company: "He lies about everybody. Even when he
tells the truth it is half a lie when he tells it!"

Mrs. Tonelli got to her feet. "Come, my young gallant,"
she said. "You can take me home now."

The way she said it, Georgie wondered if she, too, hated
him like the rest of them did. He was watching his sister and
Martin Scully move toward one another, slowly at first, then
in a rush, colliding in each other's arms as though they weren't
ever going to break apart again. He glanced at the priest: just
putting on his Roman collar. In public.

"Are you coming?" Mrs. Tonelli demanded.

"Man, am I!" Georgie cried.

The crowd opened for them to leave and closed behind
them as though they had not been in it at all.

"It was the truth, Mrs. T.," Georgie said on the walk. "I
seen it with my own eyes."

"I believed you," she said.

27

Bassett watched Georgie and Mrs. Tonelli leave the party: he had himself, by Lodini's permission, been an unobtrusive witness to Rocco's ultimate attempt at smear: of the priest and his sister. He did not doubt that there was at least a moment's truth in the incident. It explained how Rocco had built himself an alibi the night of MacAndrews' murder, calling on his sister to bear witness for him—lest he bear witness against her.

Was he aware, Bassett wondered, that tonight he had destroyed his own alibi?

But did he need it after all?

That was the hard core of the detective's problem. He might now gather testimony that the boy was not where he said he was. But could he prove *where* he was? No witnesses, no weapon. No wonder he had been willing to shoot his final bolt!

Bassett watched from the shadows of the back porch as Mrs. Tonelli poked her way slowly up the walk, the great, awkward lug bumbling alongside her. Where would their relationship go from here, left to devices of their own? The ersatz quarterback and his canny keeper? What did she think she was getting, buying him away from his own family?

My young gallant: he could still hear her crackling out that ironic epithet. She knew his worth. Did she know more? The spider and the wasp? Was that it? Every fiber in his body tensed as he contemplated that possibility. She had been watching that night—and perhaps from the moment the priest had left his car at her door and gone down to the Rocco house. *The Italian heart but an Irish conscience*, that of the priest. She would have watched him from her door, having

211

said God knows what to him . . . and she would have seen Georgie Rocco's arrival home—hard upon having committed murder? A cold chill ran over the detective as he saw the old woman reach out and clutch the boy's arm.

"Kind of chilly out here."

Bassett swung around, not having heard anyone come from the house. It was Phil Daley.

"Not when you get used to it," Bassett said.

The tall, hard youngster lit a cigaret. "Why don't you come in and join the party?"

"Because I've got an invitation to another one." Bassett took a long chance. "Want to turn State's evidence against him?"

"I don't know what you're talking about, mister."

"MacAndrews' murder. Remember?"

"I keep forgetting it wasn't a heart attack," Daley said. "Just about everybody does—except you. And maybe you're going to have to."

There was a little more than insolence in his voice, Bassett thought, a touch of threat. Weighing him and Rocco by the same scales, he would have chosen this lad as the potential killer. But if he were, the detective felt, and Rocco the accessory, Rocco would have cracked open by now. He used the phrase that had come into his mind:

"Not a chance. Your friend's going to crack open any time now. He destroyed his own alibi tonight."

Daley shrugged. "It's no skin off my ass," he said, and went back into the house.

Bassett went to join Kearns where he was waiting in the detective's unmarked car.

Mrs. Tonelli stopped in front of the ruins of the Rocco house, Georgie silent at her side, scuffling his feet. He'd have liked to pick her up and carry her home—or pitch her down the hill. She was getting on his nerves. He had a feeling inside of him like jelly. The smell of damp burnt rubbish was turning his stomach.

"When will they clean up this ruin?" she said. The light of the half-moon made it look like a movie battlefield.

"When'll they pay for it, that's what I want to know," Georgie said.

"And what will you do then, Georgie? Tell me the truth. If you get a part of the money, what will you do?"

Georgie shrugged. "I might just go away some place—to school, I mean. I want to make something of myself, Mrs. Tonelli."

The old lady snorted. "So earnest, so hard working," she derided. "I want you to do something for me tomorrow, Georgie." She gestured with her cane. "I want you to dig up that hydrangea bush."

Georgie thought he was going to pass out. The sidewalk was like the crazy house at the amusement park. He didn't know for sure if it was his own voice, but he said, "What for?"

"Buried treasure," the old lady said, and started across the street to her own walk.

Georgie couldn't get his mind to think straight at all. It was running in all directions. She'd seen him, she must have seen him burying the tape. And him purposely not going back for it. But she couldn't know what it was. Or could she? The police could. Bassett could. They'd put that under a microscope . . . He'd been afraid to go back for it. He knew that now. Christ! He hadn't meant to kill old MacAndrews . . . It was an accident. Daley and Mike knew what he'd meant to do . . .

"Open the door," the old lady said, and gave him the key.

His hand was shaking so much he couldn't get it in the keyhole. She snapped on a small flashlight and watched his fumbling.

"Give it to me," she said.

"I shouldn't 've drunk so much wine," he said, not having touched a drop.

The old lady said nothing, opening her own door.

He finally got her to her bedroom. It was like getting a piano into a closet.

She sat down at the dressing table. "Good night, Georgie." She watched him, letting him get to the door, and then said, "If somebody burns down his own house, Georgie, there is generally evidence—if you know where to look for it. I think you are going to live with me—for a long time."

"Sure," he said. "I intended to." He gained confidence even while he talked. She didn't really know . . . Not what he'd thought. "I mean, I had a terrible choice to make, Mrs. T., between you and my own flesh and blood."

She laughed. "So did I," she said. "Good night, Georgie."

He turned on the television in the living room, lowering the sound to where it was but a faint hum. Then he smoked a cigaret. He had to wait a few minutes. He wasn't going to run right out like maybe she expected him to. But he had to know. He had to take the stinking rotten tape in his hands again and get rid of it . . . if it was there. He waited out one more commercial—Be a Two-Car Family . . . If he had a car, just . . . a one-car family. A bicycle family. He hadn't even the price of a pair of roller skates. Even Billy Skillet had that.

He went to the bedroom door and knocked. Then he opened it a crack to ask, "Is the television too loud, Mrs. T.?"

"No, dear," she answered.

At least that's what he thought she said. No dear, and thinking he'd burned his house down! She was crazy. A loony!

He went out of the house, leaving the key on the inside of the door, the door open. He dared to glance up the street only once. He was afraid to look again, just dashing across it blindly, and falling on his knees beside the bush, he began digging wildly, like a dog, with his hands among the wet, dead leaves.

Bassett got out of his car even as the boy crossed the street, leaving the door for Kearns to close. "Softly," he said, and moved in to watch Georgie from the shadows of the hedge.

He could hear the boy's breathing as he paused between one patch of digging and another, and he heard a noise from him like crying . . . It might even have been praying. But Rocco gave up, at last. He rose, his hands empty, and ran across the street, back to the house.

Bassett, following him, tried the door through which he had entered. Locked. He ran back to the car and told Kearns to get up to the Tonelli house, and went himself back to Lodini's for Scully. He tried to get him outside, arousing as little suspicion as possible. "Have you got a key to your grandmother's?"

Scully had. It was best to have Scully with them in any case. They had no warrant to enter the house, and only Bassett's intuition that something might be within the house now to justify their entry, quick. They found Kearns putting his shoulder to the door. The old lady was screaming.

"Her bedroom!" Scully said, and they started to run around the house. Kearns flashed on his torch. Inside, the woman was still screaming. Bassett took the butt of his revolver to the window and smashed it open; he tore away the shade from the inside. Mrs. Tonelli was sitting upright in her bed, her hands at her face. Nor did she stop screaming until Martin climbed in through the window to her.

"He's stolen my jewels, my purse . . . and the ball. Martin, the ball . . ."

Bassett ran from the bedroom, through the living room. The boy could have got no further than out of the house. But before he himself reached the door, a series of shots rang out. He fell back of the door for a moment, for his own safety, unsure of where the bullets were spraying. Then silence. Everywhere silence. He went outdoors. Kearns, who had stayed outside the house, had doubled back toward the door. He played his flashlight now on the fallen figure of the boy. The police chief had not drawn his gun. Other people were coming. The party had taken alarm. Bassett took the flashlight from Kearns' hand and quickly shot it around: the circle of its light picked up Phil Daley, standing a few feet away, his rifle in hand. He broke the barrel and let the empty cartridges fall out. He hadn't taken any chance of the fugitive's being taken alive.

Bassett dropped to his knees and turned Georgie over. He would tell neither truth nor lie again. The old lady's purse lay beside him—and a wadded ball of electrical tape. *The ball, Martin, the ball* . . . The detective took it.

The two priests had come. Kearns shouted to keep women away. Bassett got hold of Father Walsh who was about to kneel down at the boy's side. "Let the other priest do that, Father, will you? I need your help." To Kearns he said, "Lock up Daley. I'll be in touch with you at the station."

Father Walsh spoke to the older priest and then followed Bassett on a run to the car.

The detective opened the car up, racing to Pekarik's house.

Within ten minutes, in the priest's and his parents' presence, Michael Pekarik confessed to his part in the attempted robbery. Bassett virtually reconstructed it for him: he had but to fill in certain small details. The priest stayed on with the family when Bassett took the boy out with him.

In the car Pekarik said, his voice as small as he looked himself, "Georgie didn't mean to kill him—I don't think."

"And Daley?"

"All he did was close the safe—afterwards."

Which, the detective thought, was what he had proposed to do again tonight when he filled his friend Rocco with bullets.

"What'll they do to me, mister?"

"How old are you?" The detective glanced at him: a scared punk, accessory to homicide.

"Sixteen."

"I don't know what they'll do to you—but it can't be much worse than what's already been done."

ABOUT THE AUTHOR

Her crime novels have won DOROTHY SALISBURY DAVIS a front-rank reputation, both in the United States and abroad. For her fiction Mrs. Davis is a seven-time Edgar Award nominee, and in 1985 she was recognized by the Mystery Writers of America as a Grand Master (for lifetime achievement). Among her popular and critically acclaimed novels are *A Gentle Murderer*, *Where the Dark Streets Go*, *Death of an Old Sinner*, and *A Gentleman Called*.

MYSTERY
in the best 'whodunit' tradition...

AMANDA CROSS

The
Kate Fansler
Mysteries

Available at your bookstore or use this coupon.

___**THE QUESTION OF MAX**   35489 4.95
An accident...or foul play? Amateur sleuth Professor Kate Fansler attempts to discover the truth about a former student's death...and her elegant friend Max.

___**THE JAMES JOYCE MURDER**   34686 4.95
When her next door neighbor is murdered, Kate Fansler must investigate. Every guest in her house is a prime suspect, as she puts aside sorting through James Joyce's letters to his publisher to find the guilty party.

___**DEATH IN TENURED POSITION**   34041 4.95
Kate Fansler must get on the case when her old friend and colleague Janet Mandlebaum is appointed first woman professor in Harvard's English Department and then found dead in the men's room.

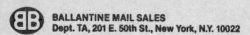 **BALLANTINE MAIL SALES**
Dept. TA, 201 E. 50th St., New York, N.Y. 10022

Please send me the BALLANTINE or DEL REY BOOKS I have checked above. I am enclosing $...............(add $2.00 to cover postage and handling for the first book and 50¢ each additional book). Send check or money order—no cash or C.O.D.'s please. Prices are subject to change without notice. Valid in U.S. only. All orders are subject to availability of books.

Name_____

Address_____

City_____State_____Zip Code_____

11   Allow at least 4 weeks for delivery.   3/90   TA-75